DEATH
ON DECK

BOOKS BY VERITY BRIGHT

THE LADY ELEANOR SWIFT MYSTERY SERIES

1. *A Very English Murder*

2. *Death at the Dance*

3. *A Witness to Murder*

4. *Murder in the Snow*

5. *Mystery by the Sea*

6. *Murder at the Fair*

7. *A Lesson in Murder*

8. *Death on a Winter's Day*

9. *A Royal Murder*

10. *The French for Murder*

11. *Death Down the Aisle*

12. *Murder in an Irish Castle*

DEATH
ON DECK

VERITY BRIGHT

bookouture

Published by Bookouture in 2023

An imprint of Storyfire Ltd.
Carmelite House
50 Victoria Embankment
London EC4Y 0DZ

www.bookouture.com

ISBN: 978-1-83790-102-9
eBook ISBN: 978-1-83790-101-2

To Hovis, my dog, who dreams of one day being as lazy and gluttonous as Gladstone.

There are no secrets better kept than the secrets everybody guesses.

~ George Bernard Shaw

1

'The very idea! Duty cannot be shirked.'

Lady Eleanor Swift's sharp-eyed and sharp-witted visitor tightened her grip on Eleanor's elbow as they partook of an afternoon constitutional around Henley Hall's manicured lawns. Despite nipping at any hint of exposed skin like a vicious terrier, the biting March wind hadn't been a deterrent to Lady Saxonby's insistence they walk and talk. Eleanor's elderly, comfort-loving bulldog, Gladstone, on the other hand, had remained firmly in his bed by the warm kitchen range.

Eleanor groaned inwardly as her visitor paused at the base of the wide stone steps leading up to the vast balustraded terrace. Fearing this was to prepare for another turn around the garden – along with another lecture – Eleanor gestured enthusiastically up the steps, only to be met with a withering look.

'One cannot skip a season. Ever, Eleanor. Byron must have lost his bearings towards the end if he didn't include such stipulations in his will. One would hope his ward, of all people, would understand such requirements!'

Eleanor bristled at the reference to her beloved late uncle, Lord Byron Henley. Initially, she'd been delighted by the prospect of meeting an old acquaintance of his, hoping to learn more about the man to whom she owed so much but knew so little. Until, that is, her butler had informed her that the very Victorian Lady Saxonby was undoubtedly calling to make sure her late friend's ward was fulfilling her duty as his heir.

And, indeed, the afternoon had turned out to be a thinly disguised diatribe on obligations, expectations and accountabilities. All of which, it had been made crystal clear, she was falling short of. In her visitor's rigid opinion, anyway.

'Actually, Lady Saxonby,' she said wistfully as they finally climbed the steps, 'I've discovered – far too late, sadly – that Uncle Byron secretly championed every path I chose in life. No matter how misjudged or misguided they turned out to be. It breaks my heart I didn't get the chance to thank him for everything before he passed away.'

Her visitor pulled them both up short as they stepped through the French doors into the drawing room. 'Don't grieve for that, Eleanor. I made your acquaintance for the first time but an hour ago. And yet you have transported me back twenty-seven years to when Byron and I were thrown together by circumstance and chance.'

Eleanor didn't miss the fleeting flush of animation that accompanied this.

'I have?' Her gaze flicked to her butler, Clifford, but his ever-inscrutable expression gave nothing away. 'How so, Lady Saxonby?'

'Because, actual physical appearance aside, you are Byron's exact double in every other regard.'

'Oh, but that's wonderful!' Eleanor breathed, staring back at her own cat-green eyes framed by her fiery red curls in the enormous mirror spanning the chimney breast.

Lady Saxonby snorted. 'Hardly! Rhinoceros stubborn and impervious to sense is fault enough in a gentleman.' She gave

Eleanor a pointed look, then swept out to the grand entrance hall. 'But they are wholly unbecoming in a lady!'

Eleanor shrugged. 'Perhaps. However, I tend to think we are who we are for a reason. But I thank you for your candour.'

Her visitor waved Clifford off from helping her into her mink coat and matching stole and stepped back to Eleanor's side.

'It will end in tears, mark my words!' She scooped up the one silver-embossed invitation occupying pride of place on the ornate marble mantelpiece. 'A female of your age and situation should have a row of these. Invitations to elegant luncheons, refined dinners, notable balls and society weddings. Not just one to,' she broke off as she scanned the card, her face falling in horror, 'to join a... a cruise to the colonies!'

Eleanor gently extracted the card from her visitor's vice-like grip. 'Actually, I declined the invitation because of other pre-existing plans. This is from my old employer, the well-respected Mr Thomas Walker, provider of renowned excursions across the globe. He is also one of the directors of Blue Star Line. The magnificent *Celestiana*, the largest and most luxurious ocean liner ever built, is the latest addition to their portfolio. Mr Walker was extremely generous in inviting me to join her maiden voyage to New York. However, as I said, I had to decline as I received an even more tantalising offer.' Her hand strayed to the silver pendant inset with a tiny emerald heart she'd been given that Christmas. 'From my beau, actually.' The vision of an impossibly handsome set of chestnut curls and deep brown eyes topping off a far too dashingly tall and athletic frame swam before her eyes.

Lady Saxonby's head jerked up. 'You have a suitor? Then maybe there remains the faint hope you will be respectably married before you reach the age of thirty-five.'

'Suitor?' Eleanor's voice faltered at the terrifying thought of marriage. Especially since her first had ended so disastrously.

'Well, perhaps, umm, our relationship being in "early days" describes us best. However, despite his fearfully important workload, he has delighted me with a wonderful birthday surprise this year.'

'If that isn't a ring for the fourth finger of your left hand, then I fail to see what interest it can possibly hold for you.'

'It isn't. It's time.' At Lady Saxonby's bewildered look, she continued. 'Time taken away from his desk. To spend with me. That means the world, especially as he had to cancel our plans last year because he was chained to that very desk.'

Lady Saxonby scoffed. 'Not a sentiment you will still hold when his business interests fail because he's frittered his hours away with you rather than tending to them.'

'Hugh doesn't have "business interests". He's a detective inspector.'

'A policeman!' Her visitor inched a delicate lace handkerchief from her tightly buttoned dress cuff and fanned her face with it. 'Oh dear, dear. I have so much more of a challenge in you than I had initially feared. However, rest assured, I shall return. For your uncle's sake. I might have failed with him, but I shan't with you!' She marched back to Clifford and slid into her waiting coat. 'Let us be grateful for small mercies. This... policeman person has at least ensured you will not be so irresponsible and foolhardy as to take the trip to New York. Oh, the very idea!'

Eleanor's Oxford heels clipped across the marble flooring of the grand entrance hall as she followed her visitor to the double-fronted oak door. 'Whatever is wrong with New York?'

'Everything. And all that remains besides.' Lady Saxonby turned back in the doorway. 'Unless one counts being amidst nothing but swindlers, thieves and murderers as "adventure", of course!' Tightening her gloves against her wrist, she nodded to her chauffeur waiting by the steps and then pointed a finger at Eleanor. 'Think hard, my girl. A woman's wits need be her greatest asset. Until I return, do try and sharpen yours. I shall bid you good day.'

Her butler closed the door as the stately hum of tyres receded. Eleanor held up a hand. 'Clifford. Kindly save your usual round of respectful admonishments for later. I did my best with her, genuinely. But she is rather...' – a polite version of the word burning on her tongue popped into her mind – 'prickly.'

Her butler's lips twitched with amusement. 'Actually, my lady, I was about to offer you my heartfelt commendations for emerging relatively unscathed. You did his lordship proud.'

She stared at the full-length portrait of her late uncle smiling down from the top of the carved staircase. 'You mean Uncle Byron received similar treatment from the eminent Countess of Saxonby?'

'If one were to consider being rubbed down with the coarsest grade sandpaper and then buffed with a paste of broken glass as "treatment", then yes.'

She laughed and shook her head. Clifford had been much more than her late uncle's batman while he was in the army. And far more than his butler when he'd left. Despite their class difference, he'd been his confidant, friend and ally. Just as, after her uncle's passing, he'd increasingly become hers.

He led her towards the door leading into the small sitting room referred to as 'the snug'. 'A well-deserved restorative, my lady?' His eyes twinkled. 'Perhaps it may also serve as an early celebration tipple?'

Her shoulders rose with glee. 'The prospect of seeing Hugh for more than just a few snatched minutes is so delicious. Promise you won't let on how excited I am because it will feel like too much pressure for him and he's already as hopelessly awkward with me as I am with him.'

'An easy promise to give, my lady.'

'I know, I know. Because you're a butler, which equates to the epitome of discretion.'

He shook his head. 'I was rather meaning that I fear your face will have betrayed you long before I should get the chance.'

She laughed. 'You're quite right. My face gives me away every time. Except it won't on this occasion! Kindly set aside an hour in your schedule to teach me your signature poker face!'

Replying only with a bow from the shoulders, he straightened quickly at the jangle of the telephone. 'Excuse me, my lady.'

Absent-mindedly tapping her chin with the invitation, she followed him back out into the marbled hall.

'Little Buckford 342,' he intoned into the receiver. After a pause, he added, 'I will see if the lady is home, Chief Inspector.'

'Of course I'm home!' She hurried forward and grabbed the handset her butler held out. 'I'll deal with you later, you terror!' She composed herself. 'How lovely, Chief Inspector Seldon, a surprise call.' She waited, then cocked her head at the silence from the other end.

'Blast it!' the familiar deep voice she was waiting for finally rumbled out and delighted her ear. The sound of a hand rubbing over a chin that had been too overworked to see a razor in the last twenty-four hours followed.

'Hugh, are you alright?'

'I am, yes. As, of course, I hope you are, Eleanor? Sorry, this infernal apparatus still trips me up every time I speak to you. But, I'm troubled that we might not be alright. After... this, that is.'

She frowned at the handset, then over to where Clifford had retired to a respectful distance. 'After this *what*, Hugh?'

'This call. I can't even manage it in person, which is so much worse of me.' A long groan came down the line. 'Eleanor, there's no easy way to say it. I feel an absolute and rotten heel, but I have to... to cancel our plans for your birthday. Sorry,' he ended quietly.

No, Ellie, this isn't happening!

'Cancel? *Again?*' she said more forcefully than intended. 'I mean, it was the same last year!'

'Y-e-s, but this... this is different.'

'But, Hugh, you'd actually taken time off! You never do that. You said you'd arranged a special birthday breakfast somewhere deliciously romantic and then we were going to go on a surprise trip and then dinner and dancing.' She softened her tone. 'What can possibly have come up? You promised that even if a fearfully important case dropped on your desk, you'd pass it to another officer and still show up. Whatever.'

'I know. I feel wretched. But as I said, this is... *different.*'

Unable to stop her heartache from showing in her voice, she shook her head at the handset so hard it made the invitation fly out of her hand and slide across the highly polished hallway floor. 'No, Hugh, it isn't. It's sadly, and disappointingly, familiar.'

'Eleanor, please. It's... oh blast, it's a question that eats me up to ask you, but can you just trust me on this? *Please?*'

'I always do, Hugh. Which I thought you knew. But what I also want to be able to do is *rely* on you. However, that appears not yet to be the case. And for one reason I think I know, but do not wish to hear today, thank you. So, off you pop to whatever is more pressing.' Her butler's gloved hand appeared in her eyeline, holding the retrieved invitation. 'And I shall choose another way to celebrate my birthday.'

'Eleanor, please believe that I'm beyond sorry.'

She sighed. 'I do, Hugh. Good day.'

She replaced the receiver, shaking her head sadly.

Back in the sitting room, Clifford materialised. 'A stiffer tipple than previously suggested, perchance?'

'I think so.' A sudden wave of indignance elbowed her

disappointment aside as she ran over the last of the conversation with her beau. 'Actually, no. I shouldn't think I'll have time for crying into my drink.' She shrugged. 'Hugh is what he is. He's married to his job and an important one it is, too. And much as he still makes my insides skip, his unreliability – however forced on him it may be – feels just a bit too wearing this time. So.' She clapped her hands overenthusiastically. 'I've no time for moping around because who knows, maybe I'll do what would delight the countess and succumb to the charms of a better catch aboard.'

Clifford looked unconvinced. 'Aboard?'

'Come on! There's a fearful amount of ugly tripe to organise and pack for all of us.'

'Aboard, my lady?' He scanned her face and then arched a single brow. 'Pack... for *all* of us?'

'Of course. I'll send a telegram to Mr Walker and tell him I'll accept his invitation so long as there are tickets available for my staff. Naturally, I won't expect him to pay for those, but I need to know there is space on the *Celestiana*. There should be. She's the largest liner ever launched. And I got the impression from his last letter that they were having no trouble filling first and third class, but there was still space in second. Now, please tell the ladies to grab their cases, and you, my faithful butler, do likewise. If I can't spend my birthday with Hugh, I can't think of anyone I would rather spend it with than my wonderful staff.'

'Too gracious, my lady. But are you *sure*?'

'Of course, Clifford. Anyway, according to Lady Saxonby, all the swindlers, thieves and murderers are in New York, so we should be fine!'

2

Eleanor had thought her staff had been bubbling over with excitement when she'd left them to take a train to Southampton Docks, while she and Clifford followed by taxi. But as she stepped out of the taxi which, for the last fifteen minutes, had been crawling along the jammed two-mile stretch to the quayside, she realised she'd been wrong. They had been fit to burst. And now, much to her delight, they had.

Above an ocean of bellowing porters, whistling barrow boys, and hollering passengers, she could clearly hear her staff even though they were still a way off. Holding hands, they were singing and dancing in a huddled ring around a pile of cases. Almost as if to complete their quintet, Gladstone whirled in uneven circles at Clifford's feet, adding a flurry of woofs to the already deafening cacophony assaulting their ears.

She glanced impishly at her butler. 'You're welcome to dash over there and do a turn around the cases with the ladies, if you wish?'

He eyed her sideways. 'If I might be excused the indignity of making a spectacle of myself on this occasion, my lady?'

'Of course.' She bit back a smile. 'Don't fret though. I'm sure there will be plenty of other opportunities for us all to make a public spectacle of ourselves during our time aboard.'

He closed his eyes momentarily. 'Doubtless, my lady, if experience is anything to judge by.'

Even with Clifford valiantly trying to protect her from getting battered by the chaos, it was heavy going as they walked towards the ladies. She felt like she was navigating her way across a boxing ring while the opponents were still slugging it out.

So much for an elegant start, Ellie!

She dodged the swarms of passing carts and barrow wheels, all perfectly placed to run over an unwary foot or bash a careless elbow or rib. Likewise, she ducked around the many tripod-mounted cameras swinging dangerously close to her head, each one shouldered by an eager-eyed reporter. Long before she reached the rest of her staff, she'd retrieved her hat three times and narrowly avoided being the victim of a last-minute laundry delivery. All the while, Gladstone wiggled in Clifford's arms, his stumpy tail wagging in time with his wide-eyed panting.

'Oh, my stars! 'Tis the mistress,' Eleanor heard Mrs Butters, her housekeeper, cry as she and Clifford navigated the last barrier of moving bodies.

The four of them jumped into line and bobbed a curtsey, Polly, her youngest maid tripping over her own feet as she did so. Clifford shook his head but said nothing.

Eleanor looked fondly along the line, which rose and dipped as much with their differing heights as their decreasing ages. The diminutive, soft-curved and grey-haired motherly Mrs Butters headed up the line. Beside her was her taller, perfect English-pear hipped counterpart, Mrs Trotman, Eleanor's no-nonsense cook. Next was the petite Lizzie, the sweet-faced seventeen-year-old maid whom she'd rescued from an unhappy employment the Christmas last up in Scotland. And then there was Polly, who at fifteen still showed no sign of growing into her gangly arms and legs. Or of growing any less clumsy, much to Clifford's despair. However, Eleanor's uncle had taken her in years before, and none of them could imagine life at Henley Hall without her. Her other staff, Joseph, the gardener, and Silas, her gamekeeper-cum-security guard, had opted to stay at the hall as a safer option than accompanying 'them women' afloat.

Eleanor beamed across to them. 'Ladies. How are we all doing?'

Mrs Butters stepped forward. 'Oh, 'tis the greatest day we'll ever live, m'lady! Thank you to the heavens and back for being so kind and generous as to bring us along.'

The others all nodded vociferously, Lizzie bobbing another curtsey, her soft Highland burr even more enchanting in the earnestness of her tone. 'To think, the likes of us aboard that miraculous machine of an ocean-travelling boat. We'll none of us know ourselves for having our heads filled with seeing so many heart-fluttering wonders.'

This drew a deep chuckle from Mrs Trotman who bumped her hip against the housekeeper's and muttered, 'Especially the ones in sailors' uniform, Butters!'

Eleanor's sharp ears caught her cook's words, but she hid her smile as Clifford pursed his lips.

'Ahem! Her ladyship is present. Even when that is not the case, I do not wish to remind you again—'

'Lady Swift! Lady Swift!' a coarse-voiced porter with a loaded handcart bellowed behind Clifford, his head swivelling in every direction but theirs.

'Here, my good man. HERE!' Clifford called through cupped hands and then reached out to clamp the man's green uniformed shoulder. Running a scrutinising eye over the cart's contents, he shook his head sharply at the white-haired and thickly whiskered face before him. 'That is but five cases.

Where are her ladyship's other steamer trunks? And hat boxes? Well, where are they, man?'

The porter held his hands up. 'This is all I've been sent out with, guv. Maybe you marked 'em "Not Wanted On Voyage" by mistake? 'Cos they'll already be stowed in the hold if as you did.'

Whipping out his pocket watch, Clifford looked troubled as his eyes flicked over the time. 'There has indeed been a grave mistake made. But not on my part.'

'They'll turn up, Clifford,' Eleanor said in a consoling tone.

'They will, my lady. Because I shall retrieve them myself from wherever they have been misplaced before the *Celestiana* sails.' He gave the porter a firm stare. 'Or misappropriated.' He turned back to her. 'Might I respectfully suggest you make your way to the first-class section of the quay to ensure your birthday week is not further marred by missing the ship's departure?'

She folded her arms. 'I was brought up on a boat, remember, Clifford. I know perfectly well how to board one!'

'True, my lady, but a forty-five-foot yacht hardly equates to...' He indicated the towering presence of the *Celestiana*.

She laughed. 'Also true.' She took Gladstone's lead from him. 'And don't worry, I'll find where to go just fine and I'll even listen to what I'm told to do for a change. But know this. I'd rather have my favourite butler aboard than my cases when she leaves.'

Acknowledging her heartfelt sentiment with a bow, he spun back to the porter. 'You. Come with me. And swiftly, my man.'

Her staff waved her off as they started toward the gang-planks, second class boarding before first. Like Clifford and the porter, in a blink they were swallowed up by the seething mass of humanity.

Feeling alone amongst thousands of oblivious others, Eleanor bent to pick up her far too cumbersome bulldog. 'Gladstone, old chum. Somehow we're going to have to find a way to run some of this excess belly off you on board.' She pulled back one of his pig-like ears and whispered, 'But what you really need to do is distract me from thinking about Hugh. I'm still catching my breath at the sight of every broad-shouldered, dark-haired man I see. Hopeless, Ellie!' she said aloud. 'No more lovesick schoolgirl. It's birthday time!'

As she approached the end of the throbbing crush of eager passengers, the glistening, arrow-point blue-and-white bow of the *Celestiana* caught her eye. It rose with an exquisite angular beauty to such a height that she had to crane her neck to follow the line to its four soaring, sky-piercing blue-and-red funnels.

Finally she spotted the waiting lounge on the quay. As first-class passengers boarded last, the cruise company had provided them with a luxurious place to wait. A few moments later, she was reclining on a plump sofa with a cup of tea, nibbles and a bowl of water for Gladstone.

Now, Ellie, that's more like it!

Another cup of tea and several delectable nibbles later – *well, it is your birthday cruise* – a man in a smart Blue Line uniform announced it was the final call for remaining passengers to board.

The first stop was the custom sheds, opposite the lounge. The crowd in front of her eventually thinned, and she headed for the gangways. It was only then that she really took in just how awe-inspiring the *Celestiana* was. She jerked to a stop, causing the portly man behind to bowl into her, dislodging his maroon silk-banded boater, which bounced off Gladstone to land at her feet.

'First time then, madam?' His over-trimmed, fair-haired moustache twitched as he grumbled in her ear.

She beamed back at him, offering his retrieved hat. 'I couldn't be any less captivated if it was my hundredth voyage. I've got actual goosebumps. Look at her! She's eight hundred and sixty-seven feet long, as I've been reliably informed by my butler, which is only just shy of two and a half Buckingham Palaces. And every inch of her is beyond breathtaking.'

'Pfoof! Nothing more than a floating dining room and cigar salon for those of us on endeavours of merit, not frivolity. That' – he jabbed a manicured nail at the vast edifice of blue-and-white steel before them – 'is a means to an end. Transport, that is all.'

'What a shame,' she said, hoping their paths wouldn't cross again. 'However, enjoy your worthy endeavours.'

'Enjoy frittering your time aboard, madam.' He begrudgingly doffed his boater and then readjusted the angle before pushing past her. Gladstone growled and pulled at his lead.

'Relax, old friend!' She ruffled the bulldog's ear, still rooted to the spot, staring at the beautiful craft as the last few hats and coats hurriedly passed her by. 'We'll be aboard for six days and all we have to do is avoid him. Easy.'

'First class this way, ladies and gentlemen. FIRST CLASS. THIS WAY!' a smart-uniformed officer called through a shiny brass loudhailer. The gangway was already clearly marked as such by an enormous banner, making her wonder if her butler hadn't organised the loudhailer especially so she didn't blunder past.

Joining the line of impressive fur wraps over cashmere skirts and tailored cloaks over bespoke suit trousers, she started up the suspended gangway. As it swung, the passengers gripped the steadying chain rails and tried not to trip on the wooden runners, which acted as a foil to the slipperiness created by the damp March sea air. After growing up aboard, albeit on her parents' very modest sailing boat, she had no need of the rail or to stare at her feet so as not to trip. Instead, she scoured the other gangways, which were already being dismantled by an army of efficient crew.

'LAST CALL. ALL ASHORE WHO ARE GOING ASHORE! ALL ABOARD WHO ARE BOARDING!' four commanding voices called in shiny-buttoned uniformed unison from the quay. She could hear the call being repeated along the decks.

A wave of disquiet washed over her. Even with all his unfathomable wizardry, surely Clifford would have to be a real-life sorcerer to have sorted her luggage, cleared customs and navigated the throng to be ahead of her? She spun around, scanning the remaining crowd of hundreds for his face. However, as they were all waving handkerchiefs at various decks and port-holes, calling final farewells to loved ones, seeing anyone clearly was impossible.

'Lady Swift?' a smooth and educated voice interrupted her thoughts.

'My butler?' she blurted out.

The immaculate navy-blue uniformed man with an outstretched hand faltered. His attractive features, sculpted by the elements, broke into a broad smile. 'Actually, I am the captain. Captain Miles Bracebridge. Welcome aboard the *Celestiana.*' He cocked his head. 'I can see we are in for a delightfully interesting voyage together.'

She smiled. 'Thank you, Captain. And my apologies. What I meant was, there is someone who hasn't boarded yet but who we cannot leave behind.'

He shook his head. 'I'm sorry, but we are shortly leaving berth. The *Celestiana*'s maiden voyage will be nothing but auspicious from start to finish under my experienced watch. Not least because the world's press are panting for even a hint of misadventure, as usual.' His expression turned more steely. 'So she sails on time.' He nodded to her and strode away as two long blasts of the ship's horn sounded.

She hurried to one of the few clear sections of bow rail. On all sides, passengers waved lace handkerchiefs or newspapers to the still throbbing quayside of relatives, well-wishers, reporters and wide-eyed gawpers. Craning perilously far over, she was amazed to catch sight of her staff on a lower deck. She craned even further in the hope of spotting Clifford's impeccably groomed form.

Suddenly the rail shuddered, and she felt the ship move, the electrified atmosphere starting a series of tingles down her spine. The gap between the ship and the quay widened slowly until she leaned back and groaned. 'Dash it, Gladstone! I've already lost my beau this birthday. And now it seems I've lost my butler!'

3

Eleanor spread her hands. 'I really have no idea.'

The young sailor she'd accosted stared nervously at Gladstone, who was panting wildly with excitement by her side. 'Your cabin number should be printed on your ticket, miss, erm, ma'am.' He tugged an anxious hand at the unruly tuft of blond hair poking from the peak of his smart, navy-banded cap.

She stepped beside him so they could scour the ticket together.

'*Lady* Swift?' His eyes turned to saucers as he ran a finger under her name. 'Apologies, m'lady!' He jerked up, ramrod straight. 'You are in Stateroom Number One on Upper Deck A. Opposite the Regal Suite.'

'Gracious.' She felt herself colouring at how grand that sounded.

'Through those gold doors into the oval room and up the main staircase until you see the sign to the staterooms. I would take you, but I'm needed—'

'More urgently elsewhere? Don't worry. I can find my way, thank you...?'

'Eric.' He slapped his forehead. 'Ordinary Seaman Pilbeam, I mean.'

'Thank you, Eric.' She half turned to go. 'Incidentally, you haven't seen my butler, have you? About six feet, dressed impeccably as... well, a butler?' At his shaking head, she shrugged. 'Oh, well, I'd better find my cabin.'

As he left, she stepped through the gold doors he'd referred to and was pulled up short. 'Oh my, Gladstone!'

The 'oval room' was the size of a concert hall. It rose two stately floors to an eighty-foot vaulted glass dome of pure indigo peppered with a thousand silver stars, which twinkled above the most elaborate double staircase she had ever seen. Designed so passengers could simultaneously ascend and descend without bumping into each other, marble cherubs holding lit lanterns adorned the base. The theme was echoed in smaller cherubs lighting the way under the ivory ostrich plumes flanking each step. Seemingly free-standing and curved around its own sweeping scrollwork-panelled banisters, it was an unparalleled feat of architectural construction and illusion.

The indisputable centrepiece, to her mind, however, was the magnificent brass clockwork model of the solar system suspended below the dome. Each planet was represented by a different coloured glass orb, even the smallest being at least three feet in diameter, and all seeming to pulsate with a mesmerising inner glow as they orbited the sun in a mesmerising ballet. She recalled Clifford had told her the name 'Celestiana' had been chosen for the ship as her designers said she contained all the wonders of the heavens.

Another wave of panic that he had been left ashore gripped her. 'Come on, Gladstone, there'll be someone assigned to the cabins on our floor who we can ask to check if he made it aboard.' She bit her lip. 'Not that I know what to do if he hasn't.'

Hurrying across the acres of white and black chequerboard

flooring, she admired the glass lifts artfully built into the rear sweep of the staircase. Her pulse skipped at the glimpse of a dark-suited set of broad shoulders. She shook her head.

Forget about Hugh on this trip, Ellie. He's always going to be chained to that desk of his. You'll have to learn to enjoy birthdays on your own. If your relationship ever actually progresses, that is!

She hurried Gladstone up to the galleried landing lit by crystal chandeliers where settees and chairs upholstered in blue and silver velvet were set among classical statues and exotic palms.

'Staterooms, this way,' she eventually read aloud, her hand flying out to the frosted and gilt-latticed double French doors before her. 'This is us, apparently, boy. Come on!'

But as she bowled through, she jerked to a stop again. Her route was blocked by an army of porters flanked by uniformed crew, all intent on ferrying a raft of smart travelling trunks into what had to be the Regal Suite opposite hers.

'Can even a royal need that much luggage?' she whispered to Gladstone. 'Assuming it is a royal.'

At that moment, Captain Bracebridge strode out of the suite accompanied by a man whose uniform had only slightly fewer gold stripes than his.

'Ah, Lady Swift. Forgive me one moment, if you will.' He turned to the other sailor. 'Carry on.'

With military-like precision, the man nodded and ordered the porters to wheel the last of the fiercely padlocked luggage into the Regal Suite. Bracebridge eyed her for a moment and then broke into that easy smile he'd first graced her with.

'No need to concern yourself at all with our other notable guest, Lady Swift.' The man who she assumed was his second in command nodded as he passed. 'Your paths are unlikely to cross on this voyage.'

'Of course,' she said, having no idea how to converse appropriately with any member of the royal family, anyway. She'd only spoken to one once, and ten minutes later she'd witnessed him die at the mercurial hand of another.

Bracebridge bade her good day before disappearing after the last of his crew through a door she hadn't seen set within a carved plaster panel at the far end of the corridor. As it clicked closed, she took a deep breath.

'Finally! Cabin ahoy, Gladstone.'

The first thing she saw as she stepped inside made her heart sink. Her steamer trunks and hat boxes stood in a neat row under the nearest window. 'Blast it! I don't need flouncy evening gowns, too many shoes and a mountain of fripperous hats. I need—'

'Adhering to a strict on-board dress code not on your agenda then, my lady?' an invisible voice called.

'Clifford!' She rushed forward. 'You made it!'

His morning-suited form appeared from the open doorway in the far-right corner. 'Indeed, I did.' He bent to accept Gladstone's exuberant and over-licky welcome with a wince. 'And with all of your luggage too. Unnecessarily, however, I overheard you say. Six days in one's travelling tweeds some might consider a bold decision aboard the most luxurious cruise liner to date.' His eyes twinkled. 'However, as I aim to please, would you prefer I hurl your luggage overboard now?'

She smiled at his teasing. 'No, thank you. No sense wasting your efforts in finding it after all. So, since you've somehow performed this miraculous feat of not only rescuing my luggage but also beating me aboard, you've probably had time to assess my accommodation. Suitable for an elegant and refined lady of the manor on a birthday jaunt, in your opinion?'

'A traditional lady of the manor, indubitably. However, I fear she is the one passenger who definitely failed to board.'

She laughed. 'You total terror! Now, come on, what's what in here, then?'

He gave his customary bow from the shoulders. 'Welcome to your home for the next six days, my lady.' He gestured around the sumptuous furniture, which added a homely grandeur to the room. 'All made from the finest hand-carved oak from Waddington and Sons, the most eminent cabinetmakers in London, including the mounted globe. Adorning the rose wool carpet is a choice of two velvet settees, or wingback armchairs. Though I suspect it might be the petite buttoned chaise longue which pleases you most?'

'If I can fight Mr Wilful for even an inch.' She pointed at Gladstone, who was already waiting with his front paws up on the chaise longue, his stumpy tail twitching.

'Perhaps first, my lady, an extra travelling blanket might be procured by the cabin boy that Master Gladstone can slumber in princely style without destroying the upholstery as he is wont to do at home.'

She nodded and waved around the room. 'Good idea, Clifford. But you didn't mention the exquisite seascape paintings I shall enjoy losing myself in for hours. Nor all the beautiful porcelain figures dotted about. And what's through here?' She reached for the ornate china doorknob.

'Your, ahem, facilities, my lady.'

She stared around the bathroom. 'Oh, look! A darling half-size clawfoot bath with the prettiest tile surround, a basket of toiletries and the fluffiest towels ever.' She returned to the main room. 'So, sitting room for elegant languishing, bathroom for—'

'That which we might be gracious enough not to detail, perhaps?' he said quickly.

She hid a smile. 'Of course. Propriety first and all that. So that just leaves my bedroom then. Which must be where you were rooting about before you popped out through the door over there, yes?'

He ran a horrified finger around his starched white collar.

'Categorically not, my lady. Your resting quarters, I believe you will find through' – he gestured to the left – 'the double doors.'

'Oh, Clifford,' she called from inside. 'Rest assured, it measures up to even your exacting standards. There's the most inviting silk-quilted bed I've ever seen, enough drawers and built-in wardrobes for even all my luggage. Oh, and the most exquisite cushioned window seat under the row of portholes.' She returned to the main room. 'What's in there where you emerged from, then?'

'This' – he stood to one side to let her through – 'is the butler's pantry.'

'Ah!' She looked around the beautiful white-and-indigo tiled space, noting the impressive range of equipment set along the pristine woodwork surfaces. 'It's like the most wonderful kitchen afloat – there's even ice buckets! And, I notice, port at the ready, thank you. Any umm... accompanying snacks, perhaps?'

He sniffed but his eyes held a teasing sparkle. 'Hardly necessary aboard the world's most luxurious collection of floating dining rooms. However, I came prepared since experience whispered it might be wise.'

'Excellent! This is a birthday cruise, after all.' She bounded over to the chaise longue and sprawled out on it, groaning as Gladstone hurled his top half into her lap. 'Without a cumbersome bulldog, this would be rather more elegant. And comfortable. Oh, hang on though.' She jerked up onto one elbow. 'As you've even managed to change, Clifford, you must have found your cabin. Are you going to be comfortable in your little billet aboard?'

He pursed his lips. 'Disgracefully so, my lady. For I am sharing a cabin, it seems, with Monsieur Voltaire, an eminent gentleman philosopher who died, I believe, in 1778. You have purchased the second ticket, at great expense, purely on my account.'

She shrugged. 'Don't be cross, Clifford. I only wanted you to have a treat and the chance to relax. You're such a private and precise man that I feared being forced to share a cabin with a stranger who might have any number of shudder-inducing habits would spoil your whole trip. Instead, as you do usually retire with one of Voltaire's works of an evening, I thought it fitting you should share a cabin with him.'

'Beyond thoughtful, my lady. However, it is also beyond inappropriate for a mere butler to have a cabin to himself.'

She sighed. 'Maybe one day you'll realise you are far from a mere butler to my mind. Just as you were to Uncle Byron's.'

'Thank you sincerely, my lady. The household accounts, nevertheless, will take some time to recover.'

She spread her hands. 'Then you can delight in saving up all your chidings for when we return and you insist I go through the ledgers.'

His lips twitched. 'Thank you sincerely, my lady. For both treats.'

'Excellent! I'm so impressed with what I've seen so far, I can't wait to see the rest of the ship. It has everything one needs for the perfect impromptu birthday celebration. I think I might almost be glad Hugh cancelled!'

He raised a brow but said nothing.

'Well, almost,' she muttered.

He coughed. 'Actually, I must say I am not pleased with one item. The cabin boy called to say a number of them were taken sick just yesterday and he will have to do duty for several cabins. I remonstrated...' He stopped and scanned her face. 'Perhaps that is for another time. If, instead, I were to regale you with the long list of extremely diverting on-board activities available, might you forget a certain gentleman for a while?'

She shook her head. 'Is my face betraying me again? Never mind, it is a splendid idea. Go ahead.'

He cleared his throat. 'The *Celestiana* has all that one could require to savour the time on one's way to New York. Indoor and outdoor games, including shuffleboard, cricket, deck quoits, bull board and tennis are available and there is a "Sports Challenge" that runs for the duration of the voyage.' He continued on down his memorised list of the ship's facilities as he handed her a glass of port and set a trio of dried fruits, walnuts and olives beside her. 'There is also a squash court, swimming pool and Turkish baths as well as a gymnasium furnished with the very latest exercise equipment.'

She waggled a finger at him. 'All sounds fabulously invigorating, but I thought I was expected to languish about elegantly, exerting myself about as much as a dying duck? Even I've grasped that ladies of the manor on glamorous cruises are not supposed to maraud about with their hair stuck to their foreheads, looking all drippy and sweaty in gymnasiums.'

He groaned quietly. '"Glistening." Ladies "glisten" whilst gliding around a sports court or gymnasium, my lady. Perhaps, therefore, I might hasten on to the more ladylike pursuits available, such as enjoying any of the three films shown daily at the particularly fine cinema. There is also a programme of events, which includes a host of concerts and a grand ball.' He placed a card in her hand. 'The full list of which has been printed in the ship's own print room. However, the ultimate diversion I have yet to detail. The meals.'

She sat up. 'Now that's more like it!'

'Indeed. The kitchens aboard the *Celestiana* are run by a highly renowned restaurateur who insisted that this remarkable craft be fitted with a custom-made oven range. It is over one hundred feet in length and incorporates seventeen ovens. And at the helm of this feat of culinary engineering is' – he nodded approvingly – 'none other than Chef Pierre Barsalou.'

'Should that mean something to me?'

'Yes, my lady,' he replied wearily. 'If, that is, you had

conceded to join high society at any point since acquiring Henley Hall.'

'I will, I will. One day.' She avoided his gaze. 'It's all just a bit formal.'

'Which,' he said drily, 'is entirely the point.'

4

Clifford's suggestion that Eleanor take a stroll around the deck while he finished unpacking had been more of an entreaty than a suggestion. He was the master of the meticulous, the absolute chalk to her cheese. So her following behind him, reminding him she'd travelled for years with only a pair of saddlebags for her clothes and a worn bicycle saddle for comfort, had started to chafe the very starch from his collar.

In truth, the sea air had been calling to her since the first salty whisper had wafted through the taxi window as they'd arrived in Southampton. After growing up aboard her parents' boat, even the merest hint of that familiar tang transported her back. Back to the young girl who would be found every morning hanging over the bow rail in her pyjamas, delighting in the waves of white horses – and sometimes dolphins – breaking left and right below.

On deck she soon realised, however, that she was alone among the other first-class passengers in finding the sea anything of a draw. They seemed to find the opening event of the Sports Challenge a far greater attraction. Many, in fact, had thrown decorum to the wind and were already competing in earnest, accompanied by vivacious music miraculously spilling from four electrified pole-mounted loudhailers. And in a dance contest at that, the object of which seemed to be to cavort and strut as outrageously as one dared.

Her gaze was drawn to a dark-haired set of curls fluttering below a rakishly low fedora snaking across the dance floor with bewitching grace and speed. Arms dipping and swirling, his feet were a blur, yet, as his unbuttoned suit jacket fanned out after his every turn, what she could see of his torso remained entirely still.

Intrigued, she slid along the handrail until she had drawn level with him, which she instantly regretted. As he danced towards her, his broad shoulders flexing and contracting above a tantalising trim waist and swirling hips, it dawned. He was the man whose rear view she'd caught in the lift. The one whose strikingly athletic form had given her the sharpest reminder of her absent beau.

Forcing herself to gaze out at the grey-green March sea, she chided her overwhelming desire to do nothing but watch this man dance. But not just because he resembled her beau. What she'd been able to see of his face was harder-jawed, his lips thinner, his chin split with a deep dimple. There was something else about him. Something so magnetic, it was drawing her to him like a hummingbird to nectar.

'Talk about fickle affections, Ellie!' she muttered as she failed to resist peeping back at the dancer. It had been less than ten minutes ago that she'd told Clifford she'd come on the cruise to enjoy herself. Not to dwell on the fact that the man she had fallen for seemed more wedded to his work than he ever would be to her. But forgetting about him so quickly in giddy attraction to another felt beyond shameful.

It was at that moment she noticed a curvaceous raven-haired woman close to her in age, standing arms folded only a few feet away. Her elaborately dressed dark tresses and silver mink draped around her swan-like neck framed her flawless olive skin. She seemed to be watching the dancer with admiration as well. Suddenly, she looked at Eleanor, tossed her head and strode off.

Did she catch you staring at her, Ellie?

Before she could decide, she noticed someone else was also studying the star of the Sports Challenge. A middle-aged woman of rather overbearing stance summoned the nearby steward with a beckoning finger. Eleanor tried not to gawp as the woman hid that she was dropping coins into his waiting hand. This was followed by a nod in the dancer's direction who she now realised had flopped into a deckchair, the music having stopped. In a trice, the steward set up two deckchairs beside the man.

'Two?' Eleanor muttered to herself.

As the older woman marched towards the seats, a girl of barely twenty came into view and trailed after what Eleanor was sure was her mother, given their similar build. Shaking her head, Eleanor returned to her cabin.

Back in her suite, she found everything unpacked and in meticulous order. Which was just as well, as she had to decide what to wear to that evening's pre-dinner champagne reception. Settling on her new emerald-green crossover beaded gown, she relaxed until it was time to attend the reception.

And what a reception it was. The first-class lounge was the peak of refined luxury, although her first impression of it was one of... chairs! They must surely have been breeding while the captain's back was turned. Plump settees, luxurious armchairs, leather wingbacks, upright reading chairs, reclining colonial seats and even tempting daybeds were dotted around a plethora of polished tables. And all were upholstered in matching jade, indigo and silver velvet stripes.

Gracing the centre of this vast, but still homely, space, was an ebony grand piano and above it the room's masterpiece – its ceiling. The central oval was a work of art in ivory plaster relief as cherubs flew among billowing clouds and angels danced across the heavens. On one side was a curved stained-glass canopy and on the other nine individual domes in the ship's signature indigo.

Taking a flute of champagne from the smart, white-jacketed waiter, she glanced at her fellow passengers, recognising several famous faces. Thinking she needed to start introducing herself around, she hesitantly adjusted the bodice of her dress, then turned at the sound of a pair of heels clicking softly behind her.

'Good evening, madam.' She turned to see a dark-skinned man in his early forties, as upright as the ivory column by which he stood. From his thinning black-brown dome of raked back hair, his faintly lined forehead had been abruptly interrupted by his prominent angular nose, which ended where his equally pointed chin began. Behind his grey-tinted horn-rimmed spectacles, she could just make out one of his blue-brown eyes holding her gaze animatedly. Peculiarly, the other seemed to be in a far more sullen mood.

'It is glass,' he said genially with a thick Eastern-European accent she couldn't place precisely. She flinched as he flipped up the right-hand lens of his spectacles and tapped the eye behind.

'Forgive me,' she said, embarrassed that she had been so obviously scrutinising his face.

'Not at all, dear lady. We are who we are.' The man wore a collarless, brass-buttoned, knee-length cobalt jacket over a frilled red shirt. Quickly she dragged her gaze away from his form-fitting knickerbockers and the black stockings running down to his slipper-style shoes adorned with large ornamental buckles.

'I'm sorry, I don't know your name.'

He stood even straighter. 'Forgive me. Count Ottokar Friedrich Balog presents himself. Although, unfortunately, I am currently dispossessed of my lands, so I am a count without portfolio, as it were.'

'And I am Lady Eleanor Swift.' Her curiosity got the better of her. 'Are you travelling to America to resettle then, Count Balog, after you... had trouble in your homeland? For which, my sincere condolences and sympathies. It can't be easy.'

'Actually no. And yes.' He gestured to the nearest set of chairs. She slid into one of the wingbacks, which reminded her of her beloved Uncle Byron's favourite seat in Henley Hall's library back home. He settled himself in the middle of the three-seater settee opposite, taking several moments to carefully arrange the tails of his lengthy jacket on a cushion either side. 'I say to you, Lady Swift, no, I do not wish to see America. I wish to ride only forwards and back on this wonderful vessel as I have done with the other ships. For, to continue without my lands, what endeavours do I have left? None! So' – his one good eye positively sparkled as he clapped his hands together – 'I have become the new man. Otto, the playboy!'

This made her sit back in surprise. 'Sounds fun.'

'Dear lady, it is like the whole roast beef pie with the icing on top, I think you say?'

She laughed. 'Almost. So you mostly just jolly back and forth on boats such as the *Celestiana*?'

'Jolly, no! I work. Although, work can be fun, I say. I have no shame to tell you I make a fine income taking money from your fellow English and Americans who have far, far too much. And far, far too little sense to keep it.' Now she was completely flummoxed, which obviously showed in her face. 'The card tables, dear lady! Oh yes, they are the place you will find me all the times of the day and the night.' He studied her intently for a moment. 'But, I think you are the unusual English lady, so maybe you also like to play?' Before she could reply, he tapped his imposing nose so hard she was sure she could hear it resonate. 'A warning, however. There are a pair of card sharps aboard.'

Having no idea how to ask diplomatically, she decided to just bite the bullet. 'Umm, of which you have sort of suggested you might be one?'

That drew a surprisingly high whinny of a laugh. 'No, no, Lady Swift. I have no need to cheat. I play fair. Only better!'

'And the captain doesn't—'

'Throw me off? Indeed not! I am well known on all the best liners. Gambling is between gentlemen. It is none of the business of the ship's company. They do nothing about the card sharps either except warn passengers, as I have you.'

A polite cough interrupted their conversation. They both looked up.

'Might we join your table, do you suppose?' a stiff upper-lipped man enquired from below his over-trimmed fair-haired moustache. His question had been delivered in that unique tone which was the singular preserve of old Etonians and other prestigious English boys' schools. Barely reaching his dinner-jacketed shoulder, the pale bird of a woman in all-encompassing grey silk beside him fingered her five strings of pearls and offered a hopeful smile.

'But of course,' Eleanor said more brightly than she felt, recognising the man as the one whose hat she had knocked off on the quayside.

'Take your preference, madam, sir,' Balog said, standing and gesturing at the seats nearby.

The couple lowered themselves into two stiff-backed, armless chairs on either side of Eleanor.

'Sir Gerald and Lady Caroline Wrenshaw-Smythe,' the man said.

'Lady Eleanor Swift.' She held her hand out, which was received reluctantly by him, and with all the strength of a butterfly by his wife. 'And this is Count Balog.'

'Who sees you have no champagne!' he said in a horrified tone. 'Allow me.' He waved at the gold-tray bearing waiter.

'No, thank you!' Sir Gerald said curtly. 'My wife and I abstain, naturally.'

'Naturally,' Eleanor said, trying to ignore that the count seemed to be taking inordinate delight in savouring the last of his. Lifting two more from the tray as it arrived, he set one before Eleanor and beamed at the couple.

'Pleasure or business is it that brings you to sail today?'

The husband cast him a disapproving look. 'Business, of course. One does not fritter one's time away.'

'And what line of business are you in?' Eleanor said, hoping they might find easier conversational ground.

Before they could reply, however, the count leaned forward. 'Wait! Like all men, I like to wager.' He traced Sir Gerald's facial features with his finger, ignoring the snort of disapproval his comment had drawn. Then he made them all jump as he slapped the table. 'Three guesses! Number one, your business is the theatre. Something to do with those marvellous variety hall acts?'

'Categorically not,' Sir Gerald barked. His wife looked at her husband in horrified embarrassment. Before Sir Gerald could add anything further, the count jumped in again. 'Alright then, guess number two. Literature. Those stories we read in the little serials. Oh, the name I forget! Penny something...'

'Dreadfuls!' Lady Caroline gasped.

'Sir,' Sir Gerald said in a sharp tone. 'I find the flavour of your "game" unsavoury. If we might move on?'

'Naturally,' the count said, mimicking Sir Gerald's clipped accent so well Eleanor bit her lip. 'Straight after my last guess.'

Sir Gerald rose and offered his wife his elbow. 'Please excuse us. I bid you an enjoyable evening. Just as ours will be, engaged elsewhere.'

Eleanor watched them march off towards another table at the furthest end of the lounge.

'You intended to offend them?' she said incredulously.

He looked shocked. 'Goodness, no. Only to discourage.'

She shook her head. 'But why?'

He laughed. 'So, Lady Swift is the novice of the cruise. Dear lady, we are locked in a box. A pretty floating palace of a box, yes, but a box nonetheless. We cannot get off. Neither can we choose who else is in the box that we must sit, eat and play along beside. All we can do is protect our corner from the bores, the over-chattersome who have nothing to actually say' – he nodded in the direction of the departed couple – 'and the bloated frogs.'

Eleanor laughed into her champagne, which she regretted as the bubbles tickled her nose and made her eyes water. Feeling sure she must need to tidy her face, she rose. 'Count Balog, it has been an education. And a pleasure, though it really shouldn't have been.'

Leaving him to rearrange his jacket tails once more, she hurried towards the doors she thought she had come through but then stopped to spin around. Hadn't the indigo domes been on the right side of the ceiling?

'It's confusing, isn't it?' a smooth voice called from nowhere. 'You came in that way. I noticed your entrance.' With a confident shake of dark curls, her dancing star from the sports contest appeared from behind a pillar and walked out of the room, calling over his shoulder, 'And I never forget a face as pretty as yours.'

5

The late evening wind whistling down the barely lit section of the promenade deck was bitingly cold and forceful enough to whip Eleanor's hair into her eyes. But it was also invigorating. She needed some air and a sea wind is like no other. She knew that of old. Who could say how far it had travelled or what strange sights and lands it had seen? A small frisson for the life of adventure she'd left behind ran through her.

Left behind, Ellie? Nonsense! At the end of this already fascinating boat journey, vibrant, teeming New York awaits! Who knows what adventures you'll get up to? After all, you'll be another year older.

'But will I be any the wiser?' she whispered to the wind.

At the glimmer of the crescent moon momentarily released from its screen of thick clouds, she continued forward. As she reached the section where the deck widened out, peppered with mountains of neatly lashed deckchairs between the dim lighting, she was still ruminating on her fast-approaching birthday.

Who would she be? A thirty-two-year-old woman, brought up by bohemian parents, who still felt more like the wild-spirited adolescent girl who'd jumped on a bicycle one day to explore the world? The one eternally grateful for all her wonderful blessings? Or a proper lady of the manor, throwing lavish parties and socialising with the rich and famous?

Now, she realised why she had come out to the promenade deck before heading on into the dining room. Even on a bitter March night in the middle of the Atlantic, outdoors was always her haven. The place to clear her thoughts. Or to simply hurl them into the wind in the hope they would have arranged themselves into something less confusing in the calm of the morning. With unladylike gusto, she mimed throwing overboard any notions of being sensible or making decisions until after her birthday. Peering down through the inky gloom, past the eight lower decks, she imagined how they would be swallowed up by the bottomless depths the *Celestiana* was steaming through. *Just like those poor people on the* Titanic, *Ellie.* She shuddered. It had been eleven years ago, but the legacy of the *Titanic's* tragic end still cast its shadow over every new liner's maiden voyage.

Pulling her sage-green cashmere wrap tighter around her barely covered shoulders, she shivered. But perhaps not just with the cold. There was no sign of anyone anywhere, but something was making the hairs on her neck stand up. The only sound was the low throb of the engines and the distant crash of waves far below. And as the moonlight came and went, long shadows crept up the white walls to the base of the funnels, looking like giant clawed hands with malevolent, silhouetted faces. Being alone on this vast and abandoned deck suddenly lost its appeal.

She spun on her heel but jerked to a hesitant stop. A movement had caught her eye mid-turn. Two shadows twisted and danced on the side of the nearest funnel. She glanced around the ship's deck, but it was empty except for her. Mesmerised, she watched the shadows... *fighting, Ellie!*

She tried to cry out, but it died in her throat as the shadows broke apart and the unmistakable silhouette of a revolver loomed menacingly large. The second shadow's distended hands rose slowly. Then, in a flash, the heart-stopping crack of a bullet rang out.

Eleanor's hands flew to her mouth. All she could hear now was the pounding of blood in her ears. She ran forward, watching as the taller shadow clutched its stomach before stumbling backwards. The other shadow had frozen. But as if suddenly electrified, it sprung forward to shove the staggering form over the handrail.

'NO!' Too fuelled by adrenaline to think of self-preservation, she ran around the last of the steel deck wall and past the lifeboat to where she was sure the shadow's origin had been. But there was no one. She rushed to the rail and peered down into the impenetrable blackness. Grabbing a life vest, she flung it – futilely, she knew – over the side. She stared down again, but only the same all-engulfing darkness stared back at her. She turned to sprint around to the starboard deck to throw more life vests out, but hit something solid.

'What the—'

'You alright, miss?' The sailor in front of her held up his lantern.

She steadied herself, the collision having partly winded her.

'Man overboard,' she gasped. 'Shot!'

'We know, miss. Middle watch heard the gun go off.' The moon face beneath the smart cap loomed closer, the disturbing orange from the lamp's glow picking out every weathered furrow contouring his features. 'You sure you're alright?'

The pounding of two other sets of ship's boots arrived.

'Anyone see which way the shooter went?' a salt-roughened voice called.

'No. But he didn't pass me that way.'

'Nor us, this.'

'Must have bolted down to the next deck!' The other sailors ran off into the dark.

'Bad business, to be sure,' the lantern-toting sailor said gravely. 'I should escort you inside. This way, please.'

She nodded and went to follow him, but there was the sound of more boots and shouts back the other way. The sailor hesitated. 'Please stay here, miss. I'll be back in one moment.' He turned and ran in the direction of his colleagues.

Still in shock, she went to move away from the handrail where the man had been shot, but stopped at the sound of something spinning away where she'd kicked it with the satin toe of her evening shoe. She glanced in the direction the sailor had gone and then bent down and picked it up. As she did so, she gasped. It was a revolver.

The one used to shoot the man who went overboard!

Then she blinked, her mind refusing to accept what it saw. For on the handle was a distinctive nick.

You must be wrong, Ellie! It can't be.

But even as she said it to herself, she knew it was.

6

_____

'Really, I wish there was more I could tell you, but that's everything I saw. Right up until I collided with the first of your watchmen.' She paused in pacing past the steely-faced sailor beside the door, the one she'd seen outside the Regal Suite who sported more stripes to his navy uniform jacket than any other save for the captain. 'We need to be searching the sea, as I keep saying.'

'There are men already engaged in that, as *I* keep saying,' the sailor said stiffly.

Captain Bracebridge had introduced him as the master-at-arms, the equivalent of the head of police on board the *Celestiana*.

She turned to where the captain was sitting behind his oak desk, still noting down the latest recounting of what she'd witnessed. She'd told him everything except one tiny detail. And she hoped desperately that her face hadn't betrayed her. Thankfully, it appeared that just for once, it hadn't.

The captain nodded. 'Most comprehensive, Lady Swift. And the details of your accounts match exactly. I must compliment you on your powers of observation and memory.' He smiled apologetically. 'I hope there was no feeling you were being interrogated, as that could not have been further from my intention.' He pointed to a framed photograph of himself with a military-uniformed crew aboard the deck of an iron turret ship. 'It's an old navy habit of mine to insist upon three consecutive recountings.'

'Every word of which you laboriously wrote down each time.' She cocked her head. 'So my brain would relax in the knowledge that nothing it thought pertinent had been missed by the end of the second telling and offer anything buried beneath in the third?'

'Disconcertingly shrewd of you.' He leaned forward and gestured for her to take a seat. She shook her head vehemently. 'Captain, you've ordered enough of your men to search for the shooter. The rest of them should be scouring the sea for any sign of—'

The captain raised his hand as the master-at-arms went to speak. 'At the risk of sounding insensitive, Lady Swift, I repeat, I have turned the *Celestiana* around. Against my better judgement, I might add, as the man not only fell overboard without a buoyancy aid as far as we know, but more to the point he had been shot in the stomach. You yourself reported this. Still, I have dispatched a lifeboat crew to search as well as they can in the dark. However, at the twenty-two knot speed we were motoring – and with the thick fog created by the convergence of the warm and cold currents along that stretch – there is no guarantee we are within miles of where his body is likely to be. With apologies for being so blunt, Lady Swift.'

He's right, Ellie. And you know from your sailing days that a healthy man overboard in cold, choppy seas might survive a few hours at best with a lifejacket. He might even be found. But at night without any aid and injured...

'Actually, you're wrong.' The wobble in her voice gave away the guilt already coursing through her at having been too rooted in horror to have intervened in time. 'He didn't topple over like a lifeless corpse would have. Therefore, he's still alive until we know otherwise and not "a body".'

The captain stared at her oddly. 'Lady Swift, please forgive my saying that I anticipated finding something of the unexpected in you. Especially after Mr Walker contacted me to expound on why he was so delighted you had accepted his invitation. But in person, you are, well, surprising in the extreme.' He tailed off, holding his hands up. 'Primary example. You have not succumbed to anything even on nodding terms with a fit of the vapours after what you witnessed. Nevertheless, a restorative to quell the shock, perhaps?' With a sharp tug, he opened the left-hand drawer of his desk and produced a half bottle of brandy and a glass.

'No, thank you,' she said firmly. 'I am fine. However, I imagine my butler might think otherwise.'

The master-at-arms snorted. 'Your butler. Six foot in stature, commanding demeanour, won't take no for an answer?'

'Now that's astute,' she said.

The master-at-arms shook his head. 'No, Lady Swift. It was he then, who buttonholed me on my way to the bridge the moment we slowed the engines to turn around. He demanded in no uncertain terms that I furnish him immediately with confirmation of your safe whereabouts.'

'Then do not let me detain either of you any further.' She turned back to the captain's desk to collect her dress purse. 'I'm sure you will have a lot of explaining to do once the passengers realise what's happened.'

Captain Bracebridge rose. 'My job is to make up the time the *Celestiana* has lost. This is her maiden voyage and she will reach New York on schedule. In the meantime, my master-at-arms will discover who is missing, but that will take at least until late tomorrow morning, I would imagine.'

'And until then?'

'For all the passengers, life aboard will continue as normal. Only you and the middle watch could have heard the shot. The master-at-arms has confirmed no one else was in the vicinity. Apart from, that is, the two persons involved in the incident, of course. Therefore, the passengers will be told we stopped to check if someone had fallen overboard, nothing more.' He held her scrutinising gaze. 'Lady Swift, no one aboard the *Celestiana*'s crucial maiden voyage will have their wonderful experience tainted by unsavoury news. I have assured Mr Walker that there will be no blemish on the ship's first – and most important – journey.'

She nodded. 'I understand Mr Walker's concern – and your position, Captain. Now, I really must return to my cabin to reassure my butler that it wasn't me overboard!'

Her door sprang open before she reached it. 'My lady, that seemed an age. It is a quarter to one in the morning. Are you alright?' Clifford ushered her inside. Beside the blanket on the chaise longue, a crystal brandy decanter and glass, a jar of tablets, and a large bar of chocolate stood in a meticulous line like a regiment of nursing staff.

'I'm fine, thank you.' She sat and ruffled her bulldog's ears as he scrabbled up her legs.

Clifford leaned down to scan her face as he passed her a warmed brandy. 'Hmm, "fine" as in, "deeply perturbed by more than whatever necessitated the captain detaining you for such an inappropriate length of time?" But please do not consider I am prying.'

'Thank you, Clifford. For caring enough to pry and for so ferociously accosting the master-at-arms to check I wasn't the one shot and pushed overboard.' She held a hand up at his startled look. 'I don't have time to explain further, but I'll be good and stay here until you return. If I can press you into

completing a task, that is? One you must undertake with absolute discretion.'

'Most assuredly. However, might I have your absolute word
that you will remain locked in here? And open the door only on
an agreed signal?' The firm look that accompanied this request
made her smile. She knew it was driven purely by his desire to
fulfil his promise to her beloved uncle in his final moments. The
one that he would do all he could to keep her safe.

After all, Ellie, you have just told him someone was shot!

'I promise, Clifford.'

'Then I shall hasten to my task. Which is, my lady?'

'I need you to...' She beckoned him forward so she could
whisper the rest of her request in his ear, more to hide her
sudden rush of emotion than out of any chance they might be
overheard.

He pulled back, a brow arched. 'You are sure?' She
shrugged. He nodded. 'I understand. As expeditiously as I can,
then. Though you may need to entertain patience. It may not be
a speedy task, my lady. Particularly at this hour of the morning.'
With a bow from the shoulders, and a whispered, 'Henley
Hall's telephone number as our safety signal,' he was gone in a
swish of suit tails.

The gift of patience had been in very short supply the day
Eleanor was born. And, as Clifford had often hinted at, the little
she'd been granted she had used up long before the age of ten.

'Almost two hours he's been gone, Gladstone, old chum,' she
muttered. 'He's the epitome of efficiency, I know. But—' The
tapped out 'three-four-two' code she'd been holding her breath
for interrupted her.

'Oh thank heavens! It's Clifford.' She tugged him inside by
his jacket sleeve, ignoring his disapproving tut. 'Success?'

'Indeed, my lady. Second class seemed the best bet, so I

started there and it turned up trumps. I also discreetly engaged the help of our ladies in the name of expediency. Mrs Butters being the one to cleverly discover that the cabin number you seek is E34. And it seems, like my own, it is single occupancy.' He shook his head. 'I fail to understand, however, how you knew—'

She held up her hand. 'As I said before, there's no time to explain. Let's go.'

The full awfulness of the situation Clifford had now unwittingly confirmed made her stomach clench as they hurried along silent corridors towards the second-class cabins.

'The last cabin door on the left,' Clifford said sotto voce, indicating yet another narrow passageway. 'I shall wait outside, my lady. To check the coast is clear, please knock once when you are done.'

She nodded and, knowing that no amount of deep breaths or prevaricating would help, marched determinedly to the door. She tapped on it quietly, given the early morning hour and the clandestine nature of her task.

Only silence answered. She knocked again, as loudly as she dared this time.

After a few moments, the door was unlocked and opened a crack.

'Eleanor?' an unfamiliarly weak voice croaked. 'Tell me I'm hallucinating?'

'It's good to see you too, Hugh!' she said drily.

Play fair, Ellie. You've appeared out of nowhere.

The door swung open more widely revealing Chief Inspector Hugh Seldon, his skin pallid and tinged with seasickness, his eyes sunken. She'd forgotten what a terrible sailor he was.

But why is he on board at all, Ellie?

He glanced hurriedly up and down the corridor, acknowledging Clifford's presence with a nod, then beckoned her in.

Scanning back along the corridor, he closed the door quickly, leaning against it.

'Eleanor, you... you shouldn't be here!'

She shrugged. 'Clifford's playing chaperone outside, as you just saw. It's fine.' Her gaze took in the two narrow bunks dressed simply with cream linen and blue blankets occupying either side of the modest white-walled space. His eyes followed hers.

'That's not what I meant. I meant why on earth... I mean how on earth...' He broke off, following her gaze. 'And there is no one else in here. Second class wasn't full, so I took the whole cabin for myself. For... for some extra pounds.' He winced through the last of his words, leaning against the wall, swallowing repeatedly. With evident effort, he shook himself and turned one of the two simple wooden chairs towards her. 'Please, have a seat. And forgive my initial horror... my... my surprise. Oh blast it!' Not moving from her side, he ran his eyes over her face. His expression softened, offering a glimmer of the hopelessly awkward man who'd made her heart skip long before he'd stammered out any suggestion he had feelings for her. 'Let me start again,' he said more gently. 'It's always the best treat in the world to see you. More than that, actually. It's become the only thing I look forward to, in truth.' A flush of colour momentarily infused his drawn cheeks. 'But, Eleanor, you really shouldn't be h—'

'Neither of us should be here, Hugh,' she said as calmly as she could. 'We had other plans. Plans you cancelled for something fearfully more important.'

He closed his eyes with a sigh. 'For which I will be forever sorry. Truly.' He reached out again and this time, his hand closed over hers, his strong fingers caressing her palm. 'It wasn't more important, but something I couldn't... leave undone.'

'Hugh, please sit before you fall over,' she said in concern, as he paled even further. 'And then tell me why, instead of being at home packing ready to whisk me off for a birthday treat away with you, you're on the *Celestiana*, sailing to New York?'

He nodded. 'An explanation is the very least I owe you. And then maybe you could reveal how you come to be here!' He took the other chair, failing on even his third attempt to fold his long legs underneath.

Whatever the explanation was, it seemed to require a deep breath and an uncharacteristic inability to hold her gaze for more than a second. When it came, it was blurted out more gruffly than any words she'd ever heard him utter. 'I'm on an undercover assignment to shadow a complete wretch we are extremely suspicious of but can't arrest yet on account of insufficient evidence against him. I'm shadowing him in the hope I... *we* can find that evidence before he reaches America and' – he swallowed hard – 'we lose him. For good.' He seemed lost in his own thoughts for a moment. Then he shook his head and shuffled forward. 'Your turn. What the dickens are you doing here, halfway across the Atlantic?' At her hesitation, he sighed. 'Are you wondering, perhaps, if you paced the entire journey on deck in your favourite green Oxford flats with the leather detailing, you might have calmed down enough to consider still talking to me when you return?'

This clearly unintended revelation that he'd quietly taken so much notice of her shoes made her smile. 'Not far off, if I'm honest. Thomas Walker sent me a complimentary ticket, you see, and I was thinking of accepting until I got the much better offer to spend my birthday with you. And once you cancelled, well...' She shrugged. 'I thought rather than mope around, I'd come after all.'

'Ah, your old boss. I see.' He managed a wan smile, but it faded as he leaned forward again, his stance suddenly every inch the detective chief inspector she'd first fallen foul of a few years back. 'Now, tell me how on earth you knew I was on this boat? It's not supposed to be common knowledge, blast it!'

'I didn't, Hugh.' His already rather haunted expression fell even further as she pulled away from him. 'Not until I witnessed a... a murder.'

He jerked out of his seat to reach for her hand. 'A *murder?*' He frowned. 'Of course! The ship slowing down. The crew running around outside.' He glanced back at her. 'I thought it was just a man overboard.'

She nodded grimly. 'It was, Hugh. But he didn't fall. He was shot.' She pulled out the revolver she'd picked up off the deck. 'With your gun.'

7

Eleanor's eyes jerked open. 'Oh, gracious!'

Forcing herself to sit up in her bed, she shuddered as she rubbed her face vigorously, imagining she was washing away the horrifying image. The image of a man callously shot and pushed overboard. She rubbed her eyes again, wishing she could equally erase her deeply unsettling conversation with Seldon. Her now more unfathomable-than-ever beau. The one who lived such a different life to her. But also the one who had made her heart skip and her stomach clench in equal measure. Especially when she'd gone to leave his cabin and he'd pulled her gently against his chest with a whispered, 'Good night' without being able to meet her gaze.

She shook her head and groaned. It wasn't that she didn't believe his explanations the night before. It was just that they were so obviously part-explanations. She had got the impression that the parts he'd left out were what she really needed to hear, and that worried her.

Swinging her legs reluctantly to the floor to meet the day, she draped her cashmere shawl over her silk pyjama-clad shoulders. Padding out into the sitting room, she was met only by disappointing silence. Before she'd had a chance to take in the innovative electric heater throwing out golden rays of warmth, she cocked her head at a sudden realisation. Gladstone hadn't been in his bed in her room.

At that moment, a solid whirlwind of delighted bulldog appeared from nowhere and bowled her backwards into the nearest velvet armchair.

'Morning, old chum,' she panted as he pressed her into the seat.

'My sincere apologies, my lady,' called an invisible measured voice. 'I have just returned from Master Gladstone's perambulation around the deck.'

'Why are you apologising for that, Clifford?'

'Because, I'm afraid I come as the bearer of bad news.'

'Oh no!' she gasped, trying to wrestle herself upright and out of the bulldog's licky reach at the same time. 'Not another unthinkable happening?'

'Regrettably so.' There was an excruciating pause. 'You have slept right through the last serving of breakfast.'

'You total terror!' She knew his teasing was intended to ease her depressed mood. 'Please emerge from wherever you are hiding so I can play the outraged mistress card properly.'

This received only questioning silence in reply.

She rolled her eyes. 'Yes, Mr Chivalrous, I am suitably over-attired despite having just blundered out of bed disgracefully late. However, to save your blushes, I'll put my robe on as well.'

When she popped back out, he was gone, but a note poked out from the top of the bathroom door's brass plaque:

Desperate breakfast foraging mission underway, my lady. Bath prepared.

As she pulled back the first four slats of the concertinaed

wood panel covering the bath, a cloud of rose and lavender-scented steam swirled up to cup her face.

When she re-emerged from the bathroom and then bedroom, her spirits had regained a fair amount of their usual bounce, as had her red curls, which now skipped like sun-burned summer clouds. They were also even more striking against her new sea-green silk knit dress which flattered her slender figure, its emerald velvet piping highlighting the drop-waist pleated skirt and fashionable sailor's collar.

'Welcome back, my lady,' Clifford said approvingly. He gestured her towards the marquetry inlaid breakfast table he'd set with a charming centrepiece of three linen napkins folded into a flotilla of little sailing boats. 'Will rich roast coffee, crème de cassis infused fruit compote and honey Vienna rolls topped with smoked salmon curls be acceptable?'

'Acceptable, no. Perfect, yes.' She took a sip of coffee and then, not knowing where to start on unburdening her jumbled thoughts, just started.

Clifford stood, hands behind his back, listening attentively. When she'd finished, he arched a brow.

'It was, perhaps, not your easiest conversation with the chief inspector, my lady?'

She smiled ruefully. 'Ever the master of understatement, Clifford! It was, in fact, distressingly awkward. I mean, as if finding out Hugh had cancelled our plans for my birthday so he could maraud across the high seas on the *Celestiana* wasn't bad enough, it seemed he was also more horrified than pleased to see me. Although maybe not so much by the end. But more discon-certing is the business of him refusing to divulge anything other than that he's here on an undercover mission.' She bit her lip. He'd been a shadow of his former self. 'He's in terrible shape, Clifford. And that was before I blurted out that I'd found his gun at the murder scene. I confess as I said it, it made me wonder if he hadn't been the one to... to pull the trigger...' She tailed off as her cheeks coloured in shame at the thought.

'Ah!'

'Ah, what?'

'It is your wish that I render an opinion, my lady?' At her nod, Clifford held up four white-gloved fingers. Starting with the fourth, he counted them off. 'One. Pirates are the only reprobates to "maraud" the high seas, not policemen in my experience, especially those of the inspector's eminent reputation. Two. The surprise of your highly unexpected and late-evening appearance at his cabin door would have clouded the effusiveness and delicacy of any gentleman's response. We both saw first-hand on the Scotland sojourn last Christmas how significantly the inspector suffers with seasickness. Three. If the gentleman had been the one to, ahem, dispatch the man you regrettably witnessed being shot, he would have had the highest moral reason to do so.'

'I never questioned that. And I believed him on the spot when he stuttered out in horror that he hadn't been the one to pull the trigger. And when he said he was completely unaware anyone had even been murdered. It's just that... well, as he wouldn't expound even a little on his supposed undercover mission, I felt as though he was fobbing me off.'

'Reticence can have many rationales, my lady. Not least of which the muzzle of being a senior detective on a highly sensitive case, I would suggest.'

'True, but I sensed it was more than that.' She shook her head. 'A lot more. Anyway, number four?' She pointed her spoon at his un-ticked off fourth finger. But as he mimed buttoning his lip, she sighed. 'I know. Number four. I could have broken the news of finding his gun far more sympathetically, you're thinking?'

'I really couldn't say, my lady.'

She groaned. 'You just did. But rightly so, dash it! I bungled the whole conversation, didn't I? And probably made him feel worse than any seasickness could.'

Clifford topped up her coffee and shooed the eager-eyed Gladstone out from under her table. 'Perhaps consolation might be drawn that no "bungling" occurred during your conversation with Captain Bracebridge at least.'

'Really? You think so? Even after I'd relayed the whole thing to you before we eventually retired last night.'

'This morning, actually. And I do think so. Most pertinently, your non-disclosure of the gun found at the murder scene was particularly shrewd. As was ensuring you left the inspector's cabin entirely unobserved.'

'But not to protect my reputation, as you probably hoped. More for prudence. Imagine the furore if it had got back to the captain's ears that I'd immediately overruled his decree that none of the passengers would be told of the events last night? And that I'd done so by running straight to a senior policeman residing among his second-class guests! It's enough of a hideous mess already.'

'Prudence, my lady?' He pretended to look under the cushions of the settee and then behind the curtains. 'Any suggestions as to where I might find her so she might accompany you on a permanent basis?' At her mock huff, he waved his pocket watch at her. 'Fifteen minutes to Sunday Service. Where I believe you are in for another restorative. Though you may consider it rather under par compared to your emergency breakfast.'

She sighed. 'Whatever it is, I'll need it. I arranged to meet Hugh at twelve.'

Ten minutes later, Clifford's predicted restorative waved nervously at her from across the crowded reception room.

'It's the ladies!' Eleanor cheered in delight.

Clifford nodded. 'Indeed. Second-class passengers are always invited to join the upper deck for Sunday Service.'

She hurried up to her staff, who were hovering uncomfort-

ably at the rear door into the first-class lounge. Turned out in
their Sunday best, the four ladies made a smart line-up in their
long black skirts and highly polished ankle boots. Their starched
white frill-necked blouses were arranged to sit perfectly above the
top button of their fitted black-collared cardigans. Except Polly's,
Eleanor noted with a smile. Quiet affection for her loyal team of
five washed over her as Clifford twitched the end of his finger in
her maid's direction. Mrs Butters and Lizzie both jumped to, the
first redoing the young girl's misbuttoned fastenings, the other
rescuing her white frills from where they'd become tangled. In
unison, the women then curtseyed. 'Good morning, m'lady.'

'Good morning, ladies,' Eleanor said. 'How are we all?'

For a moment, even her usually forthright, ever garrulous
cook seemed lost for words. But their beaming faces and
sparkling eyes spoke greater volumes than any words could.

'Crumbs to heaven and back, m'lady!' Mrs Trotman finally
managed. 'Fancy the likes of us floating about in such a beautiful silver and gold palace as this! 'Tis like walking around in a
dream all the day!'

Polly's bottom lip trembled as she stammered in a barely
audible voice. 'But surely we shall soon be chased down to the
kitchens with a horsewhip as punishment for being so brazen as
to be up here, your ladyship?'

Eleanor smiled. 'It's alright, really, Polly. Clifford has been
rather remiss and left his horsewhip in his cabin this morning.'

This drew a round of stifled giggles, except from the young
maid, who stared at Clifford wide-eyed until he shook his head
gently. 'Her ladyship is teasing... me.' He arched a brow at
Eleanor. 'Five against one is fair game now, I see.' He caught her
eye, a silent agreement passing between them.

*Not a word about the murder, Ellie. Especially not that you
witnessed it. The ladies will only fret away their holiday on your
behalf.*

'So.' She clapped her hands. 'Tell me what you've been up to so far. Ah, but the repeatable bits only, perhaps.'

Through more giggles, they described life in second class, their shared cabin and the fun of joining in with the lower deck games. The extra animation in Lizzie's tone made her Scottish burr sound all the more delightful to Eleanor's ears.

'We won the team quoits yester eve before dinner, m'lady, and I'd never even heard o' it before.'

'So much fun, your ladyship.' Polly jiggled on the spot. 'And then after the plum pudding and jelly, Mrs Trotman beat two rounds of gentlemen at rummy!'

Eleanor laughed, having seen herself how fiendish her cook could be at cards. Mrs Butters chuckled as she gave the young girl a squeeze.

'Mind, if she gawps any harder at all the fancy folks, she'll need new eyeballs long afore we get home.'

'Tsk!' Mrs Trotman slid Eleanor a cheeky glance. 'Not that Butters isn't oohing and ahhing over every stitch of upholstery and fancy wood, now. Mind, 'tis all fit for princesses and no mistake.'

'What about meal times?' Eleanor said.

'Out of this world, m'lady,' Mrs Butters said. 'But Trotters had some words to share with our chef in second class, that's for sure!' She chuckled, nudging her friend in the ribs.

This drew a purse-lipped look from the cook. 'Only to set him right on the correct way to use herbs in sauce, m'lady. Terrible waste of flavour t'otherwise.'

Mrs Butters joined in with Eleanor's laughter. 'She's being a fusspot. Everything's been delicious and we've all had bigger appetites than a house of starved wolves. Must be the sea air though, m'lady, but Lizzie and Polly have been eating for two each!'

Only Eleanor noticed the maids sharing a brief worried

glance with each other before busying themselves with the hem of their cardigans.

'Have you had a chance to explore the lower decks at all?'

'Not yet,' Mrs Trotman said. ''Twas our plan after breakfast this morning but we got that tangled up in the chatter 'bout the poor person as went overboard, we'll have to go later.'

In her peripheral vision, Eleanor caught Clifford stiffen.

'You know how folks can be, m'lady,' Mrs Butters said. 'All manner of stories there be. Wild theories flying all over the ham and eggs.'

'Would've fair soured the bacon and kidneys if as anyone knew who it was,' Mrs Trotman added. 'Strange enough, though, no one has a clue.'

Someone does, Ellie. The man who pulled the trigger!

Lizzie leaned forward. 'The two tables around us both said as the person might have jumped on purpose.'

'Couldn't be. 'Tis a sin!' Polly clapped her hand over her mouth. 'Beg pardon, your ladyship.'

'It's alright, Polly,' Eleanor said gently. 'I just hope all the rumours aren't spoiling your trip?'

'Not a bit, m'lady. Nothing could,' Mrs Trotman said. She looked thoughtful for a moment and then continued, almost to herself, 'Mind, the sailors on the stairwells a'tween second and third class weren't quite so easy on the eye this morning.'

At Clifford's immediate series of sharp tuts, Eleanor's cook waved her hands. 'Oh lawks, no, Mr Clifford, sir! I only meant as it's unnerving when men are carrying,' she covered Polly's ears and whispered, 'guns! Even when they're supposedly tucked out of sight. But I saw 'em alright.'

Eleanor was tongue-tied over any plausible explanation she could offer. A frown of concern flitted across Mrs Butters' face. Clifford seamlessly came to the rescue. 'Nothing out of the ordinary there, Mrs Trotman. Not on a cruise with such prestigious passengers.' He leaned in conspiratorially. 'If you can all be trusted to keep a secret?' The four ladies crossed their hearts and nodded, mouths agape. He lowered his voice even further. 'The Regal Suite opposite her ladyship's is not... unoccupied.'

Mrs Butters gasped. 'Oh, my stars!'

Lizzie stared back at him. 'The likes of us on the same ship as...' She tailed off, miming a crown on her head.

'Service begins in five minutes!' a voice called.

'I'd better take my seat, ladies,' Eleanor said. She turned to Clifford. 'I'll catch up with you later.'

As she walked to the seats at the front reserved for first class, her eyes swept over the other passengers. *One of them in this room might be the murderer, Ellie. But which one?*

8

Back in her cabin, Eleanor rearranged the pleats of her skirt and re-tied the delicate velvet ribbons lacing her heeled suede pumps. She then returned to fanning out her sailor's collar once more, even though it had already been lying perfectly square to her tense shoulders.

Over by the mantel, Clifford was examining an elaborate gilt clock on top of which a female figurine was holding a tele-scope-like contraption. He slid his pince-nez back into his jacket pocket and turned to her.

'It is quite remarkable, my lady.'

'That Hugh could be so late, I know!' she said more huffily than intended. 'So don't try telling me off for being unpunctual in the future.'

'It is but six minutes past. I am sure the chief inspector will have a good reason to have kept his favourite lady waiting.'

'Well, whoever she is, when he's done with her, he'd better still crawl along here to explain himself.'

She caught the amused glint in his eyes in the decorative mirror above the marble-topped bureau. 'It wasn't intended as a joke, Clifford. I think I deserve a bit more explanation.'

'Indeed, my lady. However, I meant it is "quite remarkable" in reference to Jean-André Reiche's depiction of Urania measuring the heavens.' He pointed at the clock. 'It is, of course, a copy. The original dating between 1790 and 1793, if memory serves. See the quality of the dioptra, the instrument through which she is mapping the planets? A most innovative and superlative craftsman, Monsieur Reiche was considered France's master bronzier of the Empire period.'

Her butler's fascination with clocks always made her heart soften, borne as it was from his few happy childhood years growing up under the guardianship of a fanatical clockmaker. It was a rare snippet of his past he had uncharacteristically confessed to her one troubled evening.

'Monsieur Reiche, my lady, was also renowned for striving to imbue every one of his horological works of art with his greatest gift to the world – his limitless patience.'

She laughed at her butler's mischievous humour. 'Well, it's not my fault I'm as itchy as nettle rash.'

Three short hesitant taps resonated through the cabin door.

Clifford arched a brow. 'Ready, my lady?'

She flapped a hand. 'Not a bit. But please hurry and let him in so we can get it over with.'

Not wanting to appear too eager, she shuffled into the middle of the settee and scooped up a book from the onyx coffee table and opened it on a random page. Clifford's measured tone filtered back to her.

'Please go on through, Chief Inspector. Her ladyship is at home, as it were.'

Seldon's familiar dark-grey leather brogues appeared in her eyeline. She pretended to still be reading but couldn't help her gaze following the crease of his flattering charcoal suit trousers. It ran the full length of his endlessly long legs and up to where he was turning his hat in his hands.

'Oh, it's you, Hugh,' she said airily.

'Good afternoon, Eleanor.' He lurched forward as if he was going to uncharacteristically embrace her, but then jerked to a stop. He bent and rubbed the back of his knee. 'Ouch! Gladstone, old friend. Does your enormous head have to be quite so hard?' While ruffling the ecstatic bulldog's ears and failing to dodge his wildly flailing tongue, he looked up at her. 'At least one of you is pleased to see me.'

She forced a smile. 'Why would you think he's the only one, Hugh?'

He glanced away. 'Because it's horribly obvious, I haven't exactly covered myself in glory recently.'

His crestfallen tone made her wince, but her bruised feelings stopped her refuting his truthful statement. 'Well... you look more presentable than last night.'

He ran a hand over his damp curls which he'd evidently tried to rake into groomed submission, along with the over-close shave he'd mistreated his lean cheeks and jaw to. 'But still wretched, probably.'

Clifford appeared with refreshments. He set down the large silver tray, and a two-tiered stand of nibbles. He caught her eye, then flicked his gaze to Seldon, who was still hovering awkwardly in the middle of the deep pile rug.

'Oh gracious, Hugh. Sorry, do take a seat.'

He opted for the opposite settee, which made the gulf between them seem vaster than the Atlantic Ocean itself. She sighed as Clifford poured her a small glass of sherry and then assembled a long and complicated-looking cocktail for her pallid guest, who looked enquiringly at him.

'Chamomile coconut water infusion, Chief Inspector, steeped with ginger and a dash of lime.' He added a careful measure from a soda syphon. 'Shot through with Nieder-Selters finest and then topped with three pinches of mint. Is that satisfactory?'

Seldon took it. 'Umm, I imagine it will serve fine, if you

think so. Thank you, Clifford.' He looked up as another glass appeared in front of him.

'And a warmed accompaniment, sir.'

He bowed and left them alone with a swish of suit tails.

'Umm, dig in, I suppose,' she blurted out louder than intended.

He sighed. 'Thank you for the hospitality, but I didn't come to decimate the first-class pantries. I'm sure you've been managing that just fine on your own.' He gave a weak chuckle, which held none of the deep rumble that usually tickled her ears with delight, then shook his head. 'Oh, blast it, Eleanor. I'm sorry. Truly. That came out completely wrong. Like everything I'm going to say, probably.'

She shrugged. 'It's still better to say it, Hugh. At least I hope I'll think that when I've heard whatever it is.'

He groaned. 'I don't think there's any guarantee. Still.' He held her gaze with his deep brown eyes. 'Time to be braver than ever before.'

The depth of passion in his tone pulled her up short. 'Hugh, you're a policeman and the finest there is. You're braver every day in the line of duty than the rest of us are collectively by the time we shuffle off to our final resting place.'

He shook his head vehemently. 'Don't mention that and yourself in the same sentence, Eleanor. Ever. Please.' He took a long swig of his unexpected cocktail and then turned the glass in his hand. 'It's too much to bear.'

'Apologies. I assume Clifford believes it a cure for seasickness, among other things.'

'I didn't mean the drink.'

'I know.' They looked up at each other, both breaking into an awkward smile. 'This is too hideous for words, isn't it?'

He nodded emphatically. 'Only completely. But it's not too unfamiliar with us. Unfortunately.' He patted down his jacket.

'Can I wave an imaginary handkerchief of surrender and start again?'

'Of course. Me too. So why don't you unburden yourself of whatever is eating you up while we both pretend to be busy with the odd assortment Clifford seems to have brought along?'

For a glorious minute there was agreeable silence, as they helped each other to a generous plateful, punctuated only with easy pleasantries over their joint surprise at the offerings.

'These are baked bananas, rolled in crushed walnuts, Hugh. Lashings of tiny toast squares and delectably light crackers with quails' eggs.' She added a large spoonful of green sauce to her plate. 'With mint and basil coulis. How unusual.'

'Plus apple slices dusted with sugar and, is that...' He popped an amber cube in his mouth. 'Ah! Crystallised ginger. An odd combination, but delicious.'

As a faint flush of colour suffused his cheeks, it dawned. Their peculiar fayre was clearly her butler's thoughtful way of trying to ease their discussion. Seldon had obviously just come to the same conclusion. He waved a cracker. 'Your in-house wizard's remedy picnic for awkward conversations, by any chance?'

'It must be. He is absolutely wonderful.'

'As I want to be, Eleanor.' Seldon cleared his throat and picked up the second glass Clifford had given him. 'Smells like brandy. Is that good for seasickness as well, then?'

She smiled. 'No. It's for Dutch courage. So, come on, start with the easy part.'

He sighed deeply. 'There isn't one. All I hope to salvage at the moment is that you might still talk to me after it all.'

'Try me,' she said encouragingly.

'In reverse order of importance, then.' He swallowed hard. 'My gun, which you so observantly identified from that nick in the handle before anyone else did. For which I will be eternally grateful, by the way. Assuming, that is...'

'No, Hugh! Of course I haven't told anyone. Except Clifford. The captain has no idea the murder weapon is yours.' Her cheeks coloured at how that sounded.

'Thank you.' His shoulders relaxed an inch. 'Truly. Anyway, I've hidden the infernal thing securely in my cabin this time so no one could ever guess where it is now.' He shook his head. 'Rather too late, really.'

She grimaced. 'You couldn't have known anyone would steal it and then... then use it.'

'Maybe not. But they did. And they dropped it at the murder scene, that's what's really troubling me. I mean, why not throw it overboard?'

She nodded. 'I know. I was wondering that myself. It's like the murderer wanted it found.'

He looked up at her. 'There's no other explanation. Whoever stole my gun was trying to frame me for the murder. It's that simple. Why, I don't know. And if you hadn't found my gun first, they would have succeeded.'

'But I did find it.'

He nodded wearily. 'True, but if it came to it, I couldn't, and wouldn't, lie on the witness stand.' He rubbed a hand over his eyes dolefully. 'I'm sure I've asked this before, but do you think one day, we might actually manage one entire conversation without the topics of murder, weapons or... bodies?'

'We did! Once. When you whisked me off for an evening's dancing.' Her face lit up at the memory. 'And took me by complete surprise too since I thought you found me more infuriating and impossible than anything else.'

'And now you probably find *me* more infuriating and impossible than anything else.' Before she could reply, he held up a hand. 'You need to hear the rest before you answer that.'

'Alright. But, Hugh, don't take your gun being stolen so hard. It wasn't your fault. And you're on the *Celestiana* in the line of duty.'

He shook his head. 'It was my fault. A policeman should always know the whereabouts of his weapon.' He hesitated. 'And on duty, y-e-s. But not as you are imagining.' He ran a troubled hand along Gladstone's back, not looking at her. 'My gun isn't registered with the ship's security officer because I haven't actually declared it. You see, I'm... I'm not on an official police assignment as such. In fact' – he swallowed hard – 'I'm actually... on leave.'

She was speechless.

'I'm so sorry, Eleanor.'

Somehow, she found her voice. 'On leave? The leave you booked for my birthday week?'

He nodded, his eyes cast down.

'I see.' Whilst she appreciated his honesty, the truth that he had misled her was too hurtful to hear. She rose and stepped through the narrow arch into the adjoining reading area. Throwing the porthole window open, she gulped down several lungfuls of salty air.

'I understand if you want me to leave, Eleanor,' his voice came from behind her. 'But I would like the chance to explain, if you can bear to hear me out?'

After a deep breath, she turned around and nodded. 'But only if you promise to tell me the full truth this time.'

He held her gaze. 'I promise.' He swallowed hard again. 'The truth... the full truth is... it's my wife.'

9

She couldn't help her emotions. Anger welled up inside her.

His wife again, Ellie! Your worst fears confirmed. Everything is still about his wife, who died seven years ago.

She surreptitiously wiped her tear-pricked eyes as she sat back down on the settee. Miraculously a brandy had appeared beside her plate, though she'd seen no sign of her butler. A meticulously folded handkerchief had also appeared in the crook of the cushions.

'I'm listening, Hugh,' she managed finally, in a remarkably even tone.

'Thank you.' He took a deep breath. 'Where to start? Well, the war's as good – or bad – a place as any. I joined up the moment it broke out.'

'Very noble. None of us wanted such frightening uncertainty.'

'Quite.' He glanced at his watch and caught her watching him. 'I'm sorry. My wife gave it to me as a parting gift when I went off to fight.' He swallowed hard. 'Anyway, at the same time, she went back to working for the government. She'd worked for them before we got married so she was seconded to a department which had taken up temporary quarters in a large country house used as a hotel.' He shrugged. 'Large, much like yours. When war had broken out, the owner had willingly handed it over to the government as his part helping the war effort.' He paused and shook his head. 'Anyway, the terrible years rolled on, me at the Front in Belgium and then France. My only consolation was that stuck out in the country as she was, my wife was relatively safe from the air raids. But... one late weekend evening, thieves broke into the house. And...' His deeply sorrowful eyes stared at the floor.

Eleanor's heart constricted. 'Maybe I was a bit hasty, Hugh. Perhaps you don't need to tell me every—'

'I do,' he said firmly, looking up. 'The next thing, though, was the letter.'

'The letter?'

'More of a three-line factual statement on government-issue paper sent to me at the Front. Telling me my wife had been... had been killed during the robbery.'

She couldn't hold in her gasp of horror and scrabbled for the folded handkerchief. 'Oh, Hugh! That's too awful. I always assumed your poor wife had been unwell. Or,' her voice fell, 'unfortunate in childbirth.'

'She never had the chance for either, sadly.'

Eleanor watched as he rose and turned away, running his hands through his curls.

'Since returning from the war, two years after it happened, I've been pursuing the case. But,' he said, turning back to her, 'unofficially. And in my own time, since the case was swiftly closed.' He shrugged. 'It was during the war. No one had the resources or manpower. Or desire.' He returned to his seat. 'But afterwards, that changed. There are a lot of good men on the force now as there was before. And enough of them are married themselves to understand I couldn't let it rest. They've been helping me with information whenever the slightest lead has come up.'

'In your own time? That explains why you're always so exhausted, as if your actual job wasn't too much already. And why you rarely make it home at night. Oh, Hugh, has no one caught the thief yet?'

'Murderer!' he said in a grim tone. 'Sorry, but it's true. She was... shot during the robbery. An unarmed woman, dammit!' He composed himself. 'Sorry. Anyway, to cut to now, I got a call from an officer in Southampton the day before I telephoned you to...' – he looked away – 'to cry off our plans. The officer's a good man. He'd had a case where the robbery had the same unusual method of entry as the robbery when my wife was... was killed. The officer had also picked up a man reported as acting suspiciously in the vicinity. But none of the stolen items were found on him and there was insufficient evidence to hold him. However, the officer called me as he had recognised the man they picked up as the one I was looking for.'

'So, why are you on the *Celestiana*, then?'

'Because that murdering wretch is! Somewhere. The officer followed him after they let him go and he went straight to the docks and picked up a one-way ticket to New York. A one-way ticket! I was sure I knew his devious plan. He meant – *means* – to take all the stolen goods he hasn't peddled in England and sell them in America for a fortune! He'd kept the best pieces over the years, you see. Stolen goods – especially very valuable ones – are usually the hardest to get rid of where they are stolen, as they're often the most recognisable or easiest to trace. But not so in America, especially when they're bought by private collectors and never seen again.'

'Oh, Hugh! So this man is going to set himself up for life!'

He nodded. 'An extremely wealthy life, unquestionably.'

'So you raced to Southampton and grabbed a ticket with the

idea you could arrest him aboard the ship before it reached New York?'

He nodded again. 'But only after agonising all night over cancelling my plans with you for your birthday. And' – he held his hands up – 'I'm off duty. And totally out of my jurisdiction. My "plan", hastily thrown together, was to find the stolen goods in his cabin and then persuade the ship's master-at-arms to arrest the scoundrel. Then I could drag him back to an English trial and, hopefully, finally get justice for... for my wife.'

Her heart ached for him. 'So what does this man look like? I mean, you must have a pretty good idea if your colleague in Southampton could recognise him from the description you'd passed around?'

An emotion flashed over his face too fast for her to read. 'Actually, he's quite similar in appearance to me, even build. Uncannily so. Except he's a bit harder-jawed and thinner lipped.'

Her hand flew to her mouth. *Gracious! That means the last man his wife saw before she died looked strikingly like the husband she hadn't seen since he went off to war.*

The awfulness made her wince for the pair of them. But Seldon's description suddenly registered. 'Does this wretch have the same colour eyes and hair as you then? And a rather prominent chin dimple by any chance?'

He jerked upright in his seat. 'Yes! But... but how... how did you know?'

She grimaced. 'I saw him mesmerising half the female first-class contingent with his dancing.'

'Including you?' He blushed. 'Sorry. Do you know his name? Not that it won't be an alias, of course.'

She shook her head. 'I only saw him dancing in the Sports Challenge on the top deck, so he must be in first class, I assume. That's all I know. Now, Hugh,' she said softly, 'is there anything else you need to tell me?'

He shook his head, but avoided her gaze. 'There is something, but it doesn't relate to this blasted, impossible mess. Well, not directly.' He lifted his eyes and held her gaze. 'Can you trust me to tell you when this is over?'

'Yes, implicitly.' For a moment they smiled at each other. A sharp rat-a-tat on the door made them both jump. Clifford appeared from the pantry and gestured for Seldon to duck out of sight. He then opened the door.

The master-at-arms stood on the other side, his face grim. 'Lady Swift's presence is requested by Captain Bracebridge.'

From his hidden spot, Seldon stared at her in confusion. *What now, Ellie?*

10

'Thank you for coming to my inner office, Lady Swift,' Bracebridge said with a genial smile that added a few more weather-beaten creases to those already testifying his heart had lain with the sea even before he'd stepped into long trousers. 'I appreciate you probably had other plans for this half hour.'

'Yes. But an invitation to the captain's office is always an honour. All the more so when it means I can examine this.' She waved a hand at the coffee table centred in the room. 'What a fascinating piece, inlaid with Christopher Columbus' world chart of his day, his *mappa mundi!*' Her finger traced the nine concentric circles depicting the planets of the beautiful parchment-coloured copy under the table's glass top.

Tuning in to the fact Bracebridge was watching her intently, his eyes filled with questions, she shrugged. 'My first view on waking every morning when I was a child was this exquisite symbol of adventure which I had glued to my little bunk's ceiling in my parents' yacht which we lived on.'

'And do you think that is how Columbus viewed it?' His tone had an edge of wistfulness. 'As his chart of adventure?'

'I've always believed so.'

'Me too.' His face broke into a broad smile. 'You are full of surprises, Lady Swift, if I may say.' His smile faded. 'However, I believe I might have one for you, so please take a seat.'

She settled into a deep-buttoned leather armchair, aware that the master-at-arms was all the while watching her out of the corner of his eye. Despite what seemed to be his best effort to keep his face neutral, he seemed to be about to explode with anger.

'I shall be as brief as possible.' Bracebridge pinched the smart crease of his uniform trousers before sitting down. 'I do not wish to waste either of our time. Nor mar your voyage on the *Celestiana* any more than has already regrettably happened, for which I offer my, and Blue Star Line's, most effusive apologies. So, to bring you up to speed, I contacted the ship's owner, Mr Walker, to report the incident last night.'

She winced. 'That can't have been a comfortable conversation. My sympathies.'

'As it was my duty as captain, my comfortableness or otherwise did not feature, naturally. But, thank you. Mr Walker reiterated that which I told you. This is the *Celestiana*'s maiden voyage. It cannot be jeopardised in any way. If the news that a man has been murdered on board were to reach the ears of our passengers, well!' He threw up his hands. 'The number of demands from first class to have the *Celestiana* instantly turn around and return to port would be too numerous to veto. As would the equally countless clamours for immediate transfers to other ships, mid-ocean.' His smart uniform jacket swelled with the deep breath he took. 'It would be pandemonium. Since the disaster of the *Titanic*' – he bowed his head momentarily – 'all maiden voyages have been big news on both sides of the Atlantic. A horrified fascination and hunger for a catastrophe eagerly fed by the world's press.'

Eleanor fought to keep the confusion from her face. 'But

you'll have to report the murder anyway once the *Celestiana* docks?'

'Yes. But if the murderer has been apprehended, they can be discreetly removed from the ship. Of course, it will all come out in the trial. But it is more likely then that the crew of the *Celestiana* will be seen as heroes who calmly captured a murderer without causing widespread panic aboard.'

'And if the murderer isn't caught by the time we reach New York?'

His fingers drummed on the desk. 'Then the police will detain the ship and insist all its crew and passengers remain on board until they have investigated the matter thoroughly.'

She winced. 'I can't imagine how that would go down with your more influential passengers, let alone the press.'

He grimaced. 'I can. And so can Mr Walker. It would be fatal for the *Celestiana*, and Blue Line in general.'

She bit her lip, her loyalty to her ex-boss still strong. 'I can see that.' She tried to keep her voice light. 'But what of the murdered man? What has been done to find the culprit?'

Bracebridge leaned back in his chair and steepled his fingers. 'My master-at-arms will detail what has been done so far.'

He indicated his subordinate had the floor. The master-at-arms stepped forward, went to speak and then spun around to face his superior. 'Captain, I really have to ask you again to reconsider. I am not prepared—'

Bracebridge rose from his chair, his face thunderous. 'Master-at-Arms, we have had this discussion. I do not appreciate you bringing it up again in front of one of our guests. You will stand down or be relieved of your duties!'

For a moment, Eleanor thought the two men would actually come to blows. But, instead, with what seemed a superhuman effort, the master-at-arms controlled himself. He nodded to his superior. 'Yes, Captain.'

Bracebridge sat back down. 'Good. Then proceed.'

'On board are two thousand, one hundred and seventeen passengers,' the master-at-arms barked as if trying to muster every one of them into the room. 'Plus eight hundred and sixty-three crew. Narrowing that lot down to a single suspect would see the devil to pay.'

As Bracebridge went to explain, she shook her head. 'A difficult or deeply unpleasant task aboard ship, I know. Although I would need my trusty butler and encyclopaedia-on-legs to add to whom the expression was first attributed and when. Please continue, Master-at-Arms.'

He nodded stiffly. 'Only crew assigned to first class would have been able to move about decks A to C without question. One hundred and seventy were so assigned.'

'Although perhaps only a maximum of one hundred and sixty or fewer were actually aboard for duty? Given the dearth of cabin boys?'

Bracebridge glanced appreciatively at her. 'As sharp-witted as you are sharp-eyed, Lady Swift.'

He waved the master-at-arms on, who glared briefly at Eleanor before continuing.

'Many of the first-class crew were in the dining room clearing up, except the early shift, who were all in their bunks. Which are shared, naturally. Whereabouts for all have been verified already, including the six who were on other, special duties.'

'Well done,' she said genuinely. 'That was no easy feat but speedily completed.'

He acknowledged her praise with the faintest of nods. 'Third-class passengers number one thousand and forty-one. Access to first class from third class was impossible, however, since the stairwells were locked by the time of the murder to comply with American custom regulations. Armed guards were also in position on the stairwells between first and second class soon after the murder happened. Escape from the deck the man was murdered on down to second class would be highly unlikely to have succeeded, therefore.'

'So we can all but rule out the murderer coming from third and second class then, Master-at-Arms,' she said airily, hoping her relief for Hugh but concern the killer might be missed weren't obvious.

He shook his head. 'No, Lady Swift. I have the best of my men investigating second class as we speak. Just to be sure.'

Double quick work again on his and the captain's part, Ellie.

As if Bracebridge had read her thoughts, he nodded. 'I ordered a roll call of all passengers be taken at breakfast.'

Eleanor's stomach let out an unladylike grumble at the reminder she had only eaten lightly so far that day. 'Well, you wouldn't have ticked off my name, since I missed the sittings altogether.'

'So I noticed,' Bracebridge said.

'Likewise your butler,' the master-at-arms added with a waspish edge to his tone.

She ignored it. 'So, have you found out who the poor chap was who was shoved so callously overboard with a bullet in his stomach?'

'We have,' Bracebridge said. 'A Mr Harrison Yeoman. From first class, as we suspected.' The name meant nothing to her. 'And the most likely class the murderer is from, as we have established. It has, however, only been possible so far to eliminate a few first-class passengers – elderly persons and children who were obviously not one of the shadows you saw fighting.'

She frowned. 'And yet the master-at-arms' men are concentrating on second class. Why?' She thought for a moment. 'Ah! I can see Mr Walker is concerned the first-class passengers will be ruffled if your master-at-arms asks prying and personal questions about their whereabouts and so on.'

Bracebridge smiled thinly. 'Ruffled, no. Incensed, most

definitely. However, given the location at which you unfortunately witnessed the incident, the fiend responsible can only have escaped via the left-hand front end.' He shrugged apologetically. 'Or "port side bow", as, of course, you would clearly have sufficient experience of life aboard to correctly refer to it. The doors, therefore, which the killer probably used to escape are those leading to the cabins and suites in D section of A deck.'

She looked up sharply. 'That's where my suite is.'

'Quite. Now, in D section there are twenty-three first-class passengers. The elderly and children have already been ruled out as mentioned earlier.' He stared at a sheet of paper on his desk. 'And two more, Sir Gerald and Lady Caroline Wrenshaw-Smythe have also been cleared as the steward was with them at the time of the murder. Sir Gerald had some complaint about his cabin, it seems.'

Convenient, Ellie?

'And as you yourself, Lady Swift, I must stress, are obviously above suspicion, that leaves seven possible suspects; Mrs Theodora Swalecourt and her daughter, Miss Rosamund, Miss Florentina González, Count Ottokar Balog, Sir Randolph Asquith the hotelier, Professor Daniel Goodman and Signor Enrico Vincenzo Marinelli, the renowned opera star.'

She frowned. 'So why have you asked me here?'

'To pass on Mr Walker's request.'

Her brow furrowed further at his expectant expression. Then she gasped. 'He asked you to ask me to—'

'To help undertake a discreet investigation from inside first class. Yes.' Bracebridge spread his hands. 'First-class passengers are too well travelled and worldly-wise to have any doubt who my master-at-arms is. Indeed, a great number have already called upon him regarding the safe storage of their valuables. If he starts asking them any sort of... inappropriate questions, they will raise hell.'

'And smell a rat, I'm sure. But me?' She shook her head, still in shock. 'Investigate the murder?'

'Investigate... again,' Bracebridge said firmly. 'Lady Swift, that you travelled alone by bicycle across the world, likely as many miles as I have covered at sea, was astounding enough to hear from Mr Walker. That you have also solved several murders needs no additional words.'

She smiled. 'I hadn't realised he is still following my life so closely, bless him.'

'Evidently he is. Now, to business. You would be working alongside my master-at-arms, of course.' Bracebridge ignored the man's involuntary snort. 'Lady Swift, apologies, but are you able to give me your answer now? I understand if—'

'Yes, I am,' she said confidently. 'I can see having someone inside first class who no one would suspect to be investigating would help.' She cocked her head at the captain. 'But are you genuinely happy about this?' She avoided looking at the master-at-arms.

He nodded. 'I was initially incredulous at the idea of involving a civilian, I won't deceive you. And a lady at that. But my reservations have dissipated during this conversation, however. You have left me with nothing but confidence in your capabilities.' He smiled. 'Though, I confess, I could not actually detail what they are at this juncture.'

She laughed. 'Me neither.' An idea struck. She rose and paced the length of the room, aware all eyes were on her.

No more time to think it through, Ellie. Fingers crossed it will be the right thing.

She stopped and turned to Bracebridge. 'Captain, I have a piece of information which I believe you may not. Information that, hopefully, would ensure the murder is solved not only more quickly but also more discreetly.'

He stared at her. 'Please go on.'

'I came into the knowledge recently. Very recently, in fact.

There is a most eminent and senior police detective among your passengers. One travelling incognito as he is on leave at present. If he could be persuaded to help in the investigation—'

'Captain, really, I must protest—' The master-at-arms stopped at Bracebridge's glare. Bracebridge turned back to Eleanor.

'I agree, Lady Swift. In principle, at least.' He eyed her for a moment. 'I would like to meet this detective first, however.'

'Of course.'

He rose. 'I shall endeavour to repay your kind assistance, given that you should be dealing with nothing more troubling than which among Chef Barsalou's extensive menus to choose from at dinner.'

'Well, it's not at all how I planned to be spending my birthday trip.'

He groaned. 'On your birthday too.'

'It's alright. Working with your marvellous master-at-arms to catch the murderer and see justice done will be recompense enough.'

'If you say so, Lady Swift. Now, if you will excuse me. I am behind on a great many matters.'

'One last thing, Captain. Can you invite the seven people you suggested were the most logical suspects to dine at your table tonight?'

'Yes. Along with yourself, naturally. And the master-at-arms will provide you with a description of each so you can recognise them should you meet any of them before then. Now, he will escort you back to your cabin.'

Outside in the corridor, the master-at-arms nodded curtly to her. 'This way, Lady Swift.'

No point in wasting time, Ellie

She stayed where she was. 'Tell me, have you discovered anything at the scene of the murder? Or in Mr Yeoman's cabin?'

'Not yet,' came the sharp reply.

'Then it can do no harm for myself, and the detective, to look ourselves. I'm sure you have been most thorough, but it will give us somewhere to start.'

Clearly, he was unhappy with the request but seemed unable to find a legitimate reason to refuse. 'Alright. But I must insist no other passengers' quarters will be investigated by yourselves without my approval.'

She smiled. 'Agreed. This is going to turn out fine with us working together, wouldn't you say?' He wouldn't say. She sighed. 'Your hands are somewhat tied in this matter, just as mine are somewhat forced. We'll only succeed if we work together. Please be assured, the detective I mentioned will be the one to lead my side of the investigation. Under your direction, of course. And I will also liaise with you at every step.'

He stopped and pursed his lips as if weighing up the matter. 'If you both work under my direction and report to me at every stage, then there is a slim chance it might work.'

'And obviously, I will ensure Mr Walker knows you are the one to get the credit when we catch the murderer.'

'You will?' His tone was suspicious. 'Why?'

'Because you will deserve it. And the detective is on holiday and out of his jurisdiction.' She started off down the corridor. 'And I'm supposed to be a proper lady of the manor. Heaven help me!'

She wasn't certain, but she could swear the master-at-arms let out a quiet chuckle.

11

_____

'You arranged *what* with the captain!' Seldon's jaw fell slack. 'Eleanor, for Pete's sake, what were you thinking of?' He spun on his heel and scooped her back inside her suite with him.

'Not what, but *who*.' She nudged him further in so that she could close the door and lean against it. 'You, Hugh. I was thinking of *you*.'

He looked contrite. 'Thank you. But can't you see that's the last thing I wanted you to do?'

'Alright.' She tried to hide how disappointed she felt. 'I can simply tell Bracebridge you've declined and carry on without you. Because I will. So please do me the honour of not trying to stop me. Clifford?' she called towards the butler's pantry.

Seldon took a deep breath. 'Blast it, Eleanor, what is it about you that makes me trip myself up like an oaf every time I open my mouth? I'm sorry. What I meant is, I can't bear that you put my welfare before your own safety. Again. You're supposed to be—'

'A lady?'

A glimmer of the old Seldon shone through in the smile that split his face in two. 'So I've heard your loyal butler remind you on many an occasion.' He lowered his voice. 'The one who's no doubt hiding in his kitchen or whatever it's called so I can try and make you see sense.' He stepped away from her. 'Eleanor, you are too precious to me to get mixed up in another wretched mess. Please reconsider getting involved.'

She tried to ignore the flush to her cheeks his uncharacteristically bold declaration had brought on. 'Consideration given. And my answer is no. Come on, Hugh, no matter how much we wish it was someone else's problem, or no one's actually, it's ours. We're in this together.' She raised her voice. 'Just as my errant butler is, too.'

'You rang, my lady,' Clifford said innocently as he appeared, accompanied by Gladstone, who woofed out his frustration at having been held back in the pantry.

She hid a smile. 'Only ten minutes ago.'

Without her adding anything further, he produced her sage wool coat and helped her into it. He gave Seldon a respectfully firm look. 'Return with her ladyship unscathed, if you would be so kind, Chief Inspector.'

He nodded. 'Don't worry, Clifford, I will.' He turned and hurried after Eleanor, who had already stepped out into the corridor. 'Where are we going?' he whispered to her.

'Where I've learned from England's most eminent detective chief inspector, he would go first. Even before he's got permission. Just as we haven't quite. Yet.'

The murder scene on the upper deck looked so different in the weak afternoon sun. Not intimidating. Certainly not menacing. Definitely not somewhere that a man had been murdered, as the stacks of deckchairs suggested nothing more reprehensible than lounging away the day. Not that there was anyone using them except three hardy elderly men puffing on their pipes in the chilly March air.

The scene of the crime had been cordoned off with a series of ropes, which were swinging wildly in the icy breeze. Below, a sign read, 'Closed for safety rail checking. DO NOT ENTER.'

'Our master-at-arms is certainly doing his job well,' she said. 'Despite his displeasure.'

Seldon paused in scrutinising the deck beyond the ropes. 'Why is he displeased?'

'Because he thought being ordered to work with a civilian – and a female at that – was insult enough. And then I suggested—'

'That it needed my police expertise to fill in where his falls short?' He groaned. 'Tell me that isn't how you put it?'

She shrugged. 'It wasn't. Quite.'

He shook his head. 'Smoothing over required when I meet him then. Noted.' He scanned her face. 'Can you talk me through what you saw without it upsetting you too much?'

'Yes. If you can hear it without reprimanding my every other word for being rash and impetuous.'

'I can't promise that. Besides, Clifford deserves to have someone take up that chore, poor chap. And a medal,' she caught him mutter.

She talked him through the events of last night. 'And then in a blink, the shadows rose up the side of the funnel just there.' She shook her head. 'I couldn't even tell if they were male or female. Although, as we now know, at least one of them was a man.'

And he's lying at the bottom of the ocean, Ellie.

Seldon's pen shot across the page of his notebook. He was leaning on the prow of a lifeboat as if merely staring out to sea, his coat masking his actions. She noticed he kept swallowing and seemed unsteady on his feet.

He's still seasick, Ellie, poor chap. Her eyes focused past him. 'Hmm.' She cocked her head and stared up at the enormous red funnel, encircled with three wide blue bands.

He looked up. 'What else have you remembered?'

She shrugged. 'Nothing else at the moment. I'm sorry.'

He grunted. 'Don't be. What you've relayed so far is a great start. Now, we need to slide to the other side of the ropes and look at the point on deck where the victim was actually shoved overboard.'

Beyond the ropes, she stared at the deck near the ship's rail. 'The captain organised a remarkable clean-up last night. There's no sign a man was shot. Just the suggestion this one small area of teak has been given an extra scrub.'

'From what you've described, allowing for the short time between the trigger being pulled and the victim being pushed over the side, any blood would have been on this inner wall.'

'Known as the "gunwale", which is tragically ironic on this occasion.' She sighed. 'I wish you didn't spend every day dealing with such horrors. Maybe you'd actually sleep at night then.'

'Likewise, Eleanor,' he said earnestly, 'because then, maybe I could.'

She watched as he inched his eyeline left to right, sinking lower with each sweep until his long legs were hunched up around his ears. A moment later, he stood up. 'Nothing! Still, I didn't expect the master-at-arms' men to miss anything obvious.'

She stepped to the rail itself, her hands behind her back so as not to touch the section of polished wood over which the shot man had been pushed. A shiver ran down her spine.

'You alright?' Seldon said softly.

'Yes.' She stood on tiptoe to peer over the rail. 'It's a horribly long way down. And to a hard, cold landing in that heaving slab of icy water below.' She shivered again. 'So hard. So... Gold!'

He shot her a concerned glance. '"Cold", you mean. Like you are. Come on, we need to get back inside.'

'No, Hugh! *Gold*. Look!' He craned his neck in the direction she was pointing. 'There! About a foot down. Where that rubbing strake meets the line of this lifeboat stanchion's fixings.'

He gave her a sideways glance. 'And for those of us who didn't grow up on a boat?'

'Sorry. Where this thick white bar ends, twelve inches below, caught on that slightly proud long band of black-painted steel.'

He looked hard at where she was pointing. 'I can't see anything. No, wait! There's something there for sure. Eagle-eyed, Eleanor. Well done!' He frowned as he looked over again. 'But it's nearer two than one foot down.'

'Good job I'm taller than average then.' She was already halfway out of her coat.

'No! On no account will I let you—' He broke off as his strong hands grabbed her around her waist where it was now balanced on the rail.

'Another half an inch,' she grunted. Swinging her legs back down onto the deck, she spun to face him, her words lost, however, in the soft wool of his grey suit jacket as his arms wrapped tightly around her.

'Eleanor, I beg you...' he muttered into her wind-whipped curls.

She bit back a smile. 'I promise I won't hang over this rail again.' She looked up into his deep brown eyes. 'If you don't tell Clifford that I did. Deal?'

He nodded.

'Good. Then let's go and I'll show you what I found on the way!'

12

___

She herded Seldon back into the ivory splendour of the first-class corridors. Patting her pocket, she lowered her voice. 'If the master-at-arms failed to spot this, who knows what he might have missed in Yeoman's cabin.'

Seldon stiffened. 'That... that was the name of the victim?'

'According to the captain. At least, he's the only passenger unaccounted for.' She didn't miss the anger that flitted over his face.

'Morrison Dawson. Jefferson Gifford. Benjamin Lidden. Solomon Pinner.' He ran the back of his hand across his brow. 'And Harrison Yeoman. All assumed names. And all one and the same swine I have been hunting for five years for murdering my wife!'

She gasped. 'No! And now someone's put him beyond the reach of justice. Human, if not divine, anyway.'

He shook his head. 'It makes no sense! Wh—' He closed his eyes and groaned. When he opened them again, she'd rarely seen him look so angry. 'Yes it does, damn it! Someone murdered Yeoman and is trying to frame me for it. Because when Yeoman's death comes to court, it will inevitably come out that I was shadowing him without authority. And that it was my gun used in the murder. On top of that, half the English police force know I blame Yeoman for my wife's death. Which means there's no judge, or jury, in the land that wouldn't convict me of having pulled that trigger!'

'Well, there's one person. Me! And there's one solution. Find the actual murderer. Together—'

She broke off as he pressed his fingers gently over her lips. 'No, Eleanor. Thank you from the bottom of my heart, but no! Despite anything we may have discussed before, I cannot and will not let you become involved.'

'I already am, Hugh.' She held up a hand as he went to speak. 'Don't fight me. I'll only investigate anyway, as you know. And we've proved before, we make a great team. Especially with Clifford's invaluable input. And I'll probably bungle the whole thing without your expertise.'

He seemed to wrestle with himself for a moment. Then he sighed. 'I agree. You're already involved. And I do know from our past... wranglings that nothing will stop you.'

She nodded. 'Exactly. Now, do you have any idea who knew about the history between you and Yeoman and who might want to frame you for murder? Particularly Yeoman's?'

He thought for a moment and then shook his head wearily. 'No. I can't even begin to imagine.'

'Well, at least we have something solid to go on in relation to Yeoman's murder.'

She reached into her pocket, pulling out the handkerchief-wrapped item she'd rescued from the side of the ship. They paused for a moment, both glancing up and down the corridor. Happy it was empty, Seldon's long fingers brushed her palm as he peeled back the folds. With a frown, he produced a pen and slid the item down its length before holding it up.

'A signet ring?'

She leaned over to peer at it properly for the first time. 'Not like one I've ever seen. No initials. No crest. Just a small engraved bee, I think it is.' She frowned. 'I would have thought the master-at-arms' men would have spotted it.'

'It was dark.' He placed it back into her handkerchief. 'We'd better discuss this later, somewhere more private.'

They hurried on, a question burning on her lips.

'Hugh, ignoring who might have wanted to frame you for Yeoman's murder, do you have any idea who might have wanted to kill Yeoman?'

'Aside from me? Not that I would have. But no, I don't. However, a villain like him usually has more enemies than friends.' He shook his head. 'But those sorts of people would have no trouble getting their hands on a gun. Which, again, means mine was stolen for one very specific purpose.' He groaned and thumped his forehead. 'Idiotic careless man!'

'Careless, could never be levelled at you, Hugh. You've been totally floored by your seasickness and the stress of all this.' A thought struck her. 'But wait, you told me no one knew you were on board. Would Yeoman have recognised you, though?'

He nodded. 'Possibly. I sat in on an interview over a robbery we thought Yeoman had to be responsible for. Not that we could find anything to convict him.' He laughed grimly. 'However, up to the time you somehow found me, I was incarcerated in my cabin with this wretched seasickness apart from brief trips to the... ahem.' He cleared his throat. 'It's unlikely he spotted me on board the *Celestiana*. Or while boarding. There were thousands of other people around.'

Her thoughts flew back to the ship leaving berth and how amazed she'd been to spot the ladies among those very thousands filling the decks below. His troubled expression told her he didn't need to hear that right now.

'But Yeoman *might* have seen you, Hugh. And recognised you. And he might have mentioned having seen you to whoever then killed him.' She frowned. 'Whoever that person is, it seems they realised they could turn it to their advantage by stealing your gun and pinning the murder on you.'

He nodded. 'Which still leaves the question of why Yeoman was murdered in the first place.'

The fresh-faced sailor stationed outside the cabin door flicked his eyes to Seldon and back to her. 'Apologies, Lady Swift, but the master-at-arms mentioned only as you' – his eyes flitted to Seldon again – 'might happen along, as it were.'

She smiled at him firmly. 'And how right he was to do so. But as you can see, there are two of us.'

She stepped forward, which caused the sailor to jump to one side. Opening the door, she entered the cabin, followed by Seldon. Once inside, he closed the cabin door behind them, quietly dropping the internal latch into place. Helpfully, the cabin was far smaller than her own suite. Two leather wing-backed chairs, a diminutive but elaborate writing desk, and a matching oval green card table were the only furniture in the pale blue-and-silver striped wallpapered sitting room.

The doors to the bedroom had been left thrown open, a cabinet partially visible. A tangle of vests poked from the first drawer, a muddle of shirt collars and sleeves from the next. She pointed at the telltale waistbands of male undershorts leering from the last.

'Good job Clifford isn't here. He'd be scarlet at my seeing all Yeoman's underthings.'

'Whereas I'm completely comfortable!' Seldon mumbled, turning away, the tips of his ears flushed beetroot.

She hid a smile. 'How about you deal with that and Yeoman's bunk, which must be behind that folding carved screen? And his wash area beyond that curtain, I assume. I'll tackle the sitting room for decorum's sake.'

He nodded. 'We'd better hurry. That sailor has probably gone for the master-at-arms who sounds like he'd be delighted to slap me in the ship's brig. And finding out it was my gun that killed Yeoman would give him all the reason he'd need.'

But ten minutes later, neither of them had found anything.

Seldon glanced around again. 'No hint of stolen valuables, blast it! And nothing to link him with the previous crimes.' His fists balled. 'I still need evidence to prove it was Yeoman for certain who... who killed my wife. Even though he's dead.'

She nodded. 'Of course, Hugh. I understand that.' She scanned the room. 'Wait a minute, where's the safe? Surely his cabin must have one, like mine does.'

He pointed to a painting on the wall. 'It's behind that. Unlocked. And empty. We're done here, Eleanor.'

'No.' She closed her eyes momentarily. 'There has to be a clue. Even master criminals aren't as careful as they think they are. They'd never end up shot and pushed overboard otherwise.'

He smiled wanly. 'I appreciate your determination but—'

'Grooming! If Yeoman was the man I noticed dancing in the Sports Challenge, he must have had quite the collection of things to have looked so dapper.' Seldon gave his tousled curls an uneasy tug. 'That wasn't why I noticed him, Hugh.'

'There's a leather case in there,' he said in a slightly miffed tone. 'With brushes, combs, mirror, razor, pot of shaving cream and a conceitedly large bottle of cologne. But they're just wash things.'

He led her into the small blue-and-white-tiled bathroom, where she went through the items in the bag.

'Nothing,' she muttered. But her curiosity got the better of her and she flipped off the stopper of the dark-green glass cologne bottle to take a sniff. As she placed the bottle back on the shelf, her sharp hearing caught the faintest clink from inside.

'Ah!'

13

Back in her suite, Eleanor placed the cologne bottle from Yeoman's cabin on the table. They were both examining the signet ring again when the door opened.

'Ah! Clifford, you're just in time.' She waved him over and explained where they'd found the ring. 'Any insights?'

He examined it for a moment, then passed it back to her. 'Other than the inconsistent attention to detail of the bee's depiction, I'm afraid I do not have any suggestions as to origin or the like, my lady.'

'Blast it!' Seldon said. 'We can't even guarantee that Yeoman was wearing it. The fact it was where he fell is circumstantial in essence.'

She held the ring in her hand, a frown forming. 'Something doesn't seem quite right.'

He gave her a quizzical look. She shook her head. 'Not about the ring, Hugh. About how we found it. It just seemed a little...'

'Convenient, my lady?'

'Maybe, Clifford.'

Seldon shrugged. 'It was pitch dark when the master-at-arms and his men would have searched the area, as I said. And the sea was rougher last night. Believe me, I noticed. It would have been easy to miss.'

She nodded, but her frown remained. 'I know, but you haven't met the master-at-arms yet.' She placed it back on the table. 'Like your gun, it's almost as if... someone had placed it there to be found.' She shrugged. 'If only we knew more about it.'

'I believe, my lady, there may be someone on board who could assist in regard to this ring's origin.'

Seldon tapped his notebook. 'Excellent, Clifford! I'll leave that up to you to organise.'

'I will see if I can locate the gentleman right away.'

Seldon held up his pen. 'And we'd better get the master-at-arms down here.'

'I will send a cabin boy to fetch him. If I can find one,' he muttered as he left.

Once alone, they turned their attention back to the ring for a while, but neither of them could find anything noteworthy about it. 'Clue number two, perhaps then.' She waved a hand at the cologne bottle.

Seldon picked it up, turning it in his hands. Then he shook it. A faint 'clink' came from within.

She nodded. 'That's what I heard the first time.'

He uncorked the bottle and peered inside, his stomach clearly roiling at the scent. 'I can see something, but what, I don't know.'

She took the bottle from him and poured the contents down the sink in the butler's pantry. When it was empty, she put it to her eye. 'Whatever is in there seems to be in some sort of cloth bag. But it's definitely bigger than the mouth of the bottle, so how did it get in there?' A puzzled look crossed her face. 'Clearly this was supposed to remain hidden, unlike your gun and the ring. Whoever was responsible wanted those to be found, I think, but not this.' She shrugged. 'I suppose I'll just have to smash it.' She raised her arm and started to bring it down on the edge of the sink, but it was gently whisked from her grasp.

She turned around in surprise to see Clifford standing behind her with a pained look on his face.

'Do please forgive me, my lady, but I feel the contents can be extracted the same way they were inserted. Without a petty act of vandalism.' She went to reply, but he continued. 'And there is a gentleman waiting who may be able to give us an insight into the ring you fortuitously recovered.'

Ceding to her butler's horror of mess, she re-joined Seldon in the sitting room. Clifford followed and announced their visitor.

'This, my lady, Chief Inspector, is Mr Padgett, Senior. Of Brunkton and Padgett, Hatton Garden. An elite establishment amongst London's most eminent jewellers. They have a shop in the Elysian Arcade aboard the *Celestiana*.'

The visitor, given his stooped appearance and shock of wiry, white, wispy hair, she placed in his late sixties. He wore a smart blue worsted suit and, she couldn't help thinking, incongruous florid green-and-yellow patterned neckwear given his conservative demeanour. As he nodded in greeting, his round spectacles slid off his wrinkled nose. Catching them in mid-fall, he slid them back on and waved what appeared to be a short roll of velvet.

'Godfrey Padgett, that's right, yes, yes.' He hurried forward to Eleanor in shuffling steps, his voice so taut she had to restrain the urge to reach out and loosen his necktie. 'Hoping I might be of service to you this afternoon, er, Lady Swift, I believe it is?'

She smiled warmly. 'It is. And this is Mr Seldon. Thank you for coming so promptly, Mr Padgett. Perhaps we might prevail upon your time to tell us anything you can about this.' She held out the ring she'd retrieved from the murder scene.

'Ah,' Padgett murmured. 'May I?' Whipping a pair of white gloves from his jacket pocket and sliding them on, he took it, unrolled the roll of velvet on the table, and placed the ring on it. Muttering, he ran a finger along a row of tools held in purpose-designed pockets inside the velvet. The three of them leaned forward as he chose one. After more minutes of incomprehensible mutterings, Padgett folded back the bottom half of the velvet roll to reveal a set of miniature folding scales with a line of tiny counterweights. Having weighed the ring, he straightened up.

'I fear, Lady Swift, I have only disappointing news for you. Yes, yes.'

'It's not the ring's value I'm interested in, Mr Padgett. Anything will be helpful, I assure you.'

'Very well then. Troy weight is seven ounces, as one would expect for eighteen carat gold in a signet ring of this unusually slim width. Decorative markings both chased and repoussed. Hallmark bears a leopard, letter "D", right-facing Sovereign's head and letters "WF".' He held up his hands. 'Is that all clear?'

'Actually, not at all.'

'Ah! Well, the ring's gold was graded in London. Crafted in Bloomsbury Lane between the eleventh of January and the thirtieth of April eighteen-ninety-nine, by the notable William Fladby.'

Eleanor gaped at him. 'I had no idea a hallmark held so much detail. To the novice eye, it's nothing more than a handful of indecipherable hieroglyphics.'

'Entirely as it should be, yes, yes,' Padgett said earnestly. 'But every piece of jewellery should hold all manner of other significance to its owner; nostalgia, security, investment, happiness, sorrow, remorse. A consoling symbol of bereavement, perhaps. Or a euphoric reminder of a celebratory event. Or even' – he smiled wistfully – 'proof of the depth of one's love for another. However, whether it is of great value for sentimental reasons or not, I'm afraid its monetary value is small.'

Dash it, Ellie. Nothing to help us find a killer.

She threw on a smile. 'Well, Mr Padgett, no matter. That just leaves me to thank you again. My butler will—'

Clifford cleared his throat and passed a rather wet-looking bag into Seldon's hand. Spinning around, she saw Yeoman's cologne bottle lying in two parts on the bureau. 'Clifford, you wizard!

'A most ingenious threaded design, my lady. A combined clockwise and—'

'Could we just get along, please?' Seldon said weakly. The overpowering aroma of cologne she now tuned into was clearly making the already seasick inspector feel even worse. 'Are you suggesting, Clifford, that the contents of this is something Mr Padgett might also be able to help with?'

'Absolutely, Chief Inspector.'

Seldon shrugged and tipped the bag's contents into Eleanor's eagerly waiting palm.

'Gracious!' she breathed, staring at the three-inch oval black stone she held, mesmerised by the thousand vibrant flecks of emerald green and sapphire blue, all seemingly suspended between fissures of fire. Out of the corner of her eye, she caught Padgett press a handkerchief to his mouth. 'Mr Padgett, do you know what this is?' She placed the stone carefully in his trembling hand.

The jeweller nodded, his eyes transfixed. 'Yes, yes, Lady Swift. It is the greatest day I have ever lived! That I should see... a black opal! And one of such magnificence! And that I should be so privileged to nestle her in my palm for even a moment, oh my, oh my!'

'A black opal?' Seldon said blankly. 'Is it valuable, then?'

Padgett nodded. 'Immeasurably so! More valuable carat for carat than any diamond. However, it is not her value that has thrown my heart to the heavens. It is her rarity.' He stared down at the gem. 'One had never been discovered until but thirty years ago. And other specimens have only been found sporadically since then. And only ever in one small part of Australia.'

He passed it reverently back to Eleanor, who traced its oval shape with her finger. 'But where has it come from?'

'I would hazard, Lady Swift, that this beauty has been taken from a necklace or such like of unimaginable craftsmanship, that is for sure. There can be very few in the world even similar to this.'

She looked up at the sound of boots outside.

'Perfect timing, Master-at-Arms,' she said as Clifford opened the door. 'Do come in.'

The *Celestiana*'s head of security stepped in, his two aides waiting outside. 'Perfect timing for what, Lady Swift?'

Seldon gestured to the jeweller. The master-at-arms glanced at him and then nodded back. 'Mr Padgett, I believe?'

The jeweller nodded.

'Please return to your shop and treat anything you have seen here today with the utmost discretion.'

The jeweller scooped up his things. 'Oh, absolutely, absolutely.'

Once he'd gone, the master-at-arms turned an enquiring eye on Seldon. 'The policeman, I assume?'

Seldon nodded and quickly outlined their finds, the ring and opal, and what the jeweller had told them. The master-at-arms showed great interest in the opal. In fact, he seemed to find it hard to believe until Eleanor gestured for him to hold his hand out and then placed the gemstone into it. He seemed spellbound as he stared at the stone. After a few moments, he shook his head and looked up at Seldon. 'I... I have never seen anything like this.'

'None of us have. But the murderer had, I'll bet you the

entire *Celestiana* on that. And I'm pretty sure he killed Yeoman trying to get hold of it.'

The master-at-arms slipped the opal back into the bag Clifford held out and placed it in his inner pocket along with the ring. 'I will secure these items immediately and inform the captain of developments.'

'Good.' Seldon cleared his throat. 'And I would like to request that the rest of Yeoman's luggage is brought up for thorough examination. Joint examination, of course.'

The master-at-arms shrugged. 'That would be no problem if there were any luggage to retrieve. Which there is not.' With a cool nod, he turned on his heel and left.

Eleanor grimaced as the door closed hard behind him. 'And well done, Chief Inspector, Lady Swift, for finding a major clue that my men missed!'

'You could hardly expect him to admit to that,' Seldon said.

She noticed he was frowning. 'Hugh, why did you want to see Yeoman's luggage?'

He shrugged. 'It's irrelevant now, as it seems I was wrong. It's just that, if Yeoman brought nothing with him except that opal you found in his cabin, he must have fenced all the stolen items he'd amassed over the years. And exchanged the profits all for that one gem which he was intending to sell in America, I assume. But what's troubling me is that even if you add up the possible value of the stolen items I was pretty sure Yeoman hadn't fenced, it wouldn't be enough for him to buy that opal, according to Padgett anyway. Even on the black market. Maybe especially on the black market.' He threw his hands out. 'Nevertheless, it seems however Yeoman got hold of that opal, it was almost certainly the motive for his murder.'

'So, we just need to find the murderer.' Eleanor's jaw clenched. 'And quickly!'

14

That Seldon had confessed he felt too sick to talk about the case any further told Eleanor he must be on his last legs. He wasn't one to admit defeat. Ever. Just as she never did, either. Which made his enforced cabin rest, and Clifford being absent on evidently essential errands, all the more frustrating.

'No one except you to chew over the little we've learned so far, old chum,' she huffed to Gladstone as he skipped out the door and down the corridor. Spinning around, he woofed expectantly.

'No, silly,' she chivvied him on under the wide glassed-over walkway named 'The Orangery'. 'There are no sausages here. We're just going for a stroll to clear my head.'

As they walked, she nodded to the occupants of the rattan recliners, each swathed under a sea of furs amid a proliferation of potted palms. But despite her words, when they reached the door leading to the next deck, Gladstone stopped sulkily. Stiffening his whole stocky body in mutiny, he refused to move.

She tutted. 'It's honestly not dinner time, Mr Wilful. Though I have got some of your favourite liver treats with me.' She pulled the tin Clifford had thoughtfully left with the bulldog's lead from her pocket and shook it. This galvanised Gladstone to leap through the door. She fed him three of the hard baked squares as reward, then dodged his licky thank you. 'So now you're happy, you greedy thing. But I still have to wait until my dinner time when I'll have a chance to talk to the suspects the captain promised to invite to his table.' She rounded the corner and stopped. 'Or maybe I won't!'

Huddled under a blanket each, in a semicircle of otherwise empty deckchairs, were the formidable mother and her equally sturdily built daughter. Eleanor recognised them from the excellent descriptions the master-at-arms had provided. She pursed her lips. The mother had bribed the steward to make sure they sat next to Yeoman. Why?

She looked discreetly over at the two women again. How odd. They seemed frozen to the marrow but were choosing to sit out in the stiff March breeze rather than in The Orangery.

'Maybe the daughter has a weak chest?' she mused. 'And a doctor has prescribed the sea air?' Gladstone looked up at her. 'I know, boy. No disrespect to either lady, but, like you, they look as robust as oxen!'

She wandered over, as if admiring the endless ocean view. Reaching the deckchair next to the mother, she nodded to the steward, who hurried over with a silver trolley. Selecting a laundry-fresh mint and moss green check wool blanket, she settled into the seat.

'It's really quite bracing today, isn't it?' she said brightly.

Without looking at her, the older woman replied, 'It is March. And this is the Atlantic. It is always "bracing"!' Her clipped English accent held less warmth than the winter wind.

Her daughter shook her head petulantly, her voice carrying with the resonance of a foghorn. 'I'd say it's freezing! Why do we have to—'

'Hush, Rosamund!' her mother hissed. 'You know perfectly well why.'

Eleanor smiled warmly. 'I'm Lady Swift, by the way. Lovely to meet you both.'

'Theodora Swalecourt,' the older woman replied stiffly.

'Mrs,' her younger double said pointedly.

'And this' – Mrs Swalecourt glared at the young woman – 'is my delightful daughter, Rosamund.'

From the inflection on the word 'delightful' she means obstinate, Ellie!

The three of them turned at the loud rumble of male laughter. Eleanor caught Mrs Swalecourt whipping out a hand from under her blankets to poke her daughter sharply in the leg. In unison, they both sat straighter, any sign of cold or disgruntlement lost in the winning smiles they now sported.

Ah! On the hunt for a suitor, Ellie. Hence braving the March wind.

'Men!' Eleanor tutted and threw her hands out.

'More? Where?' Mrs Swalecourt quickly looked around.

'No, I meant how is it they don't seem to feel the cold? Look at us ladies all wrapped up. That lot,' she said, pointing to where the laughter was coming from, 'would probably slide out of their coats and leap straight into the Atlantic without it even being a dare.' She gasped. 'Gracious, forgive my runaway tongue. I didn't mean to be insensitive.'

Mrs Swalecourt eyed her coolly. 'Insensitive? How?'

'Oh, because of that poor man who fell overboard. I haven't heard that he was rescued. Have you?'

There was no missing the fleetingly shared glance and then a busy rearrangement of blankets from the mother and daughter.

'No, we haven't heard,' Mrs Swalecourt said in a blunt tone. 'But we are not travelling to court gossip about our fellow passengers.'

No. Just to court anyone who will give your daughter a second look.

The, admittedly attractive, young men whose laughter had interrupted them drew level. They paused in clutching their boaters in the wind to doff them respectfully before ambling on, jostling each other good-naturedly.

The sigh Mrs Swalecourt gave as they dropped into a group of deckchairs further down made Eleanor wince.

Maybe your earlier remark was uncharitable, Ellie. Maybe she's actually trying to do her best for her daughter. Maybe she has no choice.

She knew well that if the family had fallen on hard times – perhaps the husband and breadwinner had died – marriage or destitution were sometimes the only choices for the daughter. Or living meagrely off the goodwill, or not so goodwill, of a richer relative. If, that is, you were fortunate to have one who would deign to take you in.

She shot her a sympathetic glance, but reminded herself the mother, and potentially her daughter, were suspects in a murder.

'Your husband not travelling with you?'

Mrs Swalecourt hesitated. 'No... he's busy. He runs a frightfully successful business, so has little time for... this sort of thing.'

'Sounds fascinating. What field is he in?'

'He is a renowned antiquarian. He deals exclusively in rare and precious antiques, hence the name of his business – Golden Age Antiquities.'

'Well,' Eleanor said. 'Fortunately, I do have the time for this sort of thing. I'm travelling to celebrate my birthday and make lots of new acquaintances.' She looked pensive. 'Shame I didn't have the chance to meet him before the poor fellow was lost at sea. I've been told he was quite an interesting character.'

The mother and daughter glanced at each other again and shuffled deeper into their blankets without responding.

Okay, Ellie, you'll have to push a little harder.

She caught the young girl's eye. 'Perhaps you had, though, Rosamund? Met him, I mean?'

The daughter hesitated and then nodded. 'We—'

'No,' her mother snapped. 'We did not meet him.' She gave Eleanor a hard stare. 'And we were both asleep in our cabins when he fell. According to the gossip about the time of his death, anyway.'

Eleanor kept her features neutral. *It seems strange she should offer an unasked-for alibi for the time of Yeoman's death to a complete stranger.*

Before Eleanor could respond, another woman folded her elegant curves into the deckchair beside her. It was the raven-haired beauty who, like her, had been admiring Yeoman dance on deck in the Sports Challenge. The woman flapped a dismissive hand at the steward hovering with a blanket. 'Nothing but mink for me.' Swathed from her coiffed ebony tresses down to her perfectly turned-out ankles in the silver fur that complemented her flawless olive skin, she looked between the three of them. 'Tell me you're talking of something interesting? I am so bored on this floating prison already!'

Eleanor hid a smile 'We were talking about men, actually.'

'Ugh!' The woman tossed her head. 'Rather letting our side down, aren't we? The male ego really needs no further pandering or buffing.'

The young girl let out a giggle, which earned her a furious glare from her mother. 'Actually, that topic was one we had unwillingly been pulled into.' Mrs Swalecourt shot Eleanor a pointed look.

She held her hands up. 'By me. Lady Swift.' She introduced the other two women to the newcomer, who then introduced herself.

'Miss Florentina González.'

'Delighted,' Eleanor said genuinely, since that was another

name on the captain's suspect list. 'I was merely noting how different male tolerance to the weather is compared to ours.'

Miss González laughed bitterly. 'Nothing more than bravado. Bloated pride is really a most effective overcoat.'

'A rather sweeping and tainted view,' Mrs Swalecourt snapped. 'Not one appropriate for a debutante to be subjected to, I'll thank you. There are plenty of eligible gentlemen who are decent and humble.'

'"Eligible"? Maybe. "Decent and humble", no! Marriage is erroneously considered an institution.'

Rosamund leaned forward. 'Well, if it isn't an institution, what is it, Miss González?'

'Female penance! Self-inflicted martyrdom that we might keep the world populated. Nothing more.'

Eleanor bit her tongue and settled further back into her deckchair to await the fireworks.

'Really! Preposterous!' Mrs Swalecourt fought her way out of several layers of blankets. 'Rosamund, we shall excuse ourselves from such conversation, forthwith!'

Taking her daughter's rather reluctant arm, she peered down her flared nostrils at Miss González. 'I wish you enlightenment that you might one day experience the greatest gift life offers.'

'Oh, don't worry,' she said coolly. 'I already do. It's called staying single!'

As the mother and daughter walked off, Miss González's face broke into an ugly smile. She shrugged at Eleanor's look. 'Someone had to tell the poor girl for her own good. What is she, barely twenty? And already doomed.'

Eleanor laughed uneasily, her own experience with marriage leaving her torn. 'Well, you certainly told her.'

'Excellent. Now, I'm bored *and* cold. Let's go and warm up.'

Eleanor nodded. *After all, she's ruined your chance of*

getting anything further from Mrs Swalecourt and her daughter,
so let's see what you can find out from her.

As she rose along with Miss González, for the first time she noticed the pendant the other woman was wearing was in the shape of... a bee.

15

Among the myriad facilities available on board the *Celestiana*, there were the Turkish baths. Seven intricately mosaic tiled and colonnaded adjoining rooms ranging from glacial to tropical, depending on one's preference of the moment. It was here Eleanor's companion led her.

Eleanor smiled a thank you to the attendant, who suggested Gladstone keep her company in the staff office area while they bathed. Tightening the belt on the sumptuous ivory robe she'd been assisted into by yet another starched, white-overalled attendant, she followed Miss González.

'You know, I haven't had the delight of visiting one of these since I was last in Turkey itself. This is particularly exquisite.' Her companion, however, seemed disinterested in anything other than reaching the steam room as quickly as possible, so Eleanor held back on the rest of her raptures. But ever appreciative of the luxuries afforded to her, she paused at the neatly lined up loungers around the plunge pool to admire the décor. The room's blues of every hue depicted scenes of bathing Greek gods and goddesses, running up to the domed roof. The tiled palette then ran on into the blended greens of the cooling room's tranquil fresco and the warm sandy-yellow and soft-orange tones of the temperate room.

'Finally,' Miss González huffed as they were escorted through the heavy doors into the steam room, which was decorated in more shades of gold than Eleanor could remember seeing. Nine desert-gold marble plinths, each reached by three steps, surrounded a central statue. The statue comprised nine full-sized rearing winged horses who snorted alternate jets of eucalyptus, rosemary and lemon into the hot, damp air.

Her companion stretched herself out gracefully on one of the expansive fluffy white towels and accompanying soft bolster pillows. Eleanor took her towel with a little less elegance as she sprawled on her stomach to better watch Miss González's responses to the questions she had yet to formulate.

Dash it, Ellie! Thrown into needing to think on your feet again. Actually, off them.

She laid her chin on her folded forearms. 'This would be the perfect place to recover after one of those sports challenges.'

Her companion snorted. 'If you say so. I certainly shan't be indulging, or making an exhibition of myself, which amounts to the same thing.'

'Not a sporty girl, then? Fair enough.'

The supine Miss González settled further into her pillow, obscuring Eleanor's clear view of her expression. Nonchalantly, Eleanor rose onto her elbows, pretending to admire her nails.

'The dancing contest was fun to watch though, wasn't it?'

'Can't say I noticed.'

'Oh, come on. You may not want to get married, but there's no harm in looking at some handsome chaps in their sports gear, is there?'

'If that's your sort of thing, no.'

Eleanor sighed inwardly. Getting this striking beauty to

open up was going to be no easier than Mrs Swalecourt and her daughter, although the young girl had seemed more willing to talk.

'This steam is so relaxing. Such a contrast to the plunge pool. That would be as icy as falling into the Atlantic itself.' She gasped, her hand shooting to her mouth. 'Oh gracious, like that man who fell overboard must have felt.'

Her companion hesitated before replying. 'Well, he should have been less heedless then.'

'Heedless?'

'Yes, heedless. The rest of us have managed to navigate the decks without falling or throwing ourselves overboard. Even in elegant heels.' She lifted her head an inch to hold Eleanor's gaze with fiery eyes. 'Which I can see you find a harsh observation. But it's true.'

'Is it?' Eleanor looked over at their marble horse, now bathing them with wafts of bergamot, as if considering her response. 'Everyone is entitled to their opinion. But perhaps I need to apologise for mentioning him at all. Maybe you knew him?'

'No. I didn't,' she said coldly.

That was a hurried denial, Ellie.

Before she could think of a follow-up question, her companion lay back down. 'So, will you still be sailing on the *Celestiana* on the day of your actual birthday?'

'How intriguing!' Eleanor forced a laugh, feeling a little unnerved. 'How did you know it was my birthday so soon? I mentioned it to Mrs Swalecourt and her daughter, but that was several minutes before you joined us.'

Has she been eavesdropping?

'This is the *Celestiana*. One cannot move without being assaulted by some form of astrological imagery. There is a display of the signs of the zodiac and the common characteristics of each etched into the glass next to the main staircase. I'd have thought you'd seen it. From reading it, you're obviously a Pisces.'

Eleanor hid her unease. *How did she know?* She shrugged. 'I am a Pisces. But I've no idea what strengths I supposedly embody.'

The woman lifted her head again and glared at her. 'Neither do I. But I do know one weakness of Pisces is the inability to confront reality!' She stood up. 'And the reality is, I'm bored with your inquisitiveness. Now, I'll leave you to enjoy the steam.'

Is she right, Ellie? Do you hide from reality?

'One question.' Eleanor turned onto her back, resting on her elbows as if she had little interest in what she was about to say. 'Just to satisfy my "inquisitiveness", which must be another weakness of Pisces, I presume. Why are you on the *Celestiana* if you find it so boring already?' She recalled Miss González staring longingly at Yeoman. 'Perhaps, despite your protestations to the contrary to Mrs Swalecourt, you're here to find a man as well?'

She jumped as the woman spun around, her features contorted with anger. 'Wrong! I'm here to forget entirely about men. And to have no dealings with so-called love ever, ever again!'

As Miss González strode away, Eleanor climbed off the plinth, wrapped a towel around herself and walked back to the changing room, unable to dislodge the frown on her face.

Maybe Miss González did come to forget about love, but she certainly seemed enamoured of Yeoman at the Sports Challenge. But then again, Ellie, if you're honest, he captivated you for a moment too.

She shook her head. She needed a far more logical and methodical brain than hers to work out what she'd learned, or not, from the Swalecourts and Miss González. And, luckily, she had two.

Collecting Gladstone, she headed in search of them.

16

'Miles Bracebridge.' The captain shook Seldon's hand. 'Thank you for coming to my office, Chief Inspector. As I'm sure Lady Swift has explained to you, the worst kind of brute has infiltrated my ship. I need him rounded up forthwith.'

'Or her.' Eleanor slid into the deep-buttoned velvet seat Clifford held out for her, while he restrained Gladstone with one impeccably shiny shoe. 'We have no certainty we aren't dealing with a female monster.'

'Or her, quite right.' Bracebridge tapped his wide oak desk. 'Though only being au fait with the worst of male propensities after thirty-six years in the navy, that notion does not sit easily with me, I admit.'

Eleanor didn't miss the pained clench of Seldon's jaw as he spoke. 'Even after less years in the police, sadly it sits all too easily, if equally uncomfortably, with me, Captain.'

He nodded. 'I do not need to press home how critical total discretion on your part will be, Chief Inspector, I'm sure.'

Seldon nodded. 'Lady Swift has also explained that.'

'Good. I have arranged for a room to be at your disposal. Day or night. Please consider it your base of operations.

Anything else you require...' He gave Clifford, who was standing by the door with Gladstone, an enquiring look.

'We'll arrange everything with your master-at-arms,' Eleanor said quickly, not wanting to get into a wrangle about her butler's presence. 'And Clifford will see to our routine needs.'

Bracebridge opened his mouth as if to reply, but then closed it. After a moment, he rose.

'That's settled then. I'll wait to hear from you. Now, please excuse me, Lady Swift. Chief Inspector. I'll leave you in the hands of my master-at-arms.'

He strode out.

To Eleanor's relief, Seldon had been looking a little less peaky since Clifford had plied him with more of his magical seasickness remedies. However, as they followed the master-at-arms down several corridors, his gait seemed uncharacteristically slow. Even at his reduced pace, however, they soon arrived at the room that would be their operations centre. It was dominated by a large mahogany table and floor-to-ceiling leather tome filled bookcases.

Seldon turned to the master-at-arms. 'We haven't been formally introduced, by the way. Hugh Seldon. Scotland Yard, for my sins.'

He offered his hand. This received a single tug of greeting.

'Master-at-arms. Formerly of His Majesty's Navy.'

'Excellent.' Seldon's tone suggested he was unfazed by the man's abrupt manner. 'It's good to be working with someone of your experience.'

'On your holiday, were you?' The master-at-arms' manner was a little less terse. 'Good of you to give it up. Rare as they are, I imagine.'

'True. But at least if I do get the odd day, it isn't spent incarcerated in a floating nightmare, as yours must be.'

The master-at-arms' lips pursed. 'One's man's nightmare is another's calling, Chief Inspector.'

'Which today we share in needing to hunt out a murderer. To work, then.' Seldon set off unsteadily to the mahogany table. 'Where had you planned to take the investigation next?'

Ten minutes later, the unspoken but tentative truce between the two men had resulted in several agreements being reached.

'That's brilliant, Master-at-Arms! And very reassuring,' Eleanor said genuinely. 'You'll use the *Celestiana*'s ingenious on-board radio to make discreet enquiries about our suspects. Then, when we interview them, discreetly as well, of course, we—'

He leaned forward, the stripes on his jacket cuffs reflecting in the mirror-deep polish of the table. 'Lady Swift! The chief inspector will lead you in how to conduct each, I repeat, *each* discussion with those passengers. And you'll pass all and any information you glean on to me. Immediately.'

Keen to make this awkward situation work, she swallowed the reply that this wasn't her first investigation. Nor her first collaboration with Seldon on such matters. Instead, she smiled sweetly, busying her would-be clenched fists with ruffling Gladstone's ears under the table. 'How fortuitous the inspector was aboard. Imagine how I might otherwise have unintentionally run amok, accosting suspects willy-nilly, as it were.'

The master-at-arms snorted. 'I can imagine. These things require a professional with experience.' With a nod to Seldon, he stalked out.

'Phew!' Seldon breathed as the door clicked shut, leaving the three of them alone. 'I've met some hard-boiled eggs before—'

'But he's the full ten minutes.' Eleanor flapped a hand at Clifford's disapproving arch of one brow. 'And how would you describe him then, Mr Ever-Even-Handed?'

His inscrutable expression didn't flinch. 'As hard boiled as he is headed, my lady.'

Seldon's rich chuckle made her smile.

'That almost sounded like the old Hugh. Which is good. I rather liked him.'

'Really?' His cheeks flushed. 'Er, right. That was a capital idea of yours, to get the captain to invite the suspects to his table tonight, Eleanor. But it won't be easy for you to ask much without it being obvious. However, for your first interview, please remember—'

'Third,' she corrected.

'Third what? Interview?'

She nodded. 'I couldn't let two excellent opportunities slip by, so I played the natural gossip card with Mrs Swalecourt and her daughter when I bumped into them earlier. And then with Miss González.'

Clifford placed a silver dish of assorted nibbles on the table. 'With apologies, Chief Inspector, the provided tableware is not up to her ladyship's usual standard. Perhaps one might find it easier to share from another seat?' He slid the dish further onto Eleanor's side.

'No problem,' Seldon said distractedly as he unfolded himself and made the unsteady trip to fold himself into the seat tucked in beside her. Evidently oblivious to the cloud of butterflies that his close presence had released in her, he sprawled across the table to retrieve the drink he'd left behind. They bumped hands, reaching for the olives. And again, as they both switched to the walnuts. He coughed awkwardly.

'So, you said you've spoken to two suspects, assuming we're counting the mother and daughter as one suspect?'

She nodded. 'For the moment, I assume so.'

'So who did you pounce on first?'

She hid a smile and glanced at Clifford. 'Pounced? Objection! Adjudicator?'

'Overruled, my lady,' her butler said mischievously.

Seldon held his hand up. 'It was a joke! Honest.'

She smiled. 'Well then, just to upset you, and Clifford's sense of order, I'll do them in reverse. Starting with the exquisite beauty that is Miss Florentina González. In the Turkish baths, she said—'

Seldon stared at her. 'The what?'

She rolled her eyes. 'Hugh, do you go anywhere but your ever-groaning desk and the criminal streets?'

'Chief Inspector,' Clifford said. 'Imagine a luxuriously decorated Victorian bathing house, offering a range of restorative treatments and none of the illicit activities a, ahem, *mutton shunter* would have been required for.'

Seldon nodded. 'Ah, that's clear.'

Eleanor stared between them. 'Not to me, it isn't. A "mutton" *what*?'

'Alas, as your butler, decorum forbids, my lady.' Clifford turned on his heel.

'Hugh?'

He coloured. 'A policeman who was tasked with moving on, umm, ladies of the night, as it were. Thank you, Clifford! Quickly moving on ourselves, what did you learn from speaking to this Miss González?'

'Only that she's seething over being jilted.' She seesawed her head. 'Actually, that's an assumption. She declared she's here because she's done with all men. And definitely with love.'

'Silly girl,' Seldon muttered.

'Well, silly maybe, but done with love? Plainly not, I'd say, no matter how much she protests, she was devouring Yeoman's every dance move closer than I was. Umm, than I was standing, I mean.' She coloured at his stare. 'Look, Hugh, I—'

He held up his hand. 'It's alright, Eleanor. Actually, I was just wondering... I mean, it's a long shot, but...'

Her eyes widened. 'You don't think that it was... Yeoman who dumped her?'

He nodded slowly. 'It's possible. The name's wrong. Yeoman, as far as I remember, was engaged under another false name – Solomon Pinner. But I can't remember to whom. If González *is* an alias, then if you could find out her real name, I might recall it.'

'Okay. Oh, and I forgot to mention. It might be nothing, but she was wearing a gold pendant in the shape of a bee.'

Seldon ran his hand along his chin. 'Mm, interesting. The ring we believe belonged to Yeoman has a bee on it. Coincidental?'

'They could be unusual engagement gifts to each other. A bee is a symbol of love in some cultures, my ever-knowledgeable butler informed me.'

Seldon grunted. 'Either way, *if* it was Yeoman who dumped her, maybe she was on the *Celestiana* to try and win him back. Maybe they got into a row and...'

She nodded. 'Or she was out for revenge from the start?'

'This is all assumption, but it's certainly not beyond possibility. Or even that she was a criminal herself and worked with Yeoman.'

'In which case, you mean she might not have been in love with him at all? Maybe it was a business arrangement, and she just wanted him out of the way to have the opal to herself?'

He nodded. 'It still doesn't explain how she knew to set me up for the murder if that was the case. Unless Yeoman did know I was tailing him? Maybe he did see me on the boat and recognised me?'

'And perhaps he then told Miss González, unwittingly giving her the perfect patsy for his own murder.' Her hand flew to her mouth. 'I'm sorry, Hugh, I didn't mean—'

He shrugged wearily. 'No, it was quite accurate. Someone,

whether or not it's Miss González, has done a first-class job of incriminating me. And unless we can find the real culprit...' He spread his hands.

Hugh will hang for it, Ellie.

17

Clifford swiftly poured the contents of a silver cocktail shaker into a couple of crystal-cut goblets lined with mint. He passed one to each of them.

Eleanor took a sip. 'Ooh, ginger wine. Lovely!' she said over-brightly, trying to ease the tension now filling their base of operations.

Clifford added potted lobster-topped wafers and crab saltines to the table.

Seldon took a large swig of his drink. His shoulders relaxed. 'Thank you, Clifford. Moving on again, what did you learn from Mrs Swalecourt and her daughter, Eleanor?'

She marshalled her thoughts. 'They denied knowing Yeoman. However, they also, unasked, provided an alibi for his time of death, which was rather odd. Mrs Swalecourt seemed rather on the defensive. And I'm sure Rosamund, the daughter, was about to inadvertently let something slip, but she was hushed up. Poor girl.'

'Domineering mother?'

'Very. But while watching Yeo— the dancing contest, I

noticed her bribing the steward to set up two deckchairs beside him.'

Clifford cleared his throat. 'My lady, at the risk of offering a contrary opinion, such an act is far from uncommon, thus perhaps not suspicious. Cruises such as this are quietly referred to in unrepeatable terms amongst eligible gentlemen whose voyages are plagued by predatory mothers. I would conjecture Mrs Swalecourt considered Mr Yeoman a suitable suitor for her daughter.'

Seldon let out a low growl without looking up from jotting more notes. 'The murdering swine. Some suitor!'

Eleanor nodded. 'Which shows that she really can't have known much about him, I suppose. Except that he could afford to travel first class. But she wasn't being very subtle about having Yeoman in her matchmaking sights, so it seems odd she would say she knew nothing about him.'

She shook her head. Even if Mrs Swalecourt was successful in finding her daughter a husband, would the marriage ever be a happy one? *Love just doesn't work that way, Ellie.* Mind you, she groaned to herself, who was she to judge after one disastrous marriage which had lasted all of a few months? Since then, she'd played it safe. Just as Seldon had since his wife died. She peered across the table at him. *How ironic to actually be spending more time with him on your birthday week, Ellie, than you had originally planned. Although, it's not quite how you'd have planned to spend it!*

She noticed Seldon staring at her oddly. She shook herself. 'And it seems even more peculiar if her husband is as successful in business as she says he is, that she's apparently so desperate to find a husband for her daughter. Hopefully, the master-at-arms will have some background information on them soon that will shed some light on it all.'

He grunted and then looked up at Clifford. 'Do mothers

really trawl the oceans for a husband to take their daughters off their hands?'

Clifford nodded. 'Suffice to say, a dredger might be a more suitable craft in certain cases, such as Mrs Swalecourt.'

'Mmm. Swalecourt,' she said. 'I didn't really think of it at the time, but it's an unusual name. All the stranger then.'

Seldon shrugged. 'What is?'

'Oh, nothing relevant, Hugh. Just that, I would have thought her husband would have used his surname for his business, as it's so distinctive.'

He shrugged. 'What is it called, then?'

'Mm, let me think.' She tapped Clifford's pen against her chin. 'Something Age Antiquities. Ah, Golden Age Antiquities.'

Seldon slapped the table. 'That name came up in an investigation some years ago relating to the sale of stolen antiquities. I remember it because there was a suggestion some of the items were pilfered by none other than Yeoman!'

'Do these antiquities also cover jewellery, by any chance?'

Seldon nodded. 'A connection to the opal, perhaps? Our expert thought it might have come from a necklace.'

'My lady,' Clifford said. 'Another meeting with the formidable Mrs Swalecourt, perchance?'

'Absolutely.'

She'd noticed Seldon had lost the last faint flush of colour that had suffused his drawn cheeks. Clearly, her butler had noticed it too.

'Perhaps a moment of air, Chief Inspector.' Clifford twisted the handle on the nearest porthole. But as it swung open, it let in much more than just the fresh sea breeze. A rumpus of male voices assaulted their ears.

'Got you!' barked the harshest of them.

'It's the master-at-arms,' Eleanor hissed. 'Who has he got?'

She craned her neck out of the window but could only see Bracebridge's back.

She ducked back inside. 'Quick! Both of you. Maybe they've caught our murderer!'

Even Seldon seemed to muster enough of his balance to charge out after her. Clifford followed, leaving Gladstone hoovering up crumbs under the table.

On deck Bracebridge and the master-at arms-stood in front of a burly sailor who obviously had someone in his grip. As she drew level, she could see the captured man clearly.

Only he wasn't a man. He was a rake of a child in tattered britches and a threadbare, button-shy jacket whose sleeves ended three inches short of his scrawny wrists.

'Honest, guv, I wasn't,' the boy stuttered between sobs.

She sensed Clifford flinch behind her as the captain waved at the master-at-arms. 'To the brig. The New York police can deal with him.'

'Police!' the boy cried, his bare, calloused feet slipping on the deck as he struggled. 'I ain't stolen nothin'.'

'You have stolen passage aboard my ship,' Bracebridge said firmly. 'Being a stowaway is a serious maritime crime.'

Eleanor's words tumbled out before she realised they had even formed on her tongue. 'Captain? Forgive my intervening.'

Bracebridge turned with a frown. 'Ah, Lady Swift. Et al., I see. If I might ask that you vacate the area?'

'Yes, of course.' She stepped to his side, wincing at how truly thin the boy was up close. 'But you haven't heard this young man's story.'

He held her gaze. 'Maritime law is clear on the matter of stowaways, Lady Swift.'

'I just ain't got no pennies,' the boy wailed. 'I ain't got nothin'. And no one. Empty belly and the streets is all I had for longer 'n two year after me older sister died. She was me last family.'

Her heart flew out to him. And to Clifford. Her butler was listening to his own tragic childhood tale. His guardian had died suddenly too, leaving no will, monies or shelter of any kind for his twelve-year-old ward. The streets had been his home from then on.

'Why did you stow away?' she said to the boy.

'To beg, miss. Not to pick pockets, I swear.'

'And why exactly to New York?'

''Cos everyone's rich! That's what they say. But I ain't got no way to get there other than hiding out up in that.' He jerked his head at the nearest lifeboat. 'Didn't mean to break no laws.'

'Captain. A moment, please,' Eleanor said in a low tone with a beseeching nod that they step aside.

He did as she bid. Clifford glided silently behind him.

'Captain, he's just a boy.'

'That's as may be, but I am duty bound—'

'To what?' Her cheeks flushed. 'Hurl all compassion overboard by sending a starving lad of barely twelve to jail? In a foreign country? All for the heinous crime of...' her throat clenched, 'of being orphaned and thus entirely alone in the world?'

Bracebridge avoided her gaze. 'Point taken. What are you suggesting?'

Eleanor's lips moved, but the awfulness of the boy's situation had got the better of her and no words came out. Clifford took a respectful step forward.

'Captain, if I may? Her ladyship is submitting a proposal that solves a significant failure of service on board your ship.'

Bracebridge raised an eyebrow. 'Which is?'

'The scandalous service her ladyship has received in being expected to do without a cabin boy for all intents and purposes.'

Eleanor, catching on, nodded, arms folded. 'Had I not brought Clifford with me, I would have been left entirely high and dry to fend for myself.'

Bracebridge seemed to be hiding a smile. 'Which you are eminently capable of doing, Lady Swift, after your years travelling, I'm sure. But, I agree, you should not have to do so in any regard aboard the *Celestiana*. Especially as the prestigious guest of Mr Walker.'

'Thank you. So you'll take the boy on as temporary cabin crew for food and shelter until we reach New York? If he proves himself, you might choose to keep him on permanently.' She carried on before Bracebridge could reply. 'And if not, you've lost nothing since you can still hand him over to the police in New York.'

Bracebridge ran his thumb and forefinger along his jaw. 'Supposing the boy steals or upsets one of the other first-class passengers?'

She looked at the young lad who was staring at her open-mouthed. 'I will vouch for him. Any costs, damage or trouble rendered, I shall immediately rectify.'

'Very well.' Bracebridge nodded and strode away with the lad and sailors.

Clifford permitted himself the luxury of a relieved sigh as they shared a look. 'My lady, thank you, more than words can convey. From the boy. And from myself.'

She nudged his elbow. 'It was the least I could do.' She frowned. 'You know, though. None of us had thought of that.'

'Thought of what?' Seldon said, reaching her side.

She pursed her lips. 'That our murderer could also be a stowaway.'

He nodded slowly. 'Which means they could be anywhere!'

18

Despite her outward confidence, inside, Eleanor's trepidation at the responsibility she had accepted was weighing her down. This time, more than ever, it mattered. Hugh's career – and more frighteningly, his liberty and life – were on the line.

She composed herself, smoothing down her peacock-green silk cocktail gown with its delicately beaded bodice and vivacious fringe skirt. The memory of Seldon gently holding her arms out from her sides and whispering, 'Simply too, too beautiful,' came back to her.

So, shoulders straight, head up and remember what Mother used to say. 'The more it matters, darling, the more it's worth fighting for.'

Taking a deep breath, she stepped into the palatial domain of the first-class lounge where pre-dinner cocktails were held. The air was awash with clipped aristocratic voices, foreign accents and the tinkling of grand piano keys. The impressive instrument itself had been slid gracefully to one side of its normal centre stage position. In its place were two large concentric rings of tables dressed in ivory linen with a dazzling tower of gold-rimmed champagne glasses on each. Between the two, a regiment of twenty-five pristine-aproned waiters stood poised to set the air ringing with the popping of corks. The scene of sumptuous luxury had been further adorned with over thirty waist-high purple arum lily and bird of paradise flower arrangements. And forming a breathtaking canopy over the whole room was a gossamer net strung with a thousand glass stars, which shimmered in the golden glow of the immense chandelier.

Tearing her gaze away, she scanned the lounge for any of the suspects she would recognise. But the moving sea of black velvet dinner jackets and white bow ties made it impossible to distinguish between the men. The women, equally, were a blur of silver-threaded, pearl-encrusted and gem-beaded cocktail gowns.

A hush fell over the room. Captain Bracebridge stood in front of the champagne tables.

'Ladies and gentlemen. Last night I was otherwise engaged with an emergency and therefore unable to join you for dinner. Tonight, the honour is mine to welcome you all to the maiden voyage of the miracle that is the *Celestiana*. The largest, and most luxurious, liner in the world!' As the applause died down, the army of waiters served the entire contingent of guests with a highball of translucent liquid. Bracebridge raised the one he held. 'If, before we begin with the champagne, I might prevail upon you to first humour me by joining in with an old naval tradition. Gin and water. Ladies and gentlemen. To your exceptionally good health.'

This received a near unanimous 'Hear! Hear!' The only dissenters Eleanor noted were the rather stiff couple, the Wrenshaw-Smythes, who had joined her and the high-spirited Count Balog but abstained from drinking.

As the rest of the room moved on to champagne, the hubbub of chatter resumed. She finished her gin and placed it on the tray of a passing waiter, wondering who to tackle first. The decision was made for her.

'To directly interrupt a lady so absorbed before would have been boorish.' The deep voice came from a gnarled oak of a face framed by a thick, bushy moustache and russet brown thatch of hair. The man patted his barrel of a chest, making the walking cane on his wrist swing. 'Randolph Everton Asquith. Sir.' His dark eyes held a hint of something she couldn't place as he added, 'How fortuitous to meet you, Lady Swift.'

'Ah, Sir Randolph. Good evening.' She forced an airy tone, for not only had she no idea how he knew who she was, he was also one of the very people she sought. 'You have left me rather on the back foot since we have not previously met. I believe, however, you are in the hotel business?'

He looked at her in surprise. 'I was not aware my fame had preceded me, Lady Swift. Shall we sit?'

She laughed as they made themselves comfortable in two sumptuous armchairs. 'Well, it has, Sir Randolph. Maybe I've stayed in one of your wonderful hotels myself?'

He stroked his moustache. 'It is possible. No, likely, as I have a fair few dotted around the country. Where do you reside?'

'Buckinghamshire, for my sins.'

He thought for a moment. 'My nearest three properties are in Berkshire and Oxfordshire and Bedfordshire, I think.'

'Bedfordshire?'

'Yes, Ardwycke Manor.'

'Ah! Well, I may not have stayed there, but my dear friend was married at Ardwycke Manor last year. Unfortunately, I couldn't be there, but she told me the venue was magnificent.'

He nodded in satisfaction. 'I am not surprised. It is a first-rate property with a first-rate manager, although it cost me a small fortune to bring it back to its former glory after the war.' He waved at a passing waiter and secured two champagnes. He passed one to her and raised his. 'Health has already been toasted. What would you therefore suggest we salute this time?'

She hesitated, then raised hers. 'To a long life.'

He shook his head dismissively. 'A squandered toast since the two go hand in hand, surely?'

'Only if good health is given the chance to lengthen one's life, Sir Randolph.'

She flinched as he laughed loudly. 'Cynicism or insight, Lady Swift?'

'Neither. I was just thinking about unfortunate souls such as the poor man who fell overboard.' Something flashed across his eyes. She kept her voice neutral. 'He may have been in superlative health, but it did not help lengthen *his* life.'

He grunted. 'Maybe not. I never met the fellow. I am interested only in my family and my business. And as he had no part in either...' He waved a dismissive hand.

Rather callous, Ellie.

'The *Celestiana*,' she said, taking a sip of her champagne. 'She's a true beauty, wouldn't you agree?'

His eyes flicked around the room. 'Probably. I haven't the time to analyse her trimmings and trifles.'

She groaned inwardly. *Is anyone going to make this easy?* She fixed another smile on her face.

'So, you'll be staying on in New York for a while on business then, I assume?'

She jumped as he thumped his cane on the floor. 'Certainly not! I don't intend to spend more time than is absolutely essential in that infernal city.'

That appeared to be all he had to say on the matter, so she changed tack again.

'I suppose some people just come on these liners to enjoy the journey, rather than to actually get anywhere.'

Like you, Ellie.

He nodded. 'Naturally. This is merely a floating hotel to many.' He drummed his fingers on the table. 'The bona fide business travellers are easy to identify, however.'

'What a professional and experienced eye you have. Perhaps you'll be gracious enough to teach me an observational trick or two then.' She gestured discreetly to a nervous-looking man standing at the edge of the room. 'What about him?'

'Holidaymaker. With the desire, but insufficient confidence, to truly revel away the miles as he yearns to. Too easy.'

'And the couple over there?' She indicated the stiff Wren-shaw-Smythe husband and wife, the former of whom had so vehemently declared they were there on business.

He peered over from under his protruding brow. 'Mmm. Tricky. He has the air of a man on business, but she seems preoccupied with something else altogether.'

Before she could consider this observation, she caught sight of a red, knee-length jacket and black velvet knickerbockers.

'One more.' She pointed at Count Balog and lowered her voice. 'What about this chap making his way over? Travelling for business or pleasure, would you say?'

He took a cursory glance and snorted. 'Neither. Buckled slippers on a grown man have no place on either agenda.'

The count stopped in front of them with a soft click of his heels.

'Good evening.' He nodded first to her and then to the glow-ering Asquith. 'Diverting conversation abounds in this corner, I have no doubt.'

'Good evening, Count Balog,' Eleanor said. 'Indeed, it does. Sir Randolph was kindly sharing his professional expertise.' She caught the hotel owner narrowing his eyes.

'Then, permit me to learn also.' Balog settled himself in a nearby chair, where he took great care to arrange his jacket tails.

'Firstly, have you met, gentlemen?' she said.

'Not as such,' Asquith growled.

She made the introductions.

'So, what is it you were talking about so secretly?' Balog wiggled an eyebrow at Eleanor.

She grabbed the chance to steer the conversation back to Yeoman.

'Oh, it wasn't clandestine. We were just discussing the poor man who fell overboard.'

Well, you were a few minutes ago, even if Sir Randolph wasn't.

She looked enquiringly at the count. 'Can you tell me why he was on the *Celestiana*?'

Asquith shot her a look and tapped his cane on the floor, but said nothing.

Balog turned his lips down. 'I have not an idea. I saw him around, but I shared not one word with the man.'

Asquith snorted. 'A disgraceful state of affairs.'

'That he should be able to fall overboard?' Eleanor said.

'NO!' He thumped his cane on the floor again. 'That a person of his inferior standing should be allowed in first class.'

'Ah, so you *did* know him,' Balog said animatedly. 'What did I miss by not?'

'Nothing,' Asquith grunted. 'I can assure you of that. Not that I was in any way acquainted with him, make no mistake. I merely saw him around as you did, Count Balog. I meant purely that standards have slipped to an unprecedented low if first class can be infiltrated by the lower ranks. Of which, despite his tailored attire, he was indisputably one. If I'd seen him in one of my hotels, I'd have had a close watch put on him, I assure you.'

Eleanor was confused. For someone he claimed not to have met, Yeoman certainly had made a powerful impression on Sir Randolph.

Balog was looking at the other man with an odd smile playing around his lips. 'Oh, but it is so lucky the ladder up the ranks has its feet so firmly planted in the gutter to ensure those on the middle rungs do not fall.'

Asquith glared at the count. 'Your meaning, sir?'

'Meaning?' Balog stroked his pointed chin. 'I merely observe that not long ago, men of commercial interests would not have been permitted into first class. Men such as those who make their money by owning factories or... hotels.'

Asquith launched himself from his seat. 'Character is the only true mark of a gentleman, sir!' He snatched up his cane. 'And that man was of exceptionally bad character. Most evidently, for why else would he take the coward's way out?'

With a nod to Eleanor, and another glare at the beaming Balog, he stalked off into the throng.

She stared after him, her brain whirling. *Why was Sir Randolph determined to publicly blacken the name of a man he apparently had never even formally met?*

Having finally interrupted her jumbled thoughts sufficiently to put together a plausible excuse for ducking away from Balog, she went in search of Seldon.

'Ah, there you are,' she breathed in relief, hurrying to where he was hovering stiffly outside the entrance to the first-class lounge.

'Any progress?' His sigh stopped her from replying. 'Sorry, hello, Eleanor. Did I mention that you look...' He blushed.

'Yes, you did, thank you, Hugh. And you're right to jump straight to the case.' She tugged him further around the corner. 'That's why I came to find you. Without being able to note anything down, nor having Clifford floating about, it's too likely I'll forget something important.'

'Right.' Seldon surreptitiously whipped out his notebook.

'Sir Randolph definitely seems to hold ill-feeling against Yeoman, though he protested he'd never really met him.'

'Mmm. We need to find out why. The moment you go back in—'

She shook her head. 'He's too shrewd. He'll know that something is going on. He needs to cool off until halfway through the dinner courses.'

'Fine.'

'Fine?' She smiled. 'Just like that, Chief Inspector?'

'If you say so, yes.' He smiled back.

She glowed at his confidence in her. 'But as soon as the moment is right, I'll engage him in conversation again. I know.' She clicked her fingers. 'I've got an easy lead in. I'll pretend I am thinking of holding an event at one of his hotels after the recommendation from Katarina.'

'Who?'

'The daughter of one of Uncle Byron's long-standing friends. I shall blather on to Sir Randolph about Katarina's wedding since it was held at one of his hotels. I've already mentioned she thought it an exquisite venue. Then I'll wheedle the conversation around from there somehow.'

Seldon looked down at his page. 'Which hotel, just for completeness?'

'Ardwycke Manor in Bedfordshire.' Her eyes widened. 'Gracious... Hugh?' She took his arm. 'Oh goodness, you've gone completely ashen.'

'I'm alright. Thank you.' His voice was weak, all colour drained from his face. 'It was quite a shock, that's all.'

She wrinkled her brow. 'That she got married in a hotel? It was only because...' She broke off at his solemn headshake.

'No. That one of the hotels he owns is Ardwycke Manor.' He let out a long breath. 'That was the hotel the government commandeered...' He tailed off.

Her hand flew to her mouth. 'You mean the... the one... where your wife was working?'

He nodded sadly. 'When she was... murdered.'

'You alright?' she whispered.

He smiled, which took some of the sadness from his brown eyes. 'Always.'

She was far from convinced and risked a comforting squeeze of his arm. 'Can that really be a coincidence, though, Hugh? Sir Randolph owning that hotel?'

He sighed deeply. 'I don't know. He does own a lot of them. But it's something to dig into further, that's certain. Now, you'd better get back to your epic dinner or someone will spot that you're not actually the innocent lady of the manor you're playing.'

'You mean when I make a conversational faux pas and spill the first course down my front?' she said, trying to ease his discomfort at being reliant on her.

'Unquestionably, my lady,' he teased in a remarkable impression of her butler. 'Now, go do what you do so well!'

19

Seven heralds' trumpets, each with an indigo silk banner emblazoned with the *Celestiana*'s insignia, called the lounge to attention with a stately tune she couldn't name.

For her, though, this additional pageantry only heightened the incongruity of why she'd missed last night's call and the dinner itself. She had witnessed a man being murdered. A man who himself, it seemed, was a murderer. And of the foulest kind. For a moment, she wished with all her heart that they didn't need to find Yeoman's killer. For, if she was honest, at that moment, she had no stomach for it.

Tuning out the elegant waft of silk organza, mink trim and brushed velvet, and the genteel hum of sophisticated voices, she tried to marshal her thoughts. Despite Seldon's horror that she had launched into questioning suspects before conferring with him, it meant she had now already spoken to many of the names on her list. But that still left two.

As the final notes of the fanfare died away, the toast-master cried out, 'First sitting in session, ladies and gentlemen.'

Captain Bracebridge led the way, Eleanor accepting Count

Balog's offered elbow. As they entered the dining salon, she gasped.

You're right, Ellie. You can't miss out on an experience this wonderful. It's just too... magical.

Her table, like all the others, was dressed in indigo-edged ivory linen and set with a sea of glittering glassware and floral centrepieces of purple peonies, silvery eucalyptus sprays, and alabaster orchids. Additionally, being the captain's table, five lilac roses, interwoven with tessellated fritillary and lavender, graced the centrepiece.

The room itself was a breathtaking octagon, which rose two floors to a galleried landing filled with more tables. The exquisitely tiled mosaic floor depicting the known heavens was too beautifully crafted to step on, to Eleanor's mind. While on each of the eight sides, soaring ivory statues of Greek and Roman goddesses dominated the room, their upheld hands seemingly all that supported the upper floor. Eleanor marvelled at the intricate folds of their robes and the time-honoured wisdom encapsulated in their finely carved features.

Arriving at the captain's table, she noted that the formidable Mrs Swalecourt had somehow beaten her and Count Balog, despite not being among those they'd followed to the dining salon. She now stood nudging her daughter forward and smiling smugly at the diners on the other tables. The Wrenshaw-Smythes were hovering halfway along, looking torn between enjoying the honour of being invited and their displeasure at the wine, champagne and cocktail glasses at each place setting.

She did a double take. Bracebridge said they weren't suspects, so why were they there? After all, they had an alibi for the time of Yeoman's death. She mentally slapped her forehead. Of course, you couldn't have empty places at the captain's table. They were there to make up the numbers.

The telltale clicks of a cane on marble flooring told Eleanor Sir Randolph had arrived. With a contemptuous snort as he passed Count Balog, he strode over to shake the captain's hand. Next Miss González appeared.

'Captain Bracebridge. Everyone,' she purred, nodding her pearl-studded raven tresses around the group.

'Ah, almost my full guest complement now,' Bracebridge said, looking over Eleanor's shoulder.

An evening-suited middle-aged man with a bookish haircut and conservative beard joined them.

'Professor Daniel Goodman. Psychologist.' He nodded slowly around the other guests.

Before Bracebridge could reply, applause rang out from the surrounding tables.

She turned to see Signor Marinelli, the opera star, his gold-striped waistcoat all the more striking below his box-cut ebony velvet jacket as he bowed his crown of black hair to the applauding diners.

'Ah, Signor Enrico Marinelli too,' Bracebridge said. 'Our table is complete.'

Once everyone was seated, she found herself next to Count Balog to her right and Professor Goodman to her left. By the time the first of the thirteen courses of the banquet had arrived – cubed cantaloupe melon, topped with smoked ham curls and chopped basil, misted with the finest Modena vinegar – Goodman was engaged in an in-depth conversation about the artful psychological design of the *Celestiana*'s decor.

'In vastly simplified terms, as Freud's rather outspoken paper on the rationale of religion in modern times expounded almost twenty years back, survival is at the root of all human characteristics. Thus, anything that is suggested might protect one will always be seized upon by the subconscious as a form of psychological consolation. Hence the *Celestiana*'s powerful themes, the heavens, guardian gods and goddesses and attendant angels, pacify even the deepest-seated fear of this being in any way a perilous journey across the Atlantic.'

Eleanor glanced around the table. Though every face was expressionless, it was clear there was only one thought in everyone's mind. The *Titanic*.

Goodman continued. 'Unaware, one subconsciously transfers those qualities onto the *Celestiana* herself and thus whole-hearted trust is placed in her to keep one safe. And passage is remembered only as a relaxing, joyful experience.'

Balog nodded as their second course arrived. 'Fascinating, Professor. Not just a pretty floating tin box at all, then, with everyone at the mercy of their fate. To your thinking, that is.'

'But not to yours, Count?'

'No,' Balog said firmly. He ran a thoughtful finger down the length of his impressive nose. 'Regardless of this, for my two thousand new friends, I am delighted.'

Eleanor shook her head in fascination. 'You see now, gentlemen, I feel entirely the blunt brick as I've merely been floating around the *Celestiana* admiring the beautiful decor.'

Goodman put his hands together. 'Appreciating privilege denotes a perceptive self-awareness. A refreshing attitude in a titled lady, if you will forgive my saying so.'

She smiled, trying to stop herself from just enjoying the engrossing conversation.

You've a job to do, remember, Ellie. She racked her brain while finishing her creamed chicken velouté. How could she naturally bring the conversation around to Yeoman's murder?

Soon after, the fish course arrived – ceviche of lobster with caviar garnish and lime – and just as quickly went. Courses four to six passed in a haze of mushroom vol-au-vent, pan-seared quail breasts and a palette-cleansing cucumber and lemon sorbet.

She savoured a few mouthfuls of the next course. The 'releve' comprising roasted pheasant was delicious, but the truth was, she was just stalling. Having suggested getting all their current suspects around one table, she had singularly failed to glean one single clue about any of their possible involvements in Yeoman's murder. Or even any reason for wanting him dead. And worse than that, she felt every time she asked a question, it was obvious to everyone at the table that she had an ulterior motive for posing it.

She took a deep breath.

Come on, Ellie, you're trying too hard. We all know what's at stake but getting flustered isn't helping you. Or Hugh.

She forced herself to relax over the next couple of courses, a brochette of turkey liver with bacon followed by salad, and then stared in horror as the dessert arrived.

It can't be dessert already? How many more courses are there before the end of the meal? She stared at her ice cream. *It's now or never, Ellie. You will not get everyone around the same table again.*

Taking advantage of the general lull in conversation, she spoke up. 'It's just struck me that there really should have been an empty place setting at one table as a sign of respect for the poor man who fell overboard. I mean, here we are all blithely eating...' She broke off and gazed around her now attentive audience. 'But gracious, forgive my insensitivity of mentioning such at dinner.'

'No matter,' Balog said cheerfully. 'You have not trodden on my toes with this mention as I never really met the gentleman.' He went back to attacking his dessert.

Opposite her, Lady Wrenshaw-Smythe leaned forward nervously. 'It's terribly sad when a man is driven to take his own life in that way.'

'Cowardly, you mean!' Sir Randolph's undisguised disdain rumbled from the table's far end. 'Gentlemen face down their adversities.'

'True,' Balog agreed. 'And he's likely face down now, but too late.'

'Well, really!' Sir Gerald snorted.

Who on earth started the gossip that Yeoman jumped over-board, Ellie? Perhaps the crew on the captain's orders? She nodded to herself, thinking, what better way to quell any concerns than to disguise the whole event as an isolated tragedy?

'Sadly, I did not know the man either, Count,' the professor said. He sighed into his glass of port. 'It's always hard to bear as a psychologist. A tormented mind lost before one had the chance to offer professional counsel.'

Signor Marinelli seemed less sympathetic. He turned to Miss González on his left, his strong Italian accent empha-sised all the more by his theatrical hand gestures. 'Tragedy is for discussion in operatic song only. On stage, not over dinner.'

She couldn't be sure, but she thought she saw him share a fleeting look with Mrs Swalecourt.

She turned to Goodman.

'That must feel an enormous responsibility, Professor. Every troubled person you encounter, even just those you pass in the street, would benefit greatly from your incredible exper-tise. How ever do you reconcile yourself to not being able to help them all?'

Behind his wire-rimmed spectacles, the professor blinked slowly, his intelligent grey eyes holding her gaze. 'An astute question. The answer is to have a sense of perspective, Lady Swift. Distorting one's ability to reach all helps no one.'

She nodded, thinking a psychologist's view would have been helpful on so many occasions. *Especially when trying to catch a murderer.*

Ignoring the fact that slipping away from the dinner table before the meal was concluded was a social faux pas, she made her excuses and left. She'd caught sight of a welcome face preparing drinks at the other end of the dining room.

'Clifford,' she hissed, pretending to ask for an indigestion tonic. 'How is it really that you can slide in anywhere so readily? And pinch a *Celestiana* waiter's togs unnoticed?'

He tutted over the cocktail shaker he held. 'My lady, I have not pilfered this uniform. There are other, more respectable ways to obtain what one needs.'

'Which clearly you aren't going to divulge.' She raised her voice as another waiter appeared with a list of orders. 'It must have been the oysters.'

'Which were not on this evening's menu,' Clifford muttered once they were alone again.

She flapped a hand. 'I didn't break the rules of table etiquette just to come and squabble with you, Clifford.'

His eyes twinkled. 'My error, my lady. Then how can I be of assistance?'

'Please remember five things for me, as my head is swimming as much as my stomach is.' At his nod, she whispered, 'Professor and Count denial. Rumour. Cowardly Asquith. Squeamish Marinelli.' She scrunched her eyes closed. 'And... and, dash it! I've forgotten the fifth already.'

'It will come back, my lady. Consider the others all noted.' He handed her a tall glass of a dubiously yellow-green swirling liquid.

She looked at it askance. 'I've got pretend indigestion, Clifford, not a hangover. I don't need my stomach gurgling all the way through my interviewing Marinelli. Really! How would that be?'

'Woefully familiar,' she just caught as he strode away.

20

Despite the *Celestiana*'s eminent Chef Barsalou having expertly married umpteen complementary courses, they were now genuinely squabbling in leaden layers in her stomach. She knew she was still trying too hard and needed to relax. Normally, she would walk her digestive and mental discomfort off around the deck. However, the memory of the horror she'd witnessed last time put her off. Nevertheless, she needed to get Marinelli alone now.

As the group cleared the doors leading from the dining salon, Captain Bracebridge stopped and smiled at his guests. 'Ladies and gentlemen, it has been a pleasure. Please excuse me as ship's business calls. Enjoy the rest of your evening.' He nodded imperceptibly to Eleanor and strode off.

'Just the sort of busy and professional man required. Only younger,' Mrs Swalecourt murmured after his retreating form, Eleanor's sharp hearing catching the words. As had her daughter, from the girl's eye roll. Inevitably pinned to her mother's side in a fierce elbow lock, she settled for a long sigh of defiance instead.

Eleanor looked around the group. 'Perhaps the rest of us might retire to the lounge?'

Goodman, who had excused himself a few moments earlier, reappeared. She wondered if he had indigestion as well, probably not being used to such rich food, unlike the other bona fide first-class passengers. He tapped his fingertips on his jacket front as if checking the contents of his inner pocket, his tone as mellow as it had been all evening. 'Preparation calls, I'm afraid, since I shall be delivering my talk tomorrow. Thus, I must defer. But another time I would be delighted. Goodnight, Lady Swift.'

He shook her hand.

His hands are as chilled as he is relaxed, Ellie. Woolly under-things would have been a good addition to his suitcase.

As Goodman left, she bent down to adjust her velvet ankle strap. A peculiar frisson of goosebumps caught her unawares. She looked up to find Sir Randolph's brows knitted fiercely down at her. Even though he was smiling, his words still lashed like the icy rain of a flash storm.

'I believe, Lady Swift, as we established earlier, you and I are on opposite agendas. Therefore, delightfully gracious though your suggestion is, I too shall bid you good evening.' He swung his silver-topped cane down from under his arm and nodded as if he had just settled an unspoken score.

She smiled sweetly as she bounded back upright. 'Business first, as always. You have my utmost admiration, Sir Randolph. We shall meet again soon enough, I'm sure. However, not in the cigar lounge where you are actually headed now, I believe.'

His oaken features flinched, giving away that she'd correctly called his bluff. His eyes darkened.

'A word of advice, Lady Swift. I wouldn't go poking my nose into matters that don't concern you.'

What does he mean by that, Ellie?

Before she could reply, however, Balog's irrepressibly cheery tone cut into their conversation. 'Ah, the last male bastion. The cigar lounge!' He held his hands out to Signor Marinelli and Lord Wrenshaw-Smythe. 'Gentlemen?'

The latter gave a stiff headshake, his clipped Etonian enunciation adding all the more disgust. 'I do not indulge, Count Balog.'

'Of course not,' the count said earnestly. 'But tell me, what *do* you indulge in?'

Sir Gerald glanced up sharply. 'What are you implying, man?'

'Nothing.' Balog shrugged. 'Just that you tell us you are on the *Celestiana* for business, of course, but not what business?'

Sir Gerald looked down his nose at the count as if he were a particularly offensive cockroach. 'My affairs are none of your business, man.'

'Ah! Another who pokes his nose into matters that does not concern him, I suspect!'

Sir Randolph shot the count a filthy look. 'Eavesdropping, eh?' he muttered.

Sir Gerald merely snorted and turned away from Balog.

At this rate, Ellie, there'll be no suspects left to question!

She smiled around the remainder of the group. 'Er, my offer still stands if anyone would like to retire to the lounge?'

Signor Marinelli gave several long theatrical strokes of his throat. 'My *corde vocali*, my vocal chords, they are very sensitive to smoke. I do not frequent the cigar lounge, so audiences everywhere can forever enjoy my ultimate *bel canto*. Instead, I take up your offer, Lady Swift.'

She sighed to herself in relief. *At least that's the one I wanted bagged.*

'Oh, Signor Marinelli!' Lady Wrenshaw-Smythe twittered. 'You simply have to remain vigilant. Just imagine if your unique gift was lost to the world. What a travesty.'

Her husband turned away, clearing his throat. Mrs Swalecourt shuffled Rosamund further towards the opera star. Balog threw Eleanor an amused look and clapped Sir Randolph on the back.

'Just you and I then, Sir Randolph. Let us go together and I shall treat you to the finest aged Cuban.'

'If you insist, sir.'

'I do. And over our smokes, we can swap the theories on what ladies really get up to when we are not there!' With a farewell eyebrow wiggle to Eleanor, he spun around, making the tails of his knee-length jacket fly out. 'Good evening, good people. May you win at whatever trifles you indulge in.'

The tap of Sir Randolph's cane was quickly lost to Balog's seemingly determined efforts to prattle the entire way to the cigar lounge.

Eleanor smoothed the wrinkle from her brow at her surprise. She could have sworn Sir Randolph wouldn't have passed the time of day with the count. She glanced around the five remaining.

'Mother,' Rosamund piped up. 'I have a fearful headache.'

Her mother frowned and pursed her lips. 'Take a powder when we reach the lounge, dear.'

'It's too mean for that. I need to lie in the dark.'

Eleanor felt for her. If it was true, that is. Which she doubted on looking at the young woman. Her second maid, Lizzie, suffered terribly with migraines. But on those occasions, she was a much sicklier ghost of a girl compared to the robust picture of health Rosamund presented.

'Very well,' her mother said with a rather exaggerated show of sympathy. 'Lady Swift, everyone, please do excuse us. Such a shame to have to leave you all.'

As Mrs Swalecourt led her daughter away, Miss González graced the group with a film star smile. 'I am the last to decline the delightful evening's fun on offer, it seems, so tantalising though it is.'

'And what is it that steals you from us?' Signor Marinelli said.

She batted her eyelashes. 'Why, signore, a lady must have secrets! For what is she otherwise?' Her eyes flicked over Eleanor's face. 'An open book with no mystique.'

Determined not to rise to the bait, Eleanor waved cheerily over her shoulder, hoping Marinelli wasn't now also thinking of bolting. 'Well, four of us, it is then. Very cosy.'

'Oh, quite,' Lady Wrenshaw-Smythe twittered, earning a sharp twitch of a moustache from her husband.

'Actually, I believe we must excuse ourselves, Caroline,' he grunted.

Her shoulders drooped. 'If you say so, Gerald.' She glanced at Marinelli again as she took her husband's stiffly held arm. 'Goodnight. Another time, I do hope.'

To Eleanor's relief, Marinelli threw his arms wide once they were alone. 'So much more cosy. Now we are but two left on stage.'

'Although the lounge would be more comfortable, perhaps? And without the need to perform, which frankly terrifies me.' She smiled as he laughed and offered his elbow. As each of the other dinner guests had peeled away so quickly, even her quick-fire brain hadn't had a chance to conjure up any suitable conversational openers. Wishing Clifford was there with his unwavering knack of having a ready ice breaker up his impeccably cuffed sleeves, she silently clicked her fingers. The image of her private-minded butler who thrived on his precious moments of solitude threw her the very opener she needed.

'Actually, signore, forgive my observation but I can imagine that for you every minute of every day might feel as though you are still centre stage? Never a minute's peace away from your very understandably adoring fans. No chance to simply be the man behind your remarkable charisma and extraordinary voice.'

'Fame comes at a price, it is true.' He let out a long breath.

'A very costly price.' He shook his head as if he were trying to shake a bad memory from it. 'To protect my voice is the straightforward part. But the rest...' He tailed off as they reached the first-class lounge. To her delight, he waved an imperious hand at the senior waiter. 'We will take your quietest corner and a bottle of your best champagne. And we do not wish to be disturbed.'

'Very good, signore. Please follow me.'

The screened alcove Eleanor was shown into a moment later was so private, she hesitated.

Have you just tucked yourself entirely out of view with a possible murderer, Ellie? She shook her head to herself. *Stop being so histrionic. There are hundreds of people around.* However, his intense stare still unnerved her. He seemed fascinated by her neck. Or rather, her necklace.

'Do you like jewels, signore?'

Marinelli started, his dark eyes flashing. 'Why do you ask?'

'Oh, I just noticed you'd been admiring my necklace. It's an opal. It's not rare like some types. Maybe you have a favourite?

A black opal, perhaps, Ellie!

He shrugged. 'I have no interest in jewels, but it is very... pretty.' His eyes flicked to hers. He leaned back as the waiter appeared with the champagne. After he'd poured them both a glass, he flashed her a beguiling smile. 'How are you enjoying the cruise so far?'

'Oh, enormously,' she lied. 'There are almost too many diversions to know which to pick. I keep hoping they might be distracting enough for me to forget about that poor man who went overboard. I didn't hear that he'd been found, did you?'

Marinelli lifted his glass to stare at the bubbles that obscured her view of his expression. 'Fate can be harsh, Lady Swift. I do not imagine he will ever be found.' He put his glass down and smiled. 'But please do not be offended if this sounds cavalier to your ears. I sing of tragedy every day. It is the theme at the root of so many operas.'

'But that's make-believe. This was a real man.'

He nodded. 'And in real life, I have known this before. On a cruise I was on some years ago, it happened also. A man went overboard, but his body was never recovered. It was observed later by other passengers he had been drinking. Maybe it was the same for this man, although many talk of suicide?'

Balog appeared around the screen with the senior waiter close behind. The waiter grimaced. 'My sincere apologies, signore.'

Marinelli waved the count towards a seat, throwing a bad-tempered look at the waiter. 'I said no interruptions on any count!'

Balog bowed. 'This is where you make your error, sir. I am not "any count". I am *the* Count!'

Eleanor groaned inwardly. *There goes your chance to question Marinelli on his own.*

'I thought you were partaking of a cigar with Sir Randolph?'

Balog laughed. 'It was a very short cigar.' He swirled his double measure of whisky with both hands. 'My nose, however, is tingling with the atmosphere of speculation in the air here. Let me guess the topic. Our dear departed friend?'

Marinelli's features darkened. 'Eavesdropping, I see! You scoundrel. One day you will regret such things!'

Eleanor fought a frown off her face. *Why such dramatics? We were only chatting about Yeoman.*

The count, impervious as ever, shrugged. 'Not a bit, signore. It is the talk of all of first class this evening.'

Eleanor's ears pricked up. 'Why particularly this evening?'

'Because it seems that it is now official that the man is one Mr Yeoman, a first-class passenger, as suspected. And, as the rail where he fell has been examined and found sound, that he did not fall by accident. Which leaves only the two possibilities we have already mentioned. He fell by a foolhardy act or... fell by his own hand. Suicide.' A smile played around his lips.

'Signor Marinelli, you are a man of intellect. I would wager you have a theory why the body has not been found?'

The opera star shook his head. 'It is not proper to discuss such matters in front of a lady.' He tipped his head to her.

Balog laughed with his high-pitched whinny. 'Perhaps, but I think this particular lady is used to such matters.'

She shot him a puzzled look and then turned to Marinelli. 'I confess I was already thinking about it. So please, I'm intrigued to hear.'

Marinelli shrugged. 'Mr...' He glanced at Balog who tapped the side of his nose.

'What a short memory you have, signore. The man's name was Yeoman.'

Marinelli nodded curtly. 'This man's body would have been devoured by sharks before it could be found.'

'Wrong!' Balog's cheer made her jump.

'Actually,' a gruff voice answered, 'the man's right. There are many sharks in these waters.'

She turned in surprise. 'Sir Randolph! It seems your cigar was rather short as well?'

'Very short,' Balog cut in. 'But he is wrong and right at the same time.'

Sir Randolph snorted. 'You're talking in riddles, man!'

Balog shrugged. 'It is not a riddle. You are correct that there are sharks. But they cannot have eaten Yeoman's body because they are not the man-eating ones.'

Marinelli leaned forward. 'How can you be so sure?'

Balog spread his hands. 'Because, my dear friend, all the man-eating ones are aboard the *Celestiana*!'

Eleanor's puzzled reply was drowned out by the urgent blast of the ship's horn.

21

Eleanor tried to hide her exasperation by taking a swig of champagne. Following up on Balog's puzzling remarks would have to wait. She looked around. Most of her fellow first-class passengers had already left their seats to join the throng pouring past in the corridor. Above the excited chatter, the ship's horn repeatedly brayed out its signal of two short blasts, her sharp hearing just catching an echoed refrain in the distance. An icy dread shot up her back.

We can't be sinking! Everyone's excited, not terrified. And besides, the signal would be five short blasts, not two. That means it's passing another ship on starboard, doesn't it? As usual, everyone but she seemed to know what was going on.

She was swept up by Marinelli, who was busy swaddling his throat in a white silk scarf, and Balog, who was still nursing his double whisky. 'What's happening?'

Ahead of them, a middle-aged woman called over her shoulder, 'It's the *Auriana*. She's passing the other way!'

Eleanor's eyes lit up. 'Ah! Blue Line's other flagship liner.'

Behind, a clipped voice barked out, 'It seems, my dear,

second class are allowed onto the upper decks for such a sighting. Why, I cannot comprehend. We'll see nothing but the eyesore of cloth-capped heads and collarless-shirted necks if we don't hurry.'

That means the ladies will be able to enjoy the spectacle too, Ellie. And Hugh, assuming he's feeling up to it.

She had no more time to muse, as a sea of animated humanity carried her out of the dining room and up the main staircase. But as she was swept onto the blindingly floodlit top starboard deck, the icy wind sucked all the air from her lungs.

'Oh gracious! It's bitter,' she said through chattering teeth. She was only wearing her bare-shouldered evening gown but soon forgot the cold at the otherworldly magnificence of the spectacle she could still see, despite the crowd in front of her.

'Wow!' she breathed.

In the otherwise total blackness, steaming towards them was the outline of what appeared to be a floating skyscraper, light pouring from every window, as if the whole thing was ablaze. Even over the spontaneous cheering all around her, she still caught snatches of the responding cries from the *Auriana's* passengers funnelling over the wide inky stretch between the two ships.

Thankful for her taller than average height and the additional three inches provided by her evening heels, she was able to glance over the crowd as well. It was an unusual sight. Titled gentlemen and fur-clad ladies rubbed shoulders with huddles of blue and brown wool overcoats and felt hats gripped against the wind.

It was then she realised the power of Marinelli's fame. The crowd in front parted, beckoning hands ushering him to a ringside view. He gave a gracious bow, then scooped Eleanor's arm into the crook of his elbow and strode them both forward. She felt very self-conscious. Never one to lord over others, she smiled at the second-class passengers who had given up their hard-won front row spots to accommodate her and the opera star. 'Thank you,' she called. But her words were lost as Marinelli burst into an impromptu aria. Arms thrown wide, he roared words she couldn't understand across the sea, his whole body seesawing and rolling with the passion he imbued into every note. Over her shoulder, she spotted Balog copying the opera star's movements, the whisky in his glass glinting in the deck lights as he swayed back and forth. Her eye was also caught by Sir Randolph, whom she hadn't noticed leaving the lounge with them. He was staring at the count, his face twisted in disapproval as he fought his way through the crowd.

'Oh, for some photographic equipment!' she caught an enthralled voice call from somewhere to her right.

Marinelli threw his hands to the wind as he brought his last long note to a triumphant end, the crowd breaking into spontaneous applause, Eleanor included.

'Signor Marinelli, what a wonderful surprise for everyone.'

His eyes shone, though his tone sounded wistful. 'Maybe the surprise was mine, dear lady.'

Even the bitter wind couldn't galvanise any of the passengers, including Eleanor, to move until the last of the *Auriana*'s lights had faded from view. And then there was a stampede to return to the warmth inside. This time, she noted the second-class passengers hung back, evidently their one permitted defiance of deferring to wealth and power now revoked. Balog held the door for her with an amused smile. He nodded at Marinelli ahead of them who was surrounded by star-struck admirers.

'Your eminent self excluded, and mine also, how easy it is to spellbind those who are so needy of distraction? A pretty light show and a snippet of song in a language they did not comprehend one word of is enough!'

She waggled a finger at him. 'Simply not true, Count.

Certainly not for me. I found both absolutely captivating. As did you, I would wager if I was a betting woman.'

'Well then, I wish you were.' His one good eye lit up. 'Because you would have just lost.'

'I think not.' With the show over, she needed to steer him back to the first-class lounge and his remark about 'sharks'. Fortunately, it seemed he was in no hurry to disappear off to his business at the card tables.

'Do not tease your new friend,' he said in a mock whine, slowing his pace with petulant steps of his buckled slipper shoes. 'Explain, please?'

She pointed to the crystal-cut tumbler glass he was still carrying. 'If you weren't entranced like everyone else, how come you haven't even sipped your whisky since leaving the lounge?'

'Aha!' he cried. 'A worthy opponent, Lady Swift. Let us return there forthwith that I might have a chance to trump you with an observation of my own.'

'Deal.'

Especially if it is about Yeoman. Or his death!

But as they reached the stairwell, she spotted a sickly-looking Seldon hanging on to the banister rail, head down, Clifford directing the crowd around them. Gladstone was also 'helping' by refusing to leave the next step down so he could woof exuberant greetings to everyone stumbling over him.

'Count Balog, would you wait for me in the lounge?' she said. 'I will only be a moment.'

He bowed. 'For the lady, I will wait as long as she needs. But I must first to my cabin.'

With Balog gone, she hurried up to Seldon. 'Hugh, you look dreadful!'

'Which makes me feel so much better, Eleanor.' He gingerly turned around to press one hip against the rail so he could face her. She scanned his intense brown-eyed gaze and lean chiselled cheeks. In truth, there was something about his rather more rugged than usual appearance that made him all the more handsome. A frisson of yearning that he might just scoop her into his arms shot through her. Instead, he glanced at Marinelli, just visible among his sea of female admirers in the lounge.

'He can certainly entrance the ladies!'

Was that a hint of jealousy in his tone, Ellie?

'Hugh,' she said softly. 'He's a suspect. Nothing more.' She shrugged. 'Anyway, I only meant I'm sorry that you and boats really don't seem to be a good match.'

A glimmer of the old Hugh surfaced as his face lit with a teasing smile. 'Like you and decorum, perhaps?'

She laughed. 'Rotter! Then I shall leave you to the mercy of seasickness' grim clutch, Inspector.'

Clifford glided back over with her wildly excited bulldog. 'Good evening, my lady. Is there anything you need?'

'Actually, there is.' She looked up from accepting Gladstone's exuberant welcome to jerk a thumb at Seldon. 'A Chief Inspector repair kit. Uncharacteristically slipshod of you not to have one secreted about your butlering togs.'

Seldon swayed as he replied, 'Why on earth would he? Like you, he had no idea I had foolishly boarded this infernal instrument of torture. Besides, it's only because of your wizard of a butler I made it out of my cabin at all to see why the entire boat was herding past my door. I thought the blasted ship was sinking.'

You weren't the only one!

Clifford's arm shot out to press him back against the rail as Seldon stumbled down a step.

Her sharp ears caught a horrified whisper from a familiar voice lower down the stairs. 'SINKING! TROTTERS!'

'Ladies?' she called as she hung over the banister rail. 'Pop up, please. I haven't seen you since well, last time! And no one's sinking.'

Seldon stared at her through the fingers he was now holding over his eyes. 'Ladies? Eleanor, you haven't brought your entire staff with you again, have you?'

'Whyever wouldn't I have?' She waved the ladies up from where they were now hovering down on the halfway landing. 'They deserve a holiday too.'

Her staff shuffled into a line along the step three down from where Eleanor stood. All of them, she noted with a smile, trying hard not to gawp too obviously at the policeman whose handsome frame always sent them into giddy schoolgirl fits. Except Polly, whose jaw hung slack, eyes rabbit wide.

'Ahem.' Clifford nodded towards the young maid. Mrs Butters shot a hand out and pushed the girl's mouth back up.

'Good evening, ladies,' Seldon said, clearly oblivious of the effect he was having.

'Good evening, Chief Inspector Seldon, sir,' they chorused.

'What an extra special treat, m'lady.' Mrs Trotters smiled innocently at Eleanor, then caught Clifford's firm look.

'The *Auriana* passing like that, she means,' Mrs Butters added hastily.

Mrs Trotters gave her friend a grateful look. 'And the singing from that opera man, of course.'

Mrs Butters fondly pinched the young maid's cheeks. 'Polly ran us all dry of handkerchiefs.'

The girl looked up at Eleanor with wide, bright eyes. ''Twas like being in a dream, your ladyship, to be allowed to see and hear such beautiful things. Though I'm sure we need punishing for being so brazen as to go beyond the fourth deck.'

'Oh, you silly numpty,' Mrs Trotman rolled her eyes. 'I showed you the permission note Mr Clifford slipped to me as we passed in the hall. Butters read it to you six times. We—'

A piercing scream rang out from above.

Eleanor sprinted back up the stairs towards A deck where the cry had come from. Beside her, Seldon's long stride would have kept him ahead of her if he hadn't had to press one hand along the corridor wall to stay upright. They both halted at the threshold of a cabin where an ashen-faced Miss González was staring into the interior.

Inside, Count Balog lay sprawled like a rag doll, eyes fixed blankly on the carpet, his mouth gaping open. One hand was outstretched and two playing cards lay just beyond his reach, both face down. His now empty whisky glass was clutched weakly in his other hand.

Seldon gestured for the hovering crew to keep the quickly growing crowd at bay and dropped to his knees. Eleanor watched as the inspector's long fingers searched for Balog's pulse and then pulled back each eyelid. After a moment, he looked up at her, shaking his head.

A woman gasped. '*Dead?*'

He turned to the onlookers. 'Please remain calm. And you.' He waved at a member of the crew. 'Fetch the doctor at once. And the master—'

At the look on Eleanor's face he stopped and turned around. 'Ah! Master-at-Arms. We need—'

The master-at-arms held up his hand and then addressed the passengers. 'Ladies and gentlemen, please leave so we can attend to this man properly. Thank you.' He turned to his crew who were now standing behind him obviously awaiting orders. 'Admit only the doctor.'

Once the corridor was empty of onlookers, he turned back to Seldon, his tone measured. 'What is your assessment of the death, Chief Inspector?'

Seldon hesitated. 'Well, I'm not a doctor, so perhaps—'

'Inspector?' the master-at-arms said firmly.

Seldon nodded, pulled out a fresh handkerchief from his pocket and carefully picked up Balog's glass from where it had fallen. He took a sniff. Immediately, his brow creased. He looked back at the master-at-arms whose eyes narrowed.

Without a word, he turned and left.

Seldon glanced at Eleanor. She nodded, not needing him to spell it out.

Poison, Ellie!

22

Eleanor broke the long silence. 'Perhaps if one of you two chaps were to pinch me hard enough, I could wake up and find I'm just sitting in my cabin enjoying a blissfully carefree cruise?'

Seldon groaned and continued drumming his fingers on the table.

Clifford caught her eye with the arch of one brow. 'Forgive my deferring on such a request, my lady. However, I learned the hard way in 1900 that pinching is best left as the sole preserve of incensed little girls.'

His mischievousness made her smile, especially as it was an obvious attempt to get the three of them back together.

Seldon was frowning. 'You've lost me.'

'I know,' she said. 'We all lost each other in shock for a while. Which is why Clifford and I were squabbling about a misunderstanding over him trying to extricate me from Uncle Byron's tallest apple tree when I was nine. Squabbling is still the way he enjoys communicating with me most.'

'Absolutely, my lady.' Clifford poured both of them a brandy, and then relented to add a small one for himself after

Eleanor slid another glass across the table so pointedly it clinked against the decanter.

'Chaps, we got back from Bracebridge's office just after midnight and now it's...' She broke off to fumble in her pockets.

'Five and ten minutes to two, my lady. In the morning. It is also your birthday. Happy birthday, my lady.'

'Thank you, Clifford, but I don't think this is a time for birthday celebrations – not until the murderer is caught, so let's agree to postpone my birthday until we arrive in New York. Clifford, will you please tell the ladies of this arrangement?'

Clifford nodded reluctantly and Seldon offered a muted, 'Happy birthday, Eleanor. I hope I will be celebrating it with you in happier times.'

She turned to Seldon with an ache in her heart, knowing that he feared he would not be at liberty to do so. 'Thank you, Hugh. Now, we've a murderer to catch. So, be honest. What is it about all this that is really bothering you?'

He looked up at her sharply. 'How about another dead body? Bringing the total to two in the same number of days! And we've only got three days before we dock!' His scowl changed to a look of remorse. 'Blast it, I'm sorry, Eleanor.' His fingers strayed an inch closer to hers. 'That was unforgivable of me. Especially... today.'

'No,' she said gently. 'You're just feeling the strain of this awful mess harder than Clifford and I. It can't be easy being so close to the root of it all.'

Seldon sighed deeply. 'Nor being the supposed detective who let another man be murdered during the investigation. Which I get the impression was exactly how the master-at-arms was viewing the matter when he arrived to find me crouching over the count's body!'

Clifford slid past, pretending to talk to the sleepy bulldog trailing beside him. 'You see, Master Gladstone, Oscar Wilde was particularly unequivocal when he said, "It's not whether you win or lose, it's how you place the blame."'

Seldon stared after him, then at Eleanor. 'Why do I feel I've just had my ear cuffed with a lesson in self-reproach?'

She laughed. 'Because you have. And from a scallywag butler. Are you going to take that lying down, Chief Inspector?'

Seldon's smile quickly faded. 'I wish I could. Lie down, that is. But we're up against it all the more now. It's Monday morning and we dock Thursday morning. That basically gives us three days, as I said! We left on Saturday and so far, rather than us having caught the killer, he – or she – is running rings around us!' He sighed despondently. 'If we arrive in New York with the murder – murders! – unsolved...'

She winced. *His involvement in the dreadful affair will come to light and it'll be him being led from the* Celestiana *in handcuffs!* She shook the morbid thoughts from her mind.

'I know, Hugh. And gracious! The master-at-arms didn't mince his words at all, did he? And that was in front of Bracebridge just now.'

'I can't blame him. He's the head of security and he believes he was thwarted in catching the murderer before he killed again because his authority was undermined. Undermined by a jumped-up copper who appeared out of nowhere—'

'And a toffy upstart of a lady?'

'That too.'

She grimaced. 'Hugh, neither of us felt good throughout his horribly pointed speech. Particularly as failing to save the count feels almost as awful as if I'd added the poison to his drink myself.'

He cupped his hand over hers. 'Eleanor, please.'

'It's fine. At least, it will be when we work out who the murderer is. And yes, I said "we" because I'm not bowing out now, no matter how much you or Clifford nag or implore. So, let's just get on with the job—'

A sharp rap on the door interrupted her. All three looked at each other.

Only the master-at-arms knocks like that, Ellie!

'What on earth are you thinking of?' Eleanor leapt up from her seat in the captain's office.

Bracebridge took a deep breath. 'Lady Swift, I will repeat my opening statement and the fact that I am the less than comfortable messenger. You and the inspector are off the case. By order of Blue Line's senior board. The investigation is being entrusted back to my master-at-arms and his team.'

'But surely the more experienced people you have working on this *together*,' she said pointedly, 'the more chance we'll have of catching the culprit? I mean, surely whoever murdered Yeoman murdered Count Balog? It's too much to imagine there are two murderers on board!'

'Lady Swift,' the master-at-arms barked. 'I do not question orders. And I suggest you might wish to do the same.'

She hesitated, remembering him doing just that when Bracebridge first requested her help. *Stay calm, Ellie. We must keep hold of this investigation. As much to catch the guilty party as to keep Hugh's history with Yeoman out of the spotlight until we do.* She threw Bracebridge a placating look and sat back down. 'But how did the order come through, Captain? If I may ask?'

'You may. I received a message from Mr Walker himself.'

She sighed in exasperation. 'But he was happy with the chief inspector and me investigating before!'

He shook his head. 'Mr Walker was. The other members of the board were unaware of the arrangement, it transpires.'

'Then how did it *transpire* that they know now?'

'Mr Walker did not say.' Bracebridge's brow creased as he

shot the master-at-arms a sharp look. 'Lady Swift, you must see that my hands are entirely tied on this.'

She groaned inwardly. *And you can see, Ellie, there's no point in arguing any further.*

'I do.' She rose.

'There is, of course, one more thing,' Bracebridge said. 'You are required to hand over all the evidence you have amassed so far.'

She shrugged. 'We have already handed over the ring and opal we found that, incidentally, your master-at-arms and his men had missed! That is all the evidence we have.'

Except Hugh's gun, and we're not handing that over!

Bracebridge shot the master-at-arms another sharp look and then turned back to her. 'The room I made available as your base of operations will also no longer be at your disposal from this moment on.'

As she went to leave, he raised his hand. 'Lady Swift, on a personal note, thank you for your efforts. I hope you can now return to having a pleasant journey as our valued guest.'

As she left, she caught the master-at-arms grinning victoriously.

Back in her suite, she relayed her conversation with Bracebridge. Clifford raised a brow.

'A significant setback, for sure, my lady. If you and the chief inspector would excuse me a moment?' At her nod, he left the cabin.

'And I thought the odds were against us an hour ago,' Seldon said grimly.

'They were!' Eleanor tried to tame the anger swelling inside her as she paced the sitting room. 'And they're even more so now. But, Hugh, this is far from over!'

He shook his head and grimaced. 'We'll be in New York Harbour in little over three days, as I keep repeating, I know.

There will be an investigation. It will come to light that my gun was the murder weapon and then...' He threw up his hands.

'Hugh!'

'Eleanor, Yeoman killed my wife. And I pursued him for five years, right onto this very ship, with my gun hidden in my luggage. My only alibi is that I was in my cabin, alone. That's no alibi, as we both know. No judge is going to believe it wasn't me.' Seldon ran an anxious hand through his chestnut curls, staring at her imploringly. 'Please, stay out of any more danger. This is my mess, not yours.'

'Actually, it's mine, too, as you know. I'm not just the only witness, I'm an accessory.' At his troubled groan, she pressed his arm. 'There's no point pretending otherwise. I found your gun and didn't tell the captain or the master-at-arms. A vital piece of evidence that I didn't reveal. Then I tracked you down on the *Celestiana*—'

'And handed me back the murder weapon and got me approved, on the captain's authority, to investigate the case.' Seldon buried his face in his hands.

'To steer the investigation away from the fact that you are guilty. That's how any judge or jury will view my part in this.' She jerked her head at her butler who had just returned. 'Clifford's part too.' She threw him an apologetic look. 'So we'd better put our heads together and figure out our next move.'

Seldon nodded contritely. 'Thank you, Eleanor. You too, Clifford. As to our next move, our problem is that the blasted master-at-arms will be watching us like a hawk.' He slapped his forehead. 'No, no! My notebook. It's still in our operations room.'

'It is not, in fact, Chief Inspector. Nor her ladyship's.'

Clifford's words halted Seldon's unsteady charge to the door. 'Then where are they?'

'They are both already with the master-at-arms, I believe,

since he swept them and myself from the room without cere-
mony but a moment ago.'

'But that's a disaster.' Seldon looked panic-stricken as he
stepped back over. 'I made a note about my gun having been
stolen. Agh! I can see it so clearly.'

'"How and when did the wretch break into my cabin and
steal the murder weapon, blast it?"' Clifford read out from a
sheet of narrow-lined notepaper in his hand.

Seldon whipped the paper from Clifford's fingers, his tone
incredulous. 'This is my... you tore it out before the master-at-
arms took my notebook? Without him noticing?'

Clifford tutted. 'Categorically not, Chief Inspector. I
extracted the page meticulously to leave no sign it had been
removed. Likewise, this one from her ladyship's with a similar, if
considerably less legible, note.'

Seldon grabbed his hand and shook it. 'Clifford, thank you.
I will never rag your dubious skills again.'

'Then I look forward to whatever new sport abounds
instead.'

Eleanor laughed. 'And thank you from me, Clifford. Now,
someone still tried to frame you, Hugh, for Yeoman's death and
that person has now killed again it seems. So whether we're officially on the case or not, let's get back on with the job of finding
the killer.'

Seldon scanned her face. 'The very job which is going to be
all the harder because' – he picked up a folder and waved it –
'this information on the suspects the master-at-arms passed to us
just before Balog's murder is, I believe, our last piece of
assistance from him. Or the captain.'

She bristled. 'Well, if he'd handed it over earlier, we might
have found our murderer by now. And the count would still be
with us!' At Seldon's pointed look, she collapsed back in her
chair and sighed. 'I know, that was probably unfair. I'm sure he
handed it over the minute he received it but we could so have

done with it before.' She patted his arm. 'Hugh, let's all get a few hours' sleep and then reconvene refreshed sufficiently to actually think straight. Then we can make sense of all this. And the information the master-at-arms has provided. Maybe after some sleep, hopefully even you will feel bright enough for some breakfast.'

'Alright. Two hours,' Seldon conceded, clearly too racked by exhaustion and seasickness to argue.

'Four!' she called as she headed for her bedroom door.

23

In truth, the four hours felt far too little to Eleanor as she dressed and stumbled out of her bedroom with Gladstone in slumberous tow. She hadn't been able to shake the image of Balog's lifeless stare for the first hour and had then vividly dreamed of his body being shoved overboard by a ghoulish silhouette for the rest. Still, she had risen to the unexpected treat of another steaming hot bath plus a cucumber salve for her puffy eyes. Both evidently prepared by her butler whom she hadn't yet caught sight of.

There was a knock on the door. Clifford appeared from the pantry and admitted Seldon, the master-at-arms' folder in his hand.

She rolled her eyes. 'Hugh! Have you sat up the whole four hours poring over that rather than getting some rest?'

'Actually, no.'

'Good. Straight to business then.'

With the two of them seated at the table, Seldon tapped his pen on his new notebook.

'So, we know the passengers will be told that Balog suffered a heart attack—'

'Though you're convinced he was poisoned?'

He nodded. 'Cyanide, I believe, from initial smell and observation.'

She frowned. 'But Balog would have smelt the bitter almond scent too, surely? He certainly had a prominent enough nose to do so.' Clifford gave a quiet sniff without looking up from setting out a selection of cutlery. She turned to him. 'Your point, Mr Sniffy?'

'An observation only, my lady. That neither the length nor girth of nasal passages have any bearing on the ability to detect the aroma of cyanide. Many people, myself included, simply cannot smell anything.'

Seldon nodded. 'That's true. Plus, I might be wrong about it being cyanide. Some aromas seem so strong at the moment with this wretched seasickness. We'll have to wait until the count's glass can be analysed in New York. But the expected signs were there; red flush to the neck and jawline, constricted throat and so on.'

'Poor Balog. He was so full of life,' she said sadly. 'How long does cyanide take to work?'

Before Seldon could reply, Clifford did. 'Normally within two to five minutes of ingestion, my lady. Seconds in the case of inhalation of a lethal dose.'

Despite being intrigued at her butler's in-depth knowledge of such matters, Eleanor bit back an enquiry. She guessed his answer was likely not something he would want to confess in front of Seldon.

'Mmm.' She rubbed her eyes. 'I noticed that he hadn't touched his whisky from leaving the lounge until returning from watching the *Auriana* pass. So the poison could have been introduced anytime from before he left the lounge right up until he returned inside.'

Seldon's eyes widened. 'Well observed, even for you Eleanor! So, theories as to why he was murdered next then?'

'Perhaps,' Clifford said, 'I might suggest some breakfast while doing so?'

Seldon nodded eagerly. 'Top idea, man!'

She smiled to herself. *He must be feeling better.*

Clifford bowed. 'I shall go in search of such straight away.'

As he closed the door behind him, Eleanor glanced at Seldon.

'We could sit here until he returns,' she said lightly. 'Or...'

He gave her a quizzical look. 'Check out Balog's room for any clues?'

She shrugged. 'It's pretty clear we're not going to get the master-at-arms' approval now we've been thrown off the case. So...'

'We're in!' Seldon whispered at the welcome sound of the lock clicking open. 'Rather handy that your butler happened to leave a set of picklocks behind when he went for breakfast.'

'Handy indeed,' she hissed, ducking under his arm to slide inside Balog's cabin. 'He's far too fiendish at being able to read my mind, even before I've had the thought!' She froze. Despite Balog's body having been removed, the room still had the ghoulish presence of death about it. She steeled herself, carried on in and glanced around.

'Sunshine yellow and jaunty purple decor,' she murmured. 'Irrepressibly cheerful, but slightly too much to actually live with. Just like the man himself.' The cabin itself was not that dissimilar to hers, if smaller and minus a butler's pantry. She gestured at the floor.

'Well, Hugh, aside from a couple of playing cards which must have scattered onto the floor when Balog collapsed, the place is surprisingly tidy.' She bent down and turned them over. The first card seemed very old. The illustration was what looked like a Bavarian woman in traditional dress with a fan, above which there was a red heart. From her elaborate outfit, Eleanor figured she must be a queen. The queen of hearts, perhaps? The illustration on the other card looked equally old-fashioned. It reminded her of a Germanic clown or joker, this time with a pair of giant bells above his head. Something bothered her about the cards, however.

Something about the way they've fallen, Ellie? Or is it the number or type of cards?

'We'll have to search everything.'

She looked up at Seldon and nodded in agreement. They split up, Seldon taking the bedroom and adjoining bathroom, Eleanor the sitting room.

Only a few short minutes later, he was back. 'Just routine clothes and shoes in there. Neither of which are actually routine at all. They look more like I imagine a rail of Marinelli's stage costumes does.'

She smiled, remembering with fondness the cheeky flamboyance Balog had embodied in his dress. And conversation. 'Otherwise, there's really nothing else out of the ordinary?' She sensed that he seemed to be holding something back. 'Nothing missing you expected to see?'

He looked away. 'Nothing.'

'Except a little gentleman's stimulating late night literature, perhaps? As you expected from a man of Balog's unabashed character?'

'Eleanor! For Pete's sake!' Seldon's cheeks burned as he ran his hand around his neck.

'Don't worry.' She reached into the drawer of the desk she'd found partly open while he was still searching the bathroom and scooped up one of the many packs of cards in there. 'Balog collected playing cards instead.'

'No surprise,' he gruffed. 'He was one step away from being a card fraud as far as I can make out.'

She laughed. 'Hugh, Balog might have fooled gentlemen

into emptying their wallets in a game of whatever it was he played, but he didn't do it with these particular decks.' She moved a pen and pad of paper that looked as if it had been used to record scores and fanned the cards across the desktop.

'Good lord!' He whipped them back into a pile and covered them with both hands.

'Hugh, there's nothing risqué in his bedroom because it's all in here.' She gestured at the cards. 'Naked ladies, couples, the lot. Balog collected—'

'I can see what he collected,' Seldon said hurriedly. 'No need to spell it out any further, Eleanor. Please.' He caught her peeping up at him. 'Blast it!' he muttered. 'This is hardly how I wanted to spend my time with you on your birthday. Searching a dead man's room and examining...' he waved at the cards, 'this together!'

She shrugged, feeling her own cheeks blush. 'I know. Anyway, to do Balog justice he seems to have collected decks of playing cards from all over the world. And not just naughty ones, either. Some are really quite beautiful.' She pulled out the drawer below. 'See. Packs from Argentina, France, Australia, Mexico, India—'

'Australia?' He stepped closer to her side. 'That's where Clifford's Mr Padgett said black opals come from.'

'Absolutely. Coincidence?'

He nodded. 'Probably. Balog could have simply exchanged packs of cards with other "enthusiasts" of his kind on cruises like this. Even those... other cards. He needn't ever have been to Australia.'

'"Enthusiasts?"' Despite the room's sombre air, the ridiculousness of their conversation got the better of her. She smiled. 'Delicately put, as Clifford never says to me.'

'No surprise there.' He sighed. 'Marvellous, we've learned nothing much. We can't even prove Balog visited Australia.'

'Or' – she waved at the cards in the top drawer – 'that he'd done any of the more... exotic things depicted in these.'

'OUT!' He steered her swiftly to the door.

24

Back in her cabin, Clifford was waiting with a silver trolley, the bottom of which comprised a bain marie.

'If you will forgive the liberty of my having ordered a selection.' He peered sideways at Eleanor. 'Choosing from extensive menus can be such a torment.'

She tutted. 'Not for me. I'd have simply ordered one or more of everything.'

'Precisely. And, ahem, no introductions before you "tuck in" required then, my lady?'

She dropped the salver lid back on. 'I was just appreciating the chef's efforts, thank you.'

'Doubtlessly. Perhaps I may be allowed to do the honours?' He indicated each one in turn. 'Grilled ham with kidneys, eggs – soft boiled, poached and shirred – lamb collops, mashed and sautéed potatoes, soufflés – mushroom, bacon or smoked haddock – pumpkin and ginger potage and sirloin steak slices. With toast, butter and preserves, naturally. As there was only a small amount of each remaining, I have also improvised a second, if rather unusual, breakfast course.' He indicated the top row.

Eleanor and Seldon having given their orders, he set out a tantalising selection of dishes before them. She watched him out of the corner of her eye. 'Aren't you going to ask where we—'

'Count Balog's cabin, perchance?'

She laughed. 'I thought you'd guessed. Thank you for the picklocks, but—'

'You found nothing of interest, my lady.' At her and Seldon's surprised look, he arched a brow. 'Forgive me, but your expressions as you returned made that quite clear.'

She nodded. 'You're right. The only thing of note in the room was an exotic collection of salacious playing cards.'

Seldon coughed. 'Yes, quite. Now, back to theories on why Balog was murdered.'

'Given the timing, I assume it had something to do with his "sharks" remark.'

He paused, his fork halfway to his mouth. '*Sharks?*'

'Gracious. There was that much furore last night, even before Bracebridge called me in, I hadn't time to tell you. In the lounge Balog said there were "no man-eating sharks in the Atlantic because they are all aboard the *Celestiana*".'

'Interesting,' Clifford murmured as he added cream to Eleanor's coffee.

'I know. Which is why I think he must have seen something that the murderer needed to ensure he kept quiet about. Permanently.'

Seldon's brow creased. 'But surely he would have mentioned anything nefarious he'd spotted to the master-at-arms? Or at least to one of his men?'

She shook her head. 'Honestly, Hugh, I believed Balog when he said after years of sailing around on liners, he'd learned to mind his own business. And he was also one of those people who seemed to treat life like a game.'

'I see. Was Balog looking at anyone in particular when he made his "sharks" remark?'

'Not really. He might have been referring to Marinelli, or Sir Randolph, I suppose, as they were there at the time, obviously. But he could just as easily have been referring to someone not there.'

'Perhaps to Miss González? Maybe she's a bit of a man-eater? After all, she "found" the body...'

She frowned. 'Which makes her a prime suspect, yes. Unless "sharks" was just one more of Balog's relentless jokes, of course.'

Seldon grimaced. 'My gut feeling is not, since he was murdered soon after.'

Her frown deepened. 'Talking of feelings. In Balog's cabin I felt I'd missed something.' Seldon and Clifford both stopped what they were doing, their faces attentive. 'There were only two playing cards on the floor, you see. Now, if Balog had—'

'Knocked a deck of cards off the desk, there would have been more?' Seldon said slowly. 'Unless he didn't knock them off, but purposefully pulled them out of one of the decks on the desk—'

'To try and leave a clue as to his murderer?'

'Exactly. What cards were they?'

'I think they were a joker and the queen of hearts, but they looked very old. I found the rest of the deck they were from. It's not the sort I'm used to. They seemed to have diamonds, hearts, spades and bells as the four sets.'

'Bells, my lady?'

'Yes, Clifford. Why?'

'Count Balog was from a Germanic, or Teutonic, part of Europe, I believe. The playing cards from there often use different sets in the deck. Whereas we would use hearts, diamonds, spades and clubs, they use hearts, leaves, acorns and' – he nodded at Eleanor – 'bells.'

'Interesting,' Seldon said. 'But any relevance to Balog's murder?' For a moment there was silence as they considered the possibility. Finally he shook his head. 'I can't see a connection there either.'

She frowned. 'But Balog acted the joker. And on purpose.'

'So you think that represented him? And the other card?'

'Miss González, perhaps? Of all our female suspects, I think she's the most likely Balog would have referred to as the queen of hearts. And,' she continued, frowning with concentration, 'maybe there's a reason Balog reached for an old German deck of cards?' She sighed. 'Well, we can come back to it. Let's move on.'

Having finished the first varied breakfast course, they started in on the more unusual fayre Clifford had secured. He cleared their now empty bowls and presented Eleanor with a plate of smoked salmon-topped Vienna rolls and a simpler-looking offering for Seldon.

'A light selection of the most easily digestible petits fours available, Chief Inspector. Delicate buckwheat muffin, moist sultana scone and soft-baked hominy squares.'

'Perfect, thank you.'

While they ate, Ellie flicked through her notebook. 'Right, we're definitely still assuming Count Balog's killer is the same as Yeoman's, yes?'

Seldon looked up, frowning. 'I think two murderers marauding around is unlikely. What were you talking about when Balog mentioned sharks?'

'Yeoman's "misadventure" of falling overboard.'

'Then definitely yes, let's stick with the idea we're looking for one murderer. Until proven otherwise.'

'I agree. God forbid there should be two murderers running amok on board! So all our suspects remain the same. Except Balog, obviously.'

'Yes.' He frowned. 'If, that is, any of them could have over-heard your conversation with the count?'

Her brow furrowed. 'The lounge had filled up considerably,

though we were tucked around the corner because Marinelli insisted he needed respite from his legions of adoring fans. So, equally, we couldn't see anyone else. In which case, yes, any of the other suspects could have been there and overheard Balog.'

'However,' Clifford said. 'Only Signor Marinelli or Sir Randolph would have been able to slip the poison into Count Balog's glass to begin with.'

She nodded. 'That's true. Certainly, until we went up on deck together. Then, with the crowds and everyone being so distracted, any one of our suspects could have had the opportunity. Gracious though! I did see Sir Randolph pass Balog briefly and throw him the filthiest of looks.'

'Interesting.' Seldon paused mid-forkful. 'Did you spot any of the others?'

She sighed. 'Shamefully, I got caught up in the spectacle of the *Auriana* passing and Marinelli's impromptu aria, whatever it was. Clifford?'

'I believe it was from Wagner's *Der Fliegende Holländer*, or *The Flying Dutchman*. The ghost captain berates the ocean as he and his crew are doomed to forever roam the sea due to a curse.'

Seldon stared at him in amazement. 'Impressive knowledge, as always, Clifford. But relevant at all?'

'Perhaps only for a glimmer into Signor Marinelli's state of mind. He could have chosen from a host of other, rather more, shall we say, popular language pieces.'

Eleanor shrugged. 'But the Dutch remained neutral during the war.'

'The aria, like the rest of the opera, is in Wagner's native tongue, German, my lady.'

Seldon made a note and then shook his head. 'I've no idea how that can be relevant.'

'It almost certainly isn't, Chief Inspector. My apologies.'

Seldon tapped his notebook. 'There is the possibility,

however, that Marinelli's unexpected bursting into song was less spur of-the-minute than it seemed.'

Eleanor's eyes widened. 'You mean it could have been prearranged? As a further distraction to give an accomplice a chance to slip the poison into Balog's drink, perhaps?'

He nodded. 'It's a possibility. A slim one, I admit.'

'Maybe not so slim. I just remembered, when Marinelli thought he'd caught Balog eavesdropping in on our conversation, he told him he'd regret it. But, then again, it does seem rather... unnecessary. The deck was so crowded and the lights so blinding and the distraction so, well, BIG already...'

Seldon grunted. 'True. Maybe the killer didn't really need Marinelli to distract people with a song.' He wrote a quick note in his notebook, then looked up. 'So, Clifford, did you spot any of our other suspects on deck?'

'I spotted Miss González, Chief Inspector.'

Eleanor hid a smile. 'Of course you did. She's too exquisite to miss in a crowd ten times as large, isn't she?'

Clifford sniffed. 'I was not—'

'I know you weren't. I was only teasing.'

'When you two have quite finished, shall we get back to the matter in hand?' Seldon said, obviously biting back a smile himself. 'Right then. Let's move on to the information the master-at-arms has dug up. Quickly at that.' He opened the folder. 'Balog is down first, coincidentally.' He scanned the four short lines beneath his name. 'Born in,' he faltered, 'Cekse Bud... Budejov...'

Clifford rose and stepped to the large mounted globe, which he wheeled over to them. 'Perhaps, České Budějovice?' He pointed to middle Europe with his pince-nez. 'Part of Bohemia until 1918, formerly under Austrian-Habsburg rule.'

Seldon rolled his eyes. 'Thank you for the geography lesson, Clifford.'

Eleanor laughed. 'He can't help himself, Hugh. You get used to it.'

'I have. And I've been grateful on too many occasions for it.' Seldon turned back to the list. 'Moving on. Date of birth fourteenth of February 1879, which made him forty-four. There's no reference to his having left his native country until 1921. Equally, though, there's nothing incriminating here at all, just a single address in Paris from June 1921 and subscriptions to a few apparent gentlemen's clubs that have never crossed my desk. Clifford, you, umm, might want to take a look.'

Eleanor watched her butler scan the names. He shook his head, murmuring to Seldon too quietly for even her sharp ears.

She stared between them. 'Boys?'

Clifford ran a finger around his starched collar while Seldon busied himself with his notebook.

She smiled. 'Ah, not gentlemen's clubs at all then, I see.'

'No obvious links with Yeoman,' Seldon hurried on. 'In fact, it's hard to guess how they would have met at all unless it was aboard one of these nightmare vessels.'

'Did you ever get word of Yeoman being sighted on a liner before, Hugh?'

'Never. But that's far from conclusive.' He shook his head. 'I'd have expected the master-at-arms to have come up with a little more than that. Still, on to Marinelli.' He scanned the lines, reading snippets aloud. 'Born in Italy. Trained in Milan.'

'At Teatro alla Scala, perchance?' Clifford said.

'Yes, but hardly relevant. Links with wealthy names all over Europe. No surprises there. Evidently, he cancelled several prestigious contracts a few years ago. Told the press he was semi-retiring. Well, he must have missed the limelight then, since he's made a comeback as we know. Nothing else of interest. Next—'

Eleanor frowned. 'Hang on, Hugh. Why would he stop singing at the height of his fame? Even I'd heard of him.'

He shrugged. 'No idea, but it doesn't seem relevant. However, when you next speak to him, you can always "tact-fully" enquire.'

She huffed in mock annoyance. 'As you would say, moving swiftly on...'

He looked away, but she saw the edges of his lips turn up. 'Right. Mrs Swalecourt and daughter. Evidently, they reside just outside Coventry. Husband runs an antiques business that we already know cropped up in an investigation over the sale of stolen antiques. She's a big patron of the arts, it says here. That seems to be about it.' He frowned. 'Not much again.'

She grimaced. 'Doesn't seem the giving type to me!'

He shrugged. 'Maybe not, but it's a good opener for your next conversation with her. Not you thinking her tight-fisted. Her being a patron of the arts, I mean. So, Miss Florentina González.' He scanned the document. 'Nothing incriminating or suspicious. We already know we need to follow up on that bee pendant and the possibility she was at one time Yeoman's fiancée, even though I don't recognise her name.' He looked at Eleanor, who nodded. 'Okay, Sir Randolph next then.' He studied the sheet. 'Owns an estate in Harpenfield, North Hert-ford. Innumerable hotels to his name including... Ardwycke Manor, as we also know.' He cleared his throat and hurried on. As he read down, his brow darkened. 'And, from memory, at least three of these other hotels were sites of robberies Yeoman was considered to be involved in. A little too coincidental again?'

'Although, as I'm sure you're aware, Chief Inspector,' Clif-ford said, 'criminals do often target particular chains of properties.'

He nodded. 'True. But we definitely need you to follow that up when next talking to him, Eleanor.' He held up his hands in surrender. 'In your usual inimitable style, obviously.' He made some notes and then returned to the master-at-arms' list.

'Goodman, Professor of Psychology. Lectures at Bath University. Rose to prominence on publication of his book.'

'He was very modest about that at dinner,' Eleanor said.

'Well, it seems he's moved into part-time practice on the back of its fame.' Seldon glanced back at the paper and grimaced. 'I don't know if I believe all that psychology mumbo-jumbo.'

Eleanor laughed. 'Why ever not, Hugh?'

He shrugged. 'I know, I know. It sounds rather dismissive. Even at the... the place my wife worked during the war, she mentioned they had a psychologist or someone similar seconded to military intelligence. But my evidence of human behaviour has come from the streets, not from a cosy office. Anyway,' he continued to read down the document. 'Nothing else of interest.' He closed the folder. 'Well, we've plenty of avenues to explore.'

Opening her notebook, she jotted down the suspects she needed to follow up on and anything relevant she'd learned:

Marinelli – why semi-retired and then came back?

Mrs Swalecourt and daughter, Rosamund – antiques and art

Miss Florentina González – pendant, ex-fiancée?

Sir Randolph – Ardwycke Manor, other hotels and robberies

She caught Seldon looking at her.

She smiled. 'Don't fret, Hugh. Clifford will delight in playing your stuck phonograph in your absence. "Be careful and be subtle, my lady."'

'Always,' Clifford said.

She rolled her eyes. 'And you, Hugh?'

'I shall trawl every inch of my memory together with this list for anything else which connects, however remote.' He pursed his lips. 'That feels terribly vague and inadequate though.'

'Not at all, Hugh. I tell you, though, it may sound sceptical, but the master-at arms' information on the suspects feels a bit thin overall. Like, maybe he hasn't passed on everything?'

He sighed. 'Possibly, Eleanor. Either way, it's all we have to go on.'

Clifford interrupted her thoughts. 'Chief Inspector, if I may make a suggestion?'

Seldon waved his hand. 'Go ahead.'

'Perhaps it is time to recruit some help? If not to make up for, at least to patch over the gaping wound to our investigation left by the withdrawal of the master-at-arms' assistance, however grudgingly it may have been given?'

Seldon spread his hands. 'Very possibly.'

'Then I believe I know just who to ask.'

Seldon nodded. 'Perfect, man. Don't wait. Go ask!'

As they stood up, she shook her head to herself. *Lady Saxonby was wrong. New York can't be full of swindlers, thieves and murderers because it seems they're all on board the* Celestiana!

25

Eleanor hesitated at the door, her hand dropping without knocking. Gladstone let out a huff and scrabbled at the carpet, which clearly fell short of the luxurious pile his portly frame was used to in first class.

'Clifford?' she said in a hushed tone.

'Yes, my lady, I do.' It seemed her butler had read her mind yet again. He peered at her over the rim of his pince-nez.

She shrugged. 'It just feels... wrong.'

'To deny them the honour of being asked? I think not, my lady.' He gave the door a smart rap and melted away.

A peal of laughter greeted her as it opened.

'Uniforms ahoy! Send them on in for inspection,' a cheeky voice floated out over more raucous chuckles.

'Oh, lummy!' The stunned wide-eyed face peeking out from the doorway stared back at her.

'Good morning, Polly.' Eleanor smiled at her maid as Gladstone slipped his lead from her hand and bounded inside the cabin. 'Or is it afternoon now, perhaps?'

''Tis her ladyship!' she heard her housekeeper cry. Sounds of scrambling and panic-stricken whispers came from within.

'How was I to know!' she caught her cook's hissed retort over her bulldog's exuberant woofs of greeting.

The door swung back to reveal the remaining members of her staff, mortification on their faces. Polly shuffled backwards to join the line, stumbling onto Mrs Butters' feet.

'Oh, my corns!' Eleanor's housekeeper muttered. The women all bobbed a deep curtsey.

Eleanor couldn't keep the smile off her face. 'Ladies, just so you know, I'm delighted you're doing exactly what I hoped you would be. Having fun. So, please don't stop on my account.'

The women's collective sigh of relief floated out to her like a summer breeze.

'Thank you, m'lady. But beg pardon you heard us larking all the same.' Mrs Butters flustered forward, her face aglow with the warmth of the kind-hearted aunt Eleanor had always wished she'd had. ''Tis such a treat to see you. And happy birthday, though Mr Clifford told us as not to mention it till we reach New York.'

Eleanor shook her head. 'The treat is all mine, ladies – and thank you for the birthday wishes. We shall celebrate together when we get to New York, I promise. Now, how's your holiday working out so far?'

Lizzie laughed as Polly bounced up and down beside her. 'Ach, m'lady, we're in proper heaven herself and so grateful for your kindness in bringing us all along.'

Her cook jerked a thumb at the maids with an affectionate smile. 'This pair think their lifetime of birthdays and Christmases have come all of a once.'

'Like you and me don't, Trotters?' Mrs Butters chuckled. 'M'lady, we've that many tales to tell you. If as it isn't too bold to suggest you might be interested, of course?'

Eleanor laughed. 'Yes, you must. Please. All of you.' The image of her butler's strenuous efforts to keep her excitable gaggle of female staff in order intruded into her thoughts. 'Er, at least on this occasion.'

Mrs Trotman shared a look with her friend, who nodded. 'Would it be too cheeky to ask you to come inside so as we can show you our quarters?'

'I thought you'd never ask!'

The cabin they beckoned her into was snug for four, but cosy. A long settee, upholstered in rose and vanilla twill, which matched the wall lamps, faced two low, buttoned chairs across the stretch of plum carpet. On the first of the diminutive tall-boys in either corner sat a vase of vibrant silk roses; on the second, a tray with a magenta tulip-print tea set and a smart silver Thermos flask. A pretty china mantel clock and four simple wood-framed photographs added the perfect homely touch. Intrigued, she stepped over.

'Oh, gracious.' The photographs were all of her, Clifford and the four ladies with an excited Gladstone, all delighting in one of their rare treat times away.

Mrs Trotman bustled over. 'We've a dinky kitchen that's shared with some of the other cabins, m'lady, so we can please ourselves for a little hot something whenever the mood takes us.'

Mrs Butters poked her friend in the ribs. 'Which actually means we sit here waiting to wet our whistles, while Trotters stands gossiping until the cows come home!'

'Or delivering extra tea for the two gentlemen in the cabin down the corridor,' Lizzie said with an innocent look.

'There's nothing wrong with being neighbourly, my girl,' Mrs Trotman huffed.

'No,' Mrs Butters said. ''Cept your neighbourliness is happy to let all the folks along here fend for themselves except them good-looking two!'

'And our bedroom is yet another wonderland, m'lady,' her cook said, obviously changing the subject. She drew back the cherub-print curtains behind her. Not fast enough, however, to stop Gladstone bowling through them and wearing them like a cloak.

'Little rascal!' Mrs Butters said fondly, rescuing them from the wriggling bulldog and rearranging the fabric with her expert seamstress' touch.

The bedroom itself was a restful haven of duck-egg-blue and white polka-dot eiderdowns with matching pillows. On each was a folded nightdress, and the dressing gowns she'd bought them last Christmas.

'Polly and me each have all the extra fun,' Lizzie said. 'We've this wee ladder to speel up into our beds atop the others, m'lady. And then all of us snuggle down and tear the tartan until we fall asleep.'

'She means "climb". And "chatter on", m'lady.' Mrs Trotman wagged her finger at Lizzie. 'Her ladyship doesn't understand Scottish, silly. The rest of us downstairs have only just begun learning what you're saying half the time.'

Eleanor laughed. 'It's delightful to hear you speak as if you were still up in your native Highlands, Lizzie. Please carry on teaching me more.'

'Nae bother, m'lady,' Lizzie giggled, setting them all off again.

Her youngest maid looked up at Eleanor and then quickly down.

'Did you want to tell me something, Polly?'

She looked up, her face aglow. 'I just wanted to say as how we've been walking up and down the decks like grand people and... and taking tea in a proper dining room with people waiting on us! 'Tis like a naughty dream, your ladyship. But real.'

Eleanor laughed and clapped her hands. 'Well, let's all keep dreaming a little longer, shall we? How about some tea and cake?'

This drew a rousing cheer from the ladies. Clifford covered his ears as they spilled out into the corridor.

The second-class lounge was a far cry from the palatial surroundings of its first-class counterpart. However, padded Chippendale seating for well on two hundred at a go was arranged with such artful informality, the atmosphere felt inviting rather than spartan. The walls were panelled in medium oak and hung with framed etchings of various sea creatures, real and mythical.

The ladies waited as Clifford held Eleanor's chair out until she was settled, then dived into their seats. Except Polly, whose gaze flicked over to Clifford and then down at her shoes.

'Well done, Polly, but it's alright,' he said kindly. 'Sitting in front of the mistress is permitted on this occasion.' He perched rigidly on the edge of his seat as a waiter appeared. 'Indecorous amounts of everything,' he ordered, much to everyone's delight.

'Let's have your biggest news first then, ladies?' Eleanor said.

'Oh, you'll never guess, my lady.' Mrs Butters clapped her hands. 'Trotters and I bumped into some old friends I haven't seen for nigh on ten years!'

'How exciting. And unexpected.'

Her housekeeper nodded. 'Well, it certainly was.'

Mrs Trotman took up the tale. 'Butters had no idea the poor souls had all lost their positions in service or that the family went bust... I mean lost all their money, m'lady. Imagine the good fortune to get new positions for the whole eleven together on board this boat! The butler, footman, cook, housekeeper and the housemaids. And even the hall boy. Since it was the footman's uncle as already worked for Blue Line and was able to give them a leg up in getting hired. At least them of downstairs all managed to stay together.' She dropped her voice to a whisper. ''Twas the Marchfield estate as was seized, Mr Clifford.'

'Ah! That was indeed a tragedy for a most respected family,' he said sadly.

But possibly the very insider help we need, Ellie?

Two generous tiers of cakes and pastries arrived with the largest pot of tea she'd ever seen. Clifford shook his head as Eleanor's housekeeper rose to serve. 'Thank you, Mrs Butters, but her ladyship wishes for you all to remain on holiday.' He mimed rolling his sleeves up. 'Hence, it is my turn to be mother.'

'Only you forgot your flowery pinny, Mr Clifford,' Mrs Trotman said with a cheeky grin. 'Maybe as we can borrow you one?'

This brought on rounds of laughter.

'The other news.' Mrs Trotman gave her fruit scone and jam a professional scrutiny. 'Is that your two young maids don't know the difference between kind-hearted and soft-headed. Especially gangly legs, there.' She waved a hand at Polly. 'Who needs all that chocolate and sponge and the cherry biscuits if she's ever to fill out.'

'We only wanted to help,' Lizzie murmured, staring at the table. 'Didn't mean to be thankless, giving away that what wasn't ours to offer, m'lady. Honest, we didn't.'

Noting Clifford flinch, Eleanor forced herself to sit back. He didn't need her wading in and undermining his authority over dealing with whatever mysterious misdemeanour her maids had committed.

'Lizzie? Polly?' He looked between them. 'Have you been sneaking some of your meals down to someone in third class, perchance?'

Two fat tears rolled down Polly's cheeks as she nodded. 'Humble 'pologies, Mr Clifford, sir.'

'No waterworks required,' he said gently. 'You aren't in trouble. At least not yet.'

'They're very hungry, Mr Clifford, sir,' Polly blurted out, picking up the handkerchief he'd slid across to her.

Lizzie nodded. 'They're from Leb... Leban, or some such.'

'Lebanon, perhaps?' Eleanor said.

The maid nodded. 'That'd be it, m'lady. A lovely family as has just managed to scrape the pennies to go to America by selling everything so as to try and make a new life.'

'All eight of them are crowded into one tiny cabin half the size of ours!' Polly said passionately. 'There's only six wash-rooms for the thousand-and-more people in third class. And not as much as a window for fresh air in their cabin.' Her bottom lip trembled. 'And they haven't enough food left for even half the way!'

'And they won't take any offered by the others down there,' Lizzie chimed in. 'The parents are too proud to take from those as don't have enough anyways, but we sneaked some to the children.'

Eleanor was overcome by the heartache she felt for this poor family. Before she could speak, Clifford caught her eye and nodded imperceptibly.

As they dived into a second round of tea, walnut fruit cake and miniature custard tarts, her housekeeper pointed across the room.

'Ooh! There's Wilf, the footman I mentioned.' She gave a cheery wave to a waiter emerging from the stairs. He was one of the tallest, most angular young men Eleanor had ever seen. 'It was Wilf who helped us find out the cabin number you needed afore, m'lady.' She lowered her voice. 'The one for Chief Inspector Seldon.'

'All the more reason for you to introduce me then, Mrs Butters.'

'Lawks, m'lady! If as you're sure.'

'Lady Swift,' the waiter stammered after a protracted bow. He looked to be in his mid-thirties. 'An honour to actually meet you. Butters... umm, Mrs Butters has said over and over how very kind you are.' His reedy fingers fiddled with the edge of his apron.

'Likewise, Wilf.' Eleanor cocked her head. 'But didn't she also tell you that I don't bite?'

'Not as I remember, m'lady,' he said with a hesitant smile. This drew such a round of delighted chuckles that his shoulders relaxed. 'And you must be Mr Clifford, sir.' He offered a hand. 'Beyond a pleasure.'

'Sincere congratulations, Wilfred,' Clifford said. 'Like her ladyship, I am truly delighted you all secured such dependable positions. Together.' Only Eleanor's sensitive ears caught the earnest tinge to his tone.

Staff who work together in one household become like family to each other, Ellie. Just like mine. She glanced at her house-keeper. *If Polly, or Lizzie, had to go and work in another house, it would feel to Mrs Butters like they were taking her children away!*

In fact, that was much how Polly had first come to Henley Hall. Her family could not afford to keep her and her sister. Unable to find positions for them in the same household, they'd been separated, Polly coming to work for her uncle at age eleven.

'Do enjoy your journey on the *Celestiana*, m'lady,' Wilf said, bringing her back to the present. 'And please let me know if there is anything you need.' With another bow, he wafted away.

'So you two.' Mrs Trotman raised a finger to the maids. 'Full tummies for you both from now on.'

'May we still...' Polly looked up hopefully.

'Yes,' Clifford said. 'You may still visit your new friends in third class.' He threw Eleanor a pointed glance.

He's right. Stop putting it off, Ellie.

'Ah, yes. Actually, ladies, I need to ask you something. I need to... ask for your help.'

'Help?' Mrs Butters' face lit up with delight. ''Twill be our pleasure, m'lady, whatever it is.'

Eleanor sighed. 'Actually, I'm afraid it won't.' She faltered at how to relay the terrible happenings since the *Celestiana* had left port.

Clifford stepped in and succinctly outlined events and what help they were asking for. When he'd finished, he raised his hand. 'But, ladies, none of you have anything to fear yourselves. Understood?'

They all nodded.

Eleanor nodded as well. 'Absolutely not. And all Clifford and I are asking is that you keep your eyes and ears open. Nothing more. Nothing dangerous. But I so didn't want to ask at all. This was supposed to be a holiday for you.'

'As it was for yourself.' Mrs Butters smiled that motherly smile, which made things so much better. 'Anyways, we'd a' been most upset if as you hadn't, m'lady. And cheeky of me to say, but the best part is we'll likely see a little more of you both so as we can report in, as it were.'

'Like the real police,' Lizzie said with nervous excitement.

'Police?' Mrs Trotman suddenly seemed even more animated. 'Any chance the, umm... chief inspector might need to be there to hear what we report any time?'

Clifford steepled his fingers over his nose, but his sniff of admonishment was lost in the ladies' giggles, Eleanor's included.

26

As Eleanor reached the top of the stairs linking second-class with first, she stopped and waved Clifford forward.

'Look. It's the Swalecourts over there in the Verandah Café.'

'Indeed, my lady. How unfortunate.'

She blinked. 'Why? You know I need to speak to them again about her being a patron of the arts. And about her husband's antique business.'

His lips quirked. 'I know, my lady, but the opportunity that has presented itself is within a café, and you have just partaken of tea and cake with our ladies. Pity. If only you had an unbounded capacity for cake...'

She laughed. 'Just follow me, you terror!' She took Gladstone's lead and made for the café.

Inside, under an arched glass dome, potted citrus trees and rattan chairs with cushioned seats upholstered in green and ivory gave the verandah an air of chic comfort.

'Now, moving on to the south tower drawing room at Henley Hall,' she called behind her. 'I want new everything for there, too. Furniture, furnishings, wallpaper. The lot.' She slid into the chair her butler held out for her, still holding his slim pocketbook open as if he'd been taking notes.

'Very good, my lady.' He positioned himself off to her right, as she sat one empty table away from the Swalecourts. She'd cannily chosen the next along as it was almost entirely obscured by a carved pillar and a pot of indigo clematis. She reclined in her seat to observe her quarry through the greenery.

'So that's the requirements for the west wing listed.' She paused, as if deep in thought. In truth, she was hiding her smile as Clifford ordered.

'A three-tiered stand of your finest assorted confections to accompany tea for one,' he said quietly, his expression as impassive as the waiter's was bemused.

Once her tea and lavish cake selection arrived, Clifford stopped making meticulous notes on the illusory renovations to pour her a cup. His gaze slid to the Swalecourts and back. 'Lapping up your every word,' he mouthed.

'Excellent!' she mouthed back before raising her voice. 'However, we have the... the—'

'Main recital hall to consider, my lady?'

'Oh, do keep up, Clifford. I haven't detailed the finishing touches to the ballroom yet. You know how busy a season I have arranged for this year.'

He arched a quiet brow of despair. 'Would that were true,' he murmured.

She stood up. 'I've an idea.' With her back to the Swalecourts, she waved a haughty hand at three folding silk screens printed with exotic birds. 'These. I want some like these with those carved feet and crowned corners to section off the two wings of the recital hall during my smaller gatherings. But I want them printed with musical notes and such like.'

'An excellent idea, my lady. Since invitations are now so sought after, neither of the supplementary recital rooms will suffice.'

'Quite.' She spun around as if to return to her seat. 'Oh, Mrs Swalecourt. And Rosamund. Forgive me, I didn't see you there.'

'Lady Swift,' the older woman replied with more interest than in their previous encounters. 'A busy afternoon for you, perhaps?'

'Oh, frightfully so.' Turning away, she stepped back to her table and stopped in mock horror. 'Well really, Clifford! As if any lady would gorge through three tiers of cake on her own! One does not expect such an error from the waiters on a ship the likes of the *Celestiana*. Nor from one's butler in accepting such an erroneous serving.'

'Forgive me, my lady. However, what to do since I know how you deplore waste?'

'What indeed?' She took a few steps back and smiled at the Swalecourts. 'Ladies, forgive my presumption, but I don't suppose you might care to join me in making the best of the outrageous blunder I've been subjected to?'

Rosamund leaped up. 'That sounds delightful, Lady Swift. We'd love to, wouldn't we, Mother?'

Mrs Swalecourt allowed her daughter to hustle her to Eleanor's table, where she graciously sat down. 'Of course, being country ladies, we are both very health conscious too, Lady Swift.'

Beside her, Rosamund rolled her eyes, her hungry gaze returning to the cake selection.

Eleanor accepted the miniature iced petit four Clifford proffered with a pair of silver tongs, catching the amusement dancing in his eyes. He stepped around to pour each of her guests the perfect cup of tea from the additional pot he'd sent for.

'However,' Mrs Swalecourt continued, waving for a second spoonful of sugar to be added to her tea, 'as you say, no harm in a little indulgence now and then.'

Eleanor nodded, but followed it with a gasp. 'That wasn't

the case for poor Count Balog, it seems! Such a tragedy, his passing to a sudden heart attack like that. Maybe a lot, rather than a little, indulging!'

Mrs Swalecourt sniffed. 'Hardly surprising for one of such a dissolute lifestyle. One doesn't wish to judge, of course. However,' her lips puckered in ruched disdain, 'such an undignified spectacle for the rest of us to endure!' She patted her daughter's hand, which Eleanor noted was quickly slid out of reach. 'Such lack of gallantry.'

'The Count Balog we shared the captain's table with?' Eleanor said in a puzzled tone.

'Absolutely. Not a hint of consideration for sensitive souls like Rosamund. What Captain Bracebridge was thinking in seating him beside my daughter at dinner, I cannot begin to fathom. Even the most blissfully innocent and unaware of young minds can succumb to the impressionable, you know.'

Eleanor threw Rosamund a suitably horrified look. 'Goodness, the count didn't raise any inappropriate topics with you, I trust? Like his penchant for, er, "decorative" playing cards?'

The girl's cheeks flushed. 'He didn't, no. His only conversation was a string of waggish observations and amusing, if tall, tales.' She pointed at the largest of the chocolate eclairs as Clifford turned the tiered stand for her perusal.

Eleanor took a sip of her tea and a ladylike bite of cake. 'Perhaps, Mrs Swalecourt, you are worrying unnecessarily then on Rosamund's behalf? Perhaps Count Balog was merely the high-spirited gentleman he appeared?' She leaned forward conspiratorially. 'Although with your evidently shrewd character judgement, maybe you sensed there was a darker side to his persona?'

'I am very alert to all the male attention paid to my daughter, Lady Swift,' she said evasively. 'Oh yes, it is no easy task chaperoning such a beauteous and eligible young woman.' She sat back, obviously trying to hide that she was sizing up if

Eleanor had swallowed her response. 'But perhaps that is not an unfamiliar task to you also?'

'Actually, I would have no idea where to start.' Eleanor tried to wave off the unexpected wistful shroud that tightened around her heart. 'Umm... no children, so no daughter.'

'Not yet,' Clifford mouthed to her from behind the Swale-courts. He glided to her side. 'More tea, my lady?'

'Yes. And just another of those little pistachio macaroons. Oh, and I suppose to save the disgraceful waste, you'd better add a rhubarb finger meringue and a chocolate florentine.'

Rosamund nodded eagerly to Clifford as he hovered with the tongs at her elbow. 'I'll have the same. This never happens at Mother's affairs. She's far too careful when arranging the catering for her soirées. What is it you call those deliberately over-elaborate affairs, Mother?'

'I've no idea what you are referring to, dear,' Mrs Swale-court said through a strained smile.

'It can be so time consuming, I agree,' Eleanor said quickly in a sympathetic tone. 'Planning a busy programme of social events is always so fraught, isn't it?' She let out a tinkled laugh. 'If you are prepared to share any tips from your most successful galas, I would be most grateful.'

'Galas?' Mrs Swalecourt looked puzzled. 'I have not mentioned any.'

Eleanor smiled. 'No need to have. Clearly, a lady of your standing must have great experience in hosting a large number. Especially with your husband's many clients.' She cocked her head. 'You said he was in antiques, I seem to remember?'

'Antiquities, actually. Indeed, only the finest, and rarest.'

'Does he also deal in antique jewellery?'

She hesitated. 'Yes, but again, only the best.'

'All the more so, then. I mean, the need to arrange numerous and extensive galas. Those who appreciate the finest antiquities and jewellery are almost always those who appreciate the musical arts too, I find.'

Mrs Swalecourt threw her a look she couldn't quite read. 'Of course, I support my husband's business interests. Which includes entertaining, naturally.'

Rosamund clattered her cup back onto her saucer. 'However, Mother is very creative in entertaining. Frugally so, one might think.' She ignored her mother's icy glare. 'If, that is, one wasn't aware of her charitable help for struggling artists as well.'

Eleanor jumped in. 'My, oh my! Then I am in even greater admiration. How does your work as a benefactor of the arts tie in with your husband's business, exactly?'

Out of the corner of her eye, she saw Clifford's brow twitch. *You might have led up to that better, Ellie.*

Mrs Swalecourt eyed her suspiciously. 'I do not know what you imagine you have heard, Lady Swift?'

Think, Ellie. 'Oh, only that holding musical soirées must attract the type of person who is naturally interested in your husband's antiquities and vice versa. I mean most cultured people' – *you mean rich, Ellie* – 'attend, er...' She floundered for an example. Then she remembered the adulation Marinelli had received even among the first-class passengers. 'Attend opera, for example.' She was sure Mrs Swalecourt stiffened. She cast around for a way to probe further. 'You must have held opera soirées? Perhaps... Signor Marinelli has sung for you?' He was the only opera star she knew. 'He would—'

'Would probably have no interest in such a provincial affair!' Mrs Swalecourt smiled icily.

Her daughter snorted. 'Really, Mother! Your memory is getting worse every day. Signor Marinelli sang at one of your soirées last year. Even I remember that.'

'Rosamund, come!' Mrs Swalecourt rose and reached for her daughter's arm.

The young woman stood up, but shrugged off her mother's hand. 'But I'm sure Lady Swift would be interested in—'

'Enough, Rosamund!' Her thunderous look brooked no dissent. She turned to Eleanor. 'Now I recall, Signor Marinelli did sing for me some time ago. He has a remarkable talent, as we all heard when the *Auriana* passed. However, I believe in supporting the new wave of artists. Now, please forgive our declining anything further, Lady Swift, but I fear if we indulge in any more of this unexpected yet most delightful tea, it will spoil our appreciation of dinner.' She nodded with exaggerated graciousness. 'And one does so deplore waste.'

Eleanor watched as Mrs Swalecourt all but dragged her reluctant daughter from the café. Clifford appeared at her side.

'Bravo, my lady. It seems we might, perhaps, have an unexpected ally in the young Swalecourt?'

She nodded, frowning. Her mind had flashed back to sharing a table with Marinelli and to him staring intently at her necklace. The one with the opal.

27

'Lady Swift?' a silken female voice called. 'Oh good, it is you. Perfect timing.'

Behind her, Eleanor felt Clifford slip Gladstone's lead from her wrist.

'Ah, Miss González. How are you this evening?'

'Tired.' The set of enviable silk-wrapped curves sashayed the last few feet of the deep-pile sea-green carpet to her. 'Really tired. Exhausted, actually.'

'Haven't you been sleeping well?' Eleanor asked sympathetically.

Miss González sighed. 'No. Not really.'

Eleanor shook her head. 'Do you always struggle to sleep on cruises?'

Miss González shook her head vehemently. 'No. In fact, this is my first cruise. And my last!' Her dark eyes held Eleanor's gaze too intently for it to feel comfortable. 'What have you been keeping so busy and entertained with, then?'

'Oh, nothing much.' Eleanor waved an airy hand. 'Just the usual holiday activities.'

Her brain, still caught up in her conversation with Mrs

Swalecourt and her daughter, struggled to remember what it needed to find out from Miss González.

Was she engaged to Yeoman, check out her pendant, and something to do with her finding Balog's body?

'Well, what do you say?' Miss González cut into her thoughts with an edge of petulance. 'Are you coming or not?'

She nodded. 'Yes. It sounds delightful, whatever it is.'

What it was, was the Elysian Arcade, the *Celestiana*'s own luxurious shopping centre. A hundred and fifty feet of curved glass shop fronts, spanning both sides of the exquisite indigo-and-white frescoed marble floor. The gold cursive lettering adorning the signs hanging from each boutique glinted in the shimmering lights of the thirty cascading chandeliers hanging below the impressive, vaulted ceiling. Halfway down the arcade, the water in the ten-foot marble fountain danced a mesmerising ballet that had Eleanor shaking her head.

It really is almost impossible to remember that you are on a boat. And in the middle of the Atlantic at that.

Her companion, however, seemed impervious to both the beauty and the attention to detail such as the flying cherubs Eleanor could now see suspended between each of the chandeliers. Or, between each shop, the mirrored panels adorned with a silhouette of an elegantly suited lady or top-hatted gentleman.

'So what is it you are looking to buy?' Eleanor said.

'Stimulation. Diversion. Whatever I can get.'

Eleanor laughed. 'Well, looking down this bewitching shrine to shopping, I'm sure we can find both. And a great deal more besides.'

They peeled left to the milliner's, Eleanor enticed by the display of lace, silk flowers, ribbons, sequins and feathers adorning every shape and size of hat and fascinator.

'Pointless,' Miss González said in a jaded tone. 'You'd spend your life trying to keep any of them on even in a light breeze.'

Eleanor shrugged and followed her companion as she crisscrossed the arcade, thinking it quite incredible that Miss González seemed to have no desire to admire any of the beautifully crafted gloves, gowns or even shoes they passed.

'So no more Count Balog, then.' Her words made Eleanor jerk to a stop. She quickly turned and scrutinised the array of handbags, each beautifully displayed on its own velvet-covered stand. 'Sorry, did you say something?'

'Yes. I said, so no more Count Balog, then.' Those perfect cheekbones lifted half an inch as if fighting something.

Was that the beginning of a crocodile smile, Ellie?

'So I heard.'

Miss González's jaw twitched. 'You and that doctor seemed to be getting along so well.'

Eleanor hastily turned back to the display to hide her unease at the sudden switch in conversation. *Does she really think Seldon is a doctor? Or does she know he's a detective? And more worryingly, that we are working together?*

Miss González wafted a set of manicured nails. 'That must be why you arrived so soon after Count Balog died.'

Feeling like she was the one being interrogated, Eleanor shook her head, adopting her best matter-of-fact tone. 'I'd only had two, perhaps three chance conversations with the count. And well, you know how it is when you hear a scream. Somehow you find yourself running to see if you can help.'

Miss González shook her head vehemently. 'My feet usually run in the opposite direction. One has no idea what danger might be waiting.' She gave Eleanor a sharp sideways glance. 'Didn't anyone ever tell you ladies need to be careful?'

'Constantly. But somehow, it just doesn't seem to sink in if someone is in trouble.' *Like you might be now, Ellie.* All the more unsure if she was being pumped for information, she went on the attack. 'If *you* weren't coming to the count's aid, what were you doing there? Your cabin is the other side of the main stairs to D section, I thought?'

Miss González looked daggers at her but said nothing.

Realising she wasn't going to get an answer, Eleanor strode across to the window dressed with an eye-catching collection of tailored ladies' jackets. She needed to turn the conversation around. But then again, maybe she didn't? She wandered on to the next window to buy some more time. Maybe she just needed to let the other woman rattle on in the hope she'd unintentionally reveal her real agenda? Just give her enough rope to hang herself.

Bad analogy, Ellie!

'Seriously?' Her companion joined her and stared disparagingly at the display. 'Who is going to buy linen on board a cruise liner?'

Eleanor nodded at a couple leaving the shop with numerous bags. 'Them? They look very pleased with their purchases. Anyway, isn't there anything that takes your fancy? You're always so beautifully attired. What about some lovely luggage? We passed two shops a few moments ago offering every conceivable kind of case and trunk so one could shop for England. Or America.' She glanced over her companion's flawless olive complexion.

'Or Spain. Since that's what you're angling to find out.'

Eleanor shrugged. 'Not particularly. But you sound as English as I do.'

'International boarding school. That was deathly boring too. Come on.' She urged them onwards.

'It's lovely to see so many people enjoying the chance to shop together,' Eleanor said wistfully as they passed two more shops with happy couples beaming over purchases.

'Pff! What kind of woman wants to marry a man who likes shopping as much as she does? A man should be a man.'

Eleanor looped her arm through Miss González's and steered her towards the jeweller's opposite. As they neared the door, she realised in horror the whiskered man behind the counter was Mr Padgett, the very man Clifford had arranged to examine Yeoman's signet ring. She spun them both away, shaking her head at her companion's barbed comment.

'No hope that you will actually acknowledge femininity and purchase a proper dress watch, then, instead of that terribly masculine timepiece you carry?'

'No chance. However, sorry, that was insensitive of me.'

'Aside from nearly snapping my ankle, I don't see what you mean?'

'My eye was caught by the sparkle of those sublime engage-ment rings. But you made it clear in the Turkish baths you couldn't possibly be interested in them.'

'And what about you?' her companion smirked. 'Wedding dress and organ music galloping over your horizon anytime soon, then?'

'Nope.' Eleanor spread her hands, thinking there could be no harm in letting her companion think she was opening up. 'Been there once already.'

'Ah! And I foolishly had you down as an intelligent member of our gender.'

'Isn't that a bit harsh?' Eleanor stopped outside the hosiery shop. 'Not every girl has suffered whatever has turned you against men so adamantly.'

'If you say so.'

Eleanor gritted her teeth. 'Look, Florentina, I'm sorry you had your heart broken so badly.'

Her companion scowled. 'I never said I had.'

No time to keep tiptoeing about like a silk-slippered mouse, Ellie.

'Broken by the man who died falling overboard. Yeoman, wasn't it?'

The other woman's hand flew to her mouth so hard, she reeled backwards on her heels. 'I—'

'Florentina, I saw you watching him intently at the dancing

contest.' Eleanor shook her head. 'Now I'm the one who's bored. Bored with this ridiculous game of pretence. So I'll bid you farewell aga—'

Miss González pushed her face into Eleanor's. 'Oh alright! Yes, it was Yeoman who broke off with me. So what!'

'So nothing.' Eleanor took a step backwards. 'However, extra condolences then since you must be very upset. Although you've maintained your composure like a true lady. That can't be easy at all, as you must have been horrified to see he was on the *Celestiana*.'

'Not a bit. I followed him.' Miss González folded her arms. 'Yes, I admit it. And with the laughable intention of winning him back.'

Eleanor tried to hide her confusion. 'So, you still loved him?'

'I thought I did. Even when he... he told me it was over. That he didn't... didn't love me any more. I mean, I still loved him until I heard he'd fallen overboard,' she added hastily. 'But then in a blink, it hit me. I didn't. All the grieving I'd done after he left me high and dry had obviously worn out the last of my feelings for him.'

Eleanor saw her chance. 'And did he give you that pendant? I know bees are considered a symbol of love in some countries.' *Thank you, Clifford.*

Miss González fingered the pendant sadly. 'Yes. He gave it to me when we became engaged. He had a ring with a bee on it as well.'

'Could I have a closer look? It's very pretty.'

The other woman handed her the pendant. Eleanor turned it over in her hand. Trying to keep her expression neutral, she handed it back. 'I'm sorry it didn't work out.'

Miss González twitched her shoulders dismissively. 'I probably had a lucky escape.'

'Escape! There's no escape!' a deep voice rumbled...

28

Eleanor spun around. 'Ah, Sir Randolph,' she said over-brightly, wishing he'd disappear as quickly as he'd appeared.

'Indeed, Lady Swift. And it seems there really is no escape. Wherever I go, you seem to turn up.'

Actually, Ellie, it's the other way around this time.

'Ladies.' He raised his homburg, revealing deep lines etched into his brow. 'Just window shopping?'

'Oh, we got distracted chatting. You know how we ladies do when it's just girls together on an outing,' Eleanor said as pointedly as she dared without sounding impolite.

To no avail, it turned out, as Sir Randolph stroked his bushy moustache as if weighing something up. 'Then permit me to interrupt.' He lowered his voice. 'A little feminine advice, please. If, that is, I might be forgiven for straying an inch over the boundaries of decorum with such a request?'

'Of course, Sir Randolph,' Miss González purred. 'However, Lady Swift is absolutely the one you need.' She threw Eleanor a winning smile. 'Since she is indisputably the epitome of femininity.' She nodded to Sir Randolph and sauntered away.

Eleanor sighed to herself.

Buck up, Ellie. You can always have another go at Miss González later. For the moment, let's quiz Sir Randolph about Ardwycke Manor and certain robberies at some of his other hotels.

'What advice exactly were you seeking, Sir Randolph?' She kept her voice even.

He hesitated. 'A slightly awkward matter. I wouldn't ever normally venture such. Unusual circumstances and all that.'

His silver-topped cane swung under his arm as he clasped his hands, his gnarled fingers opening and closing. 'Gift needed. For my wife, don't you know.'

His wife?

Feeling guilty for doubting it was really for his wife, she clapped her hands. 'Is that all? Where do you want to start? Looking for your wife's present, I mean?' He gestured that the hosiery shop in front of them was definitely not the place, so they walked on, Eleanor thinking on her feet. 'So, tell me, Sir Randolph, what is your wife's most delicious pleasure? What makes her shoulders rise with unadulterated glee? Except having her husband beside her, of course.'

He grunted. 'If I knew that for sure, Lady Swift, I would not have engaged your services.'

She pointed past the fountain at another handbag shop. He shook his Zeus' mane with a shudder. They continued on to a dazzling display of glassware, the centrepiece vase being taller than she was. She laughed.

'Even if your wife loves flowers around the home, getting that back to her in one piece would be a significant challenge.'

He seemed to seriously think about it. 'Yet gifts can never be practical. They must be beautiful. Just as my wife is.'

She realised he was trying to avoid staring at her striking red curls. 'How about some beautiful silk scarves? The more vibrant the better. Like your wife's colouring, I suggest.'

He nodded appreciatively. 'Lead on.'

Among the haven of silk and colour she'd led Sir Randolph into, she fought to keep her focus. Choosing three of the most exquisite scarves on his behalf was easy. Not selecting double that for herself was another matter. In the end, she settled on only a couple, purely to keep Sir Randolph engaged for longer. At least that was what she'd tell Clifford later when he baulked on entering the cost into the household accounts, which he kept as fiercely as a terrier.

'See what you've done now, Sir Randolph,' she laughingly chided. 'So much for window shopping!'

'Put them all on my account,' he bellowed at the assistant who was wrapping each of their choices in the finest tissue paper.

'Oh, no need for that,' she said. 'Goodness, no.'

'Yes there is. You helped me out of a tricky spot. Hopeless at choosing presents.'

'Nevertheless, your wife is very lucky. Most men in your position, I'm sure, would simply not have found time to buy their wives a present themselves. Which is a shame, because you never know...' The assistant handed Sir Randolph his purchases and Eleanor hers. He stood in front of her with an enquiring look on his face. She shrugged. '"You never know when will be your last day on this earth, so never leave a kind act or word till tomorrow." My mother used to tell me that.' She looked towards the stairs leading to A deck. 'I wonder if Count Balog had a wife? Poor fellow. To succumb to a heart attack just like that. You see, you never know. And he can't have been under the kind of pressure that you must face every day as a hotelier.'

Sir Randolph snorted. 'He would not have understood the meaning of the word. The man was a card sharp, nothing more.'

'Goodness, really? With the number of hotels you own and have to manage, though, Sir Randolph, don't you worry sometimes about your health? Especially with all the things you have to cope with. Angry customers. Robberies.'

He started. 'What do you mean, robberies?'

'Well, surely hotels as opulent and well known as yours must fall prey to professional thieves? Ardwycke Manor, for instance, where my friend—'

'Got married. Yes, I remember, Lady Swift.' He looked at her oddly.

Dash it, Ellie. What's wrong with you? You're normally much better at this.

Her worry, however, appeared to be unfounded as he suddenly let his guard down. 'It's true. Unsurprisingly, any establishment that attracts the wealthy and famous is bound to fall prey to the criminal element. Ardwycke Manor is no exception. There was indeed such a robbery there. When it wasn't even in use as a hotel, can you believe?'

She gasped. 'Really? Did they ever catch the man, or men, responsible?'

His brow turned thunderous. 'No, Lady Swift, they did not. But it was during the war and all sorts of dark deeds went unpunished. Now, if you will excuse me, business calls. Send the scarves to my suite,' he called to the sales assistant. 'Good day.'

As he strode out of the shop, she shook her head at his sudden change of demeanour. *You're right, Sir Randolph. Too many dark deeds...*

29

The following morning, Eleanor was in a quandary. After having taken Gladstone for his morning constitutional, should she breeze back on into her cabin as planned? Or hurriedly tiptoe away? She nudged the door open another half an inch and peeped inside again.

It was even worse than she'd first thought. Seldon sat hunched in a corner, head in his hands, fingers drumming his forehead. Clifford's pocket watch slid into her eyeline from behind.

'Eighteen minutes, my lady,' he whispered. 'Without so much as looking up.'

'Poor Hugh,' she whispered back. 'He's obviously feeling more wretched than ever! Any chance you could conjure up something even more potent for his awful seasickness?'

He bowed from the shoulders. 'Most assuredly.'

'Thank goodness.' After a beat, she held her hands out in a questioning gesture as her butler hadn't moved.

'Clifford? The seasickness remedy?'

'Would make no difference, my lady. Since that is not what is ailing the chief inspector.'

'Then what is?'

Clifford mimed buttoning his lips.

Despite the seriousness of the situation, she smiled. 'Alright, Mr Discretion. Well, since we need Hugh's brilliance and expertise to progress with this impossibly confusing investigation, he needs mending. And now. So I'll slip away and you can —' She broke off at Clifford's headshake.

'My lady, I categorically cannot be the one to ease the chief inspector's... discomfort. Men do not discuss such things. Ever.'

'But what things? Dash it, that's entirely the problem! You boys are such closed books.'

'Yet as Oscar Wilde noted, "Give a man a mask and he will tell you the truth."' His suit tails swished away, his whispered, 'Good luck,' leaving her all the more confused.

She crept into the sitting room and slid her notebook quietly onto the table. Turning to the drinks tray, she shook the coffee pot.

'Or would you prefer tea?' she said loudly.

'What?' Seldon lurched to his feet, clutching his chest. 'Eleanor! Where did you spring from, blast it?'

'Nice to see you too, Hugh. Sorry I'm late. Gladstone had to say hello to every other dog on board and I just couldn't drag him past the smell of cooking sausages coming from somewhere on the lower decks. But you didn't come here to listen to me whittering away. We've a murderer to catch.' At his groan, she glanced quickly at him and away. 'Or is that the problem?' His silence told her everything. 'Hugh, you can't beat yourself up for failing to bring your wife's... killer to justice. You weren't even assigned to the case when it happened. You were abroad fighting for king and country. And then the case was closed before you even returned. You yourself once told me failure is an everyday part of your job.'

Anger flashed across his face. 'Due mostly to those faceless men in Whitehall who constantly cut my budget and manpower!' He groaned again and rubbed his forehead. 'One in sixteen of my cases result in a conviction in an average year. And I'm only assigned to the most serious ones which makes that fact feel all the worse.'

She gaped at him. 'But, Hugh, you're one of the most eminent detectives in the entire south of England. Only one in sixteen?'

'That's actually one of the best records in the country.' He managed a momentary smile. 'And thank you for the compliment.'

'It wasn't just a compliment. It was the truth. Gracious though, some of your investigations run for years, and then—'

'Come to an abrupt end. Case closed because it's been decided it's not worth the taxpayers' money to continue pursuing it.' He frowned. 'Do they want these blasted wretches brought to justice and put behind bars where they can't harm innocent members of the public again or not!' He ran a hand around the back of his neck. 'But every detective's choice is to accept that justice may not be done in every case and march on with the next one regardless. Or lose faith in the system,' he muttered.

'Or himself?' she said gently. 'And... and likely find himself wrestling with his conscience sometimes too?'

He hesitated and then nodded with a deep sigh. 'Even I've learned some people have a justifiable reason to commit a crime.'

'If I was in your shoes right now, Hugh, I'd be entirely torn too.' Her tone softened. 'What I mean is, I'd be torn between wanting to bring Yeoman's murderer to justice. Or wanting to... shake his hand.'

He sighed. 'Too perceptive, Eleanor.' A relieved smile hovered on his lips. 'Maybe it isn't a crime to... to... you know.'

'To want revenge rather than justice, Hugh? Even if you're a policeman?' His silence told her everything. 'Well, at least you came out and said it. Well, I said it for you. But it's normally poor Clifford who has to listen to me saying all sorts of inappropriate things at definitely inappropriate times. I'm amazed his bowler hat ever stays on his head since I've bent his ears out of shape day after day.'

Seldon's unexpected roar of laughter made her heart skip.

'That's better.'

'So much better. Thank you.' He ran his thumb over her palm, his deep brown eyes filled with such unexpected tenderness it made her insides flutter.

'Speaking of Clifford, where is he? I've got a serious bone to pick with him.' He caught her questioning look. 'If he's going to teach you that unfathomably devious trick of his, of reading minds, then I'm lost!'

It was her turn to laugh. 'No chance he'd ever do that. Just imagine what dubious truths I'd find out about him if I could.'

'I so wish you could.'

They held each other's gaze for a moment, then looked away.

'To business, then,' she said reluctantly, wishing all things murder would disappear and leave them to the tender mood still hugging her shoulders and shining in Seldon's eyes.

'Regrettably, yes, let's.' Seldon opened his notebook slowly. 'Eleanor, when this is all over...'

'Whatever it is, yes please, Hugh. Right now, we need progress...'

Seldon's appreciation of her headway in questioning the Swalecourts was clear in how intently he listened to her every word as she recounted their discussion. His pen moved in those short efficient strokes of his that she found fascinating, having nothing but spidery handwriting herself, no matter how hard she tried, or Clifford despaired.

'But Rosamund sounded almost... sarcastic or mocking when she said her mother was a patron of struggling artists.'

Seldon frowned. 'Because she is embarrassed by it? Or it's a lie she's been told to repeat? Even if only to make Mrs Swalecourt seem more charitable?'

She jumped at his sudden cry. 'Agh! My shins!' He craned his neck under the table to be met by a wild-eyed bulldog poking up between his knees. 'Gladstone, old friend, do you always have to do everything with such exuberance? Like your mistress,' he whispered into one of the bulldog's stiff little ears.

Before she could refute his statement, Clifford stepped in with a loaded silver tray. He pressed the door closed behind him with one impeccably polished shoe.

'My sincere apologies for Master Gladstone's unruly greeting, Chief Inspector.'

'No problem.' Seldon rose. 'Umm, would you excuse me for just five minutes?'

He cleared the room in brisk, if still unsteady strides. The door closed behind him.

'Bravo, my lady. A remarkable turnaround in the chief inspector's demeanour.'

'Oh, that was easy.' She gave a coquettish shoulder wiggle. 'Since I could disregard any nonsense about preserving a lady's reputation as my chaperone was absent.' She let him continue running a horrified finger around his collar for a little longer. 'Clifford, Hugh is far too much of a gentleman to take advantage of us being alone as you well know. And too dashedly awkward, bless him,' she added with a wry headshake. 'Relax, my ever-chivalrous knight, I was just teasing.'

'How disappointing.'

'Clifford!'

30

She was still chuckling when Seldon returned.

'Gracious, that really was only five minutes.'

Clifford spread an exquisitely presented selection of cheeses, crackers, baton sliced salad vegetables, toasted walnuts and almonds on the table, all set around a bowl brimming with grapes, dates and figs. 'Master Gladstone, no begging required.' He beckoned the drooling bulldog out from under the table. 'You have your own treat from Mrs Trotman. A braised ham bone, dusted with baked liver sprinkles, served on pillows of carrot.'

'Talk about spoiled, old friend,' Seldon called to Gladstone. 'No wonder you're as impossible to reason with as your mistress.'

Eleanor caught her butler nodding.

She laughed. 'Rotters, the pair of you.'

Setting a sherry beside her, Clifford offered one to Seldon who sniffed it gingerly and then nodded. 'This will go down perfectly, thank you.'

Clifford cleared his throat. 'I also have some news from the ladies, Chief Inspector. My lady?' They both looked at him expectantly. 'It seems Wilf, the former footman you met, my lady, asked discreetly among the crew for any "titbits" of gossip, as it were. Well, it seems one of the nightwatch crew "accidentally" read a message sent by the master-at-arms to the board of the Blue Line. I am sure you can guess the contents.'

She slapped the table. 'So it *was* the master-at-arms who ratted on us!'

Seldon grimaced. 'I'm not surprised, but it's good to get it confirmed. At least we know who our enemies are now.' He shook his head. 'Sorry, Eleanor, where were we? I think you were going to tell me what you found out when you talked to the Swalecourts again?'

'Yes.' She conveyed the essence of her conversation. 'I'm convinced she was going to let slip something more about her mother and Marinelli, but she got instantly hushed down. And then dragged out by her hair, poor girl. I need to catch her on her own.'

'Sounds like a lot of tension between mother and daughter then. I agree you should question Miss Swalecourt alone next time. But how? You've said her mother keeps her on a very short leash.'

Eleanor shrugged.

'If I might be so bold,' Clifford said. 'I believe I may have a solution.'

Seldon raised a hand. 'Fine, just don't tell me what it involves. So long as it doesn't place your mistress in any danger, obviously, which I trust you it won't. So next we—'

'Hang on,' Eleanor said. 'What about my success with Miss González?'

'You've already questioned her again, too?'

'Of course. And not only did she confess to being engaged to Yeoman, but also to purposefully following him on to the *Celestiana* to try and win him back.'

Seldon's brow furrowed. 'Mmm. You know, the whole thing

could be a lie to hide her real reason for being on this wretched ship.'

'True. I did get a good look at her pendant, though, and on the back saw different initials to those Mr Padgett noted on Yeoman's ring. These were "BEJ".'

'BEJ... Blanche Elspeth James!' Seldon slapped his forehead. 'That was Yeoman's fiancée's name.'

'Good memory, Hugh. So it looks as if her story, part of it anyway, is true, even if she is travelling under a false name.' She caught Clifford's arched brow. 'I know, there was no alias listed in the master-at-arms' notes.'

Seldon thumped the table. 'You might have been right about him withholding some information from us then, Eleanor. But, Florentina, or Blanche as we now believe she is, does have a solid motive!'

'For killing Yeoman, yes. Assuming he did dump her and not the other way around. She is a very cool fish.'

'But either way, it still doesn't give her a motive to kill Balog.'

Clifford topped up both their plates. 'Perhaps he witnessed the lady... eliminating Mr Yeoman?'

She threw her hands out. 'But I was the only one on the deck when it happened.'

'Honestly, Eleanor, how can we be absolutely sure of that?' Seldon said gently. 'I've noted at least half a dozen hiding places up there where someone could have been concealed.'

Clifford nodded. 'Might it be prudent, Chief Inspector, to consider whether Miss González had the means or opportunity to steal the, ahem, murder weapon which dispatched Mr Yeoman?'

'My gun!' Seldon groaned.

'With apologies for raising such, but yes.'

Eleanor frowned. 'How could she possibly have recognised you though, Hugh? You haven't mentioned interviewing her.'

'I haven't. Never met the woman. She was just a name. If they were together, Yeoman could easily have told her about me, though. I interviewed him once, as I said, so he could probably have given her a reasonable description, especially as we were uncomfortably similar in appearance. All of which means we can't discount her seizing a chance to frame me for killing him.' He made a note. 'Okay, so we'll work out our next move with Miss González later. For now, any more progress?'

'Sir Randolph.'

'Talk about making a chap feel inadequate,' he grumbled, but his eyes were shining. 'I can't believe you've managed all this so quickly!'

Secretly glowing at his praise, she shrugged. 'Don't be impressed. I just happened to meet him in the shopping arcade. He wanted help choosing a present for... for someone.'

'For his wife?' Seldon said quietly. 'It's alright, but thank you, Eleanor. What did you discover?'

'That he absolutely has a guilty conscience.'

The two men shared a fleeting look.

She flapped her hand. 'That was my first thought too. But I was wrong, I'm sure. It wasn't a gift for his mistress. His guilty conscience seemed to have more to do with those robberies at his hotels. Particularly the one at Ardwycke Manor.'

'Interesting,' Seldon said. 'That might tally with the news I was going to tell you both.'

'Go on.' She eagerly leaned over to scour his notebook.

'It's not in there. Not yet.' Seldon tapped his temple. 'It's in here. And it came to me in the middle of last night. I knew some of Sir Randolph's hotels had been robbed, possibly by Yeoman, and that's when I remembered. On two occasions, a couple of notorious swindlers were spotted in the hotel lobbies only an hour or so after the robberies. And more interestingly, when Ardwycke Manor reopened as a hotel after the war, they were also spotted there by an eagle-eyed policeman.'

'What sort of swindlers, Hugh?'

'Card sharps, Chief Inspector, by any chance?'

'Among other sharp practices, yes. Spot on as always, Clifford.'

Eleanor's eyes widened. 'They could have been retrieving the stolen items then! For a, what's the street term, Clifford?'

'A "cut", my lady.' He avoided Seldon's gaze. 'Or so I have overheard.'

'I shan't ask where,' Seldon said. 'But if you're right, Eleanor, it would explain why Yeoman was always squeaky clean of any stolen items. He breaks in, steals the stuff from a safe or wherever, and then hides it in a predetermined place still on the premises. The police, if they do apprehend him at any point from leaving the scene of the crime, find nothing on him and have to let him go.'

'Then his two accomplices turn up later and retrieve the stolen stash.' Clifford raised an eyebrow. 'Quite ingenious.'

Eleanor nodded. 'So, Asquith could have been in league with Yeoman and the card sharps?'

'Maybe. But why would someone as apparently wealthy as Asquith want to rob his own hotels? And why would he then kill Yeoman, his golden goose, as it were?' He slapped his forehead. 'To cover his tracks, of course. This damned seasickness has made me so slow-witted.'

Eleanor looked thoughtful. 'Balog mentioned that there were card sharps on board this ship.'

Seldon stared at her. 'But now he's dead, how does that help?'

'Because, forgetting Sir Randolph for a moment, that's another possible motive for Balog's murder. With Balog dead, the identity of the two card sharps remains hidden. Maybe they are the same pair from Asquith's hotels.'

'Actually,' Clifford said, 'I have more progress to report from the ladies which they discreetly obtained from Wilfred.'

'A trustworthy friend of Mrs Butters, Hugh.'

Clifford nodded. 'Indeed he is, Chief Inspector. And a most upright young man, I am reliably informed. Count Balog, it seems, played cards with Yeoman the night of his demise despite his insistence to her ladyship that he had no dealings with the man.'

'Well done, ladies!' Seldon said. 'I shall thank them when this is all over.'

Eleanor thought for a moment. 'You know, maybe our link between the card sharps and Yeoman isn't Sir Randolph then, but Balog. Balog claimed he wasn't a card sharp, but not that he didn't *work* with some! How's this? He plays with all the wealthiest passengers and then passes on the names and descriptions of those who can be easily cheated or who gamble excessively to the card sharps so they can make a killing. Balog gets a cut. For some reason, there's a falling-out and the card sharps believe Balog is going to out them.'

Seldon nodded. 'That could have got him killed, alright, but it doesn't link directly to Yeoman, does it?'

She frowned. 'No, I suppose not.'

Clifford coughed. 'There is more from the ladies, however, Chief Inspector, my lady. Regarding alibis for the time of Count Balog's murder.'

Seldon glanced at Eleanor and then back at Clifford. 'Go on...'

'The ladies have been made aware of several alibis for the time of Count Balog's death. Sir Randolph and Lady Wren-shaw-Smythe spent the entire evening in the on-board cinema. I know they are not suspects, per se, but they do reside on A deck and I did not wish to discourage the ladies.'

She waved him on. 'Quite right. And you said alibis in the plural?'

'Indeed. Professor Goodman also has an alibi. He was preparing for his talk in the lecture theatre. A pair of carpenters annoyed the gentleman endlessly, it seems, as the *Celestiana* sailed without the seating in the theatre being properly finished. Disgraceful! For a boat this prestigious...'

Eleanor flapped him gently to a stop and turned to Seldon. 'So, Hugh. As the professor has an alibi for Balog's death...?'

'He's ruled out.' Seldon crossed Goodman and the Wrenshaw-Smythes' names through on his list. At her quizzical look he shrugged. 'I included the Wrenshaw-Smythes for completeness. As I noticed you had too.' He turned to a new page. 'Anyway, it's good to feel we're finally narrowing the field.'

'Absolutely! So, to summarise, who's left on our list of suspects?'

'The Swalecourts, Miss González, Signor Marinelli and the now more interesting Sir Randolph.' Seldon slapped his pen down. 'Blast it though, that's still way too long a list given the time we have available.'

She nodded. 'Yes, too long a list, I agree. But don't worry, Hugh, I've had an idea. The killer thinks he or she has outwitted us and, to be honest, even with the ladies' superb help, we're harder up against it than ever.'

'What are you suggesting?' Seldon said cautiously.

'I think we may finally have a chance to level the playing field. But first, I need to divide and conquer!'

31

'Clifford,' Eleanor whispered. 'What the devil are we doing lurking behind some wretched bamboo? I thought—'

'*Fargesia robusta*, my lady,' he said at louder than normal volume.

He stepped out from their hidey-hole and gestured down the corridor where Mrs Swalecourt was just visible turning the corner towards the main staircase.

Eleanor shook her head. 'Well done, Clifford! Whatever ruse you came up with worked a treat.'

'Actually, my lady, we have the ladies to thank again. They found out from Doris – the former maid of the Marchfield family, and Wilf the footman's fiancée now, it seems – that Mrs Swalecourt has an appointment at the hair salon today, at this exact time.'

'Excellent! But what was that you blurted out a moment ago? Honestly, you nearly gave us away before she'd gone!'

He pointed at the potted plants. '*Fargesia robusta* is the name of this particular species of bamboo, my lady.'

She threw her hands out. 'Which you felt I needed to learn at that precise moment because?'

'Because what other rationale could there be for a titled lady rustling around with her butler in inappropriate proximity behind such vegetation other than an avid desire to collect exotic plants? Only a scandalous one. Exactly as the gentleman who emerged from that door just across thought until his expression quickly soothed. Thankfully.'

'Spoilsport. He might have enjoyed being outraged. However, you skip off now and I'll snag our prey.'

He pursued his lips. 'Butlers do not "skip".'

'Silly me.' She waved her hand towards the far door. 'Trot along then. We haven't got long.'

Once Clifford had left, she headed purposefully towards the table Mrs Swalecourt had just left...

'Oh, say you will,' Eleanor implored. 'Taking tea alone is so dull, don't you find?'

Rosamund, who was sitting at the table waiting for her mother to return, let out a loud huff. 'I have absolutely no idea, Lady Swift. That never occurs. Mother doesn't like me taking tea or anything else with people she doesn't know when she isn't there.'

Eleanor smiled sweetly. 'But your mother and I are old friends. We met days ago.' Looping her arm through the bemused young woman's, Eleanor steered her off towards her cabin.

'Tea for two, Clifford,' she called as the door opened a beat before they arrived. Once inside she waved a gracious hand. 'Do make yourself at home, Rosamund.'

Her guest wandered to the centre of the sitting room's deep pile rose carpet where she turned in a slow circle, eyeing everything with hungry scrutiny.

'The attention to detail is delightful, isn't it?' Eleanor waved her onto the nearest settee. 'The *Celestiana*'s decor, I mean?'

Rosamund shrugged. 'I hadn't noticed. Everywhere we go has "delightful" decor.' She flopped into a seat. 'A country lady cannot settle for anything less. As I am constantly reminded.' She glanced around again. 'But your cabin is bigger, and fancier, than ours.'

'But that's not what caught your eye, is it?'

'No. I wondered what your husband looked like. But you've brought no photographs of him with you. Even Mother brought one of Father to sit beside her bed.'

'I didn't bring any, Rosamund, because I am not married.'

'Oh, but then you're practically an old... sorry, I didn't mean—'

'No need for apologies. You're right. I am way past the age an eligible titled lady should be married, according to convention. But that doesn't mean it won't happen later. Or sooner.' She bit back a chuckle as she caught Clifford's black-jacketed arms shoot mischievously out from his butler's pantry door, both sets of fingers crossed. 'However,' she said, loud enough for him to hear, 'I'm not sure I'm suited to anything except unfettered independence.'

Rosamund shuffled forward. 'But that's what's so unfair! I shan't have had even a moment of independence before I'm wed. Mother is absolutely single-minded on that.'

Eleanor was overwhelmed with sympathy for the young woman. And all the more grateful for the independent life she herself had been able to lead. Even if her parents hadn't disappeared when she was so young, they would never have enforced their will on her. Nor hampered any plans she made.

'I'm sure your mother is just trying to protect you, Rosamund.' She searched for any genuine solace she could offer her clearly frustrated guest. 'Honestly, too many purely independent-spirited days can become rather wearing.'

'For one's butler,' her sharp hearing caught Clifford mutter as he appeared with a large silver tray, which contained an impressive array of sweet delicacies. Their eyes met and he nodded once. She needed his perceptive eyes and ears. She turned back to her young guest.

'What would you choose to do if you had the choice, Rosamund? Maybe you share your mother's devotion to the arts, for instance?'

'As if! Lady Swift, I will be twenty in two months' time. What do you think I would choose to do? I would be out having fun with friends my own age!' She let out a sound not unlike hissing steam. 'I certainly wouldn't waste a single moment enduring any of the mizzle Mother calls entertaining!'

Clifford appeared at Eleanor's elbow, topping up her tea. 'Light but tediously endless rain, my lady.'

'Ah.' She looked at her guest over the rim of her teacup. 'So not a fan of any of the performers your mother has arranged? Although actually, now I think back over our conversation in the Verandah Café, you've intrigued me. What did you mean by "struggling artists"?'

Rosamund shrugged. 'Nothing of note.'

'It's quite the evocative term for something without note, I'd say. "Struggling artist" has such an air of the romantic about it.'

'Then we have very different views on romance!' Rosamund haughtily urged Clifford into adding a generous second round of the dainty miniature fruit scones to her plate.

'More cream and preserve, Miss Swalecourt?' he said, doing so without waiting for her to reply.

'Well,' Eleanor waved her hand at the coffee table, 'we don't differ in our view on the sublime tea my butler has put on. Thank you, Clifford.'

Rosamund stared at her. 'You know, you're not the model country lady my mother is adamant one simply cannot but be. Not being rude, but one doesn't thank the staff. Especially in front of guests.'

'Quite right. Which is one reason I shall never fit the model country lady mould. I appreciate all my staff enormously and make no bones about saying so. They're very precious.'

'*Precious?*'

'Yes.' Eleanor tilted her head. 'What's precious to you, Rosamund?'

'My right to make my own decisions.' She threw her arms wide. 'My freedom!'

Eleanor nodded. 'I can understand that. Genuinely. Maybe you need to tell your mother how much it means to you.'

The young woman looked at her pityingly. 'Lady Swift, no one can tell my mother *anything*. Not even Father. It's like rain pouring off a roof.'

'Ah, but she married a man who undeniably respects *her* freedom.'

Rosamund hastily swallowed the two cubes of Turkish delight she'd popped into her mouth. 'How do you know that?'

'Your mother said so. Not in so many words, I suppose. But she mentioned that your father has his own business, and she is a busy and successful society hostess and art benefactor in her own right.'

Rosamund rolled her eyes. 'She's never bashful in making sure everyone grasps that last part. Not that subtle and Mother have ever so much as been introduced. Every soirée is the same. I'm paraded in front of every eligible bachelor she's invited, no matter his looks, or his opinions on women.'

'Is it any solace to you that at least she stops short of including the artists from her soirées in the line-up of potential suitors, I assume? Struggling or otherwise?'

The young girl stared at her. 'You really want to know, don't you, Lady Swift? About the artists at Mother's entertainments, I mean?'

You must be losing your touch, Ellie. Every suspect you speak to on this case seems to be able to see through you like a torn veil. She sighed to herself. *You're trying too hard again.*

She forced herself not to reply, but to settle back in her seat instead. Clifford came to her rescue as he placed a fresh bowl of cocoa-dusted almonds in place of the one the two of them had already finished. 'Will I cancel your gown fitting, my lady?' he said in a grave tone.

Catching his drift, she gave a convincing sigh. 'Yes, please, Clifford. Miss Swalecourt is quite right in protecting her mother's highly sought-after invitations. It was disgracefully presumptuous of me to even hope for such.'

Rosamund's face broke into a smug smile. 'I thought you were angling for an invitation! I *can* help you with that. Though why you'd want to go to one of her events is a mystery.' Eleanor opened her mouth but closed it again as Rosamund held up a finger. 'There are conditions to me getting you an invite, though.'

She smiled at her guest. 'Bartering, I see. Well, what conditions are you proposing?'

'That you find a way for me to get some more time away from Mother during the rest of this stifling cruise.' At Eleanor's hesitation, she laughed. 'I'm not proposing to ruin my reputation, if that's your worry.'

'I'm sure you're far too sensible to do that, so it's a deal.' She took a sip of tea. 'But first, let me confess.'

Her guest started in on the cherry and almond fondants. 'Confess away. This is going to be fun.'

'Well, the truth is, I am a terrible hostess.' Eleanor didn't need to look over to know Clifford would be nodding. 'To the point, in fact, I've avoided it altogether.'

Well, that part's true, Ellie

'That's why I would dearly love to attend one of your mother's soirées. But first, I'd like to hear about them. Who she invites to perform, and what the arrangements are, as it were, so that I can emulate—'

Rosamund's curt laugh caught her by surprise. 'You won't

want to emulate the half of it! It's shameful, really. Does it say in the manual of how to be a proper lady that one must take advantage of others?'

Eleanor forced herself not to lean forward. 'Never having stumbled across the manual, I really couldn't say. But are you sure that's the case where your mother is concerned, Rosamund? She seems so... magnanimous.'

'No, she doesn't. And yes, I am. I have overheard her and Father plotting on an embarrassing number of occasions. The last one was over Signor Marinelli, can you believe? The person my mother "forgot" had sung at one of her soirées.' Now clearly buoyed up at the chance to get back at her mother, Rosamund became quite garrulous. 'He's one of the "struggling artists" she's got her claws into.'

'But he's so famous. I thought you said your mother only invites artists who are up and coming?'

'No. She said that to cover up that I let it slip. Not that she has any idea I know what's really going on.'

'And what is really going on?' She crossed her fingers under the coffee table.

'Mother lends them money.'

'Including Signor Marinelli?'

'Especially him.'

'You mean she pays the artists a princely sum for performing at her evenings?'

'No. I mean she "loans" them money.' Rosamund's tone turned conspiratorial. She was clearly enjoying gossiping about her mother. 'I overheard Mother and Father talking about Marinelli having lost his confidence. Everyone thinks he's rich, but apparently, he's practically bankrupt! That's what I heard Mother and Father saying, anyway.'

That agrees with the information we got from the master-at-arms, Ellie.

She held out her hands. 'Well, there you go. She is probably just selflessly trying to help him.'

'Pah! My mother does not know the meaning of the word "selflessly". And Father isn't much better. I mean, who else would take advantage of a man so desperate that he begged them for money? Believe me when I tell you, if Mother and Father "lend" someone money, they expect it back with interest!'

'Do you know what Signor Marinelli wanted the money for?'

'To see that psychologist man that everyone wants to know now, just because he's written a book.'

'Psychologist?' Eleanor said as nonchalantly as she could. Behind Rosamund, Clifford arched a brow.

'Yes. That stuffy man you were seated with at the captain's dinner. I did feel for you. The eminent Professor Daniel Goodman looks about as much fun as cold rice pudding.'

Eleanor thought for a moment while Rosamund devoured another cherry and almond fondant. 'You said that your parents don't "lend" money unless they expect something in return. Do you know what they expected in return from Signor Marinelli, by any chance?'

Rosamund swallowed the last of her fondant. 'Not exactly. I did happen to overhear them mentioning Marinelli again, though.'

She means she was eavesdropping again. 'And what did they say?'

Rosamund frowned. 'I only caught half of it. I think they'd been arguing for a while. Mother was saying something about the problem not being on her side with Marinelli. He'd given them spot-on information, as always. The problem was on Father's side with his wunderkind, whatever she meant by that. Anyway, in the end Father agreed. Mother always wins, you know.'

Eleanor nodded. 'I can believe that! But, er, did you by any chance catch what they were going to do? And a "wunderkind", that sounds fun! Who was it, I wonder?'

Rosamund sprang up. 'No, I didn't catch it. They went into the other room. But I do remember Mother mentioning someone called Dawson to Father before they did, so maybe he was their "wunderkind".' She shrugged. 'Now, Lady Swift, I am going to go and enjoy the rest of my free time.' She gave Eleanor a pointed look. 'Not that it will be my last, will it?'

'Absolutely not. A deal is a deal.' Eleanor rose too, hoping her usually infallible butler still had a few tricks up his impeccable suit sleeves on that score. 'It's been delightful.'

As she reached the door, Rosamund spun around. 'And if I were you, I wouldn't mention anything I've said to Mother. I'll deny everything and you wouldn't want to see her bad side!'

As Clifford closed the door behind Rosamund, Eleanor winced.

'I'm sure I wouldn't!'

32

In the lecture theatre, Eleanor was spellbound. The mesmerising voice at the lectern, which had carried her and clearly the whole audience on such an unexpected journey of discovery, was winding to a close.

'In conclusion, please take away with you the comprehension, and the wonder, that your brain, the mere two per cent of your body below your skull, weighs up to only three pounds. But the mind it houses, that incredible seat of thought, will, memory, feeling and desire – that is as infinitely powerful, yet still so vastly uncharted a phenomenon, as all the heavens. And deeper than the Atlantic herself that we are sailing across at this moment. Thank you and good evening.'

After a moment's silence, she shook herself out of her captivated trance and started the applause, which quickly swelled to a standing ovation. On the stage, Professor Goodman clasped his hands serenely.

'Ladies and gentlemen. I am indebted to your kind and unwavering attention. Go forth forever in curiosity.'

As the last of the audience straggled out of the auditorium, he tapped the edges of his notes into a neat pile before sliding them into a smart but well-travelled briefcase. Eleanor lingered, waiting until he'd finished before walking up to him.

'Gracious, Professor. No wonder you were asked to repeat your lecture. That was positively illuminating.'

He turned and nodded, his intelligent grey eyes behind his wire-rimmed spectacles shining back at her. 'Lady Swift, good evening. Kind words indeed, thank you. I am delighted you came. But all the more that you learned something too, perhaps?'

'Not something, Professor. The world! The fascinating world that is psychology. I learned that I wish I had studied it.' She shrugged. 'You've left me feeling every inch the blunt brick.'

'No, no.' Goodman swung his index finger from side to side with the precise tempo of a metronome. 'We are all laymen in every walk of life but our own. Or laywomen, of course. And after your most compelling conversation at the captain's dinner, "blunt" is definitely not an adjective I would use to describe you.'

'Thank you.' She gestured behind her. 'Actually, there's someone else I think you'd be interested to meet too.' Seldon cleared the last of the distance to the stage in what was evidently his best attempt at a straight line. 'His walk of life is one most people need never encounter.'

'Thankfully.' Seldon offered the professor his hand. 'Hugh Seldon.'

'Mr Seldon.' Goodman tilted his head. 'Not a doctor then, since few escape the need for medical attention at least once in their life. So what is it that occupies your days when you aren't battling the imbalance of holidaying aboard ship?'

'Something marginally less troubling than this nightmare. I'm a policeman.'

'A chief inspector,' Eleanor said.

'Ah!' Goodman put his hands together and pressed them to

his neatly bearded chin, then pointed them at Seldon. 'Then we are in a very similar business, are we not?'

'You'll have to enlighten me there,' Seldon said, shaking his head in puzzlement. 'Not that you haven't already with your lecture. But how do you see our jobs can have anything in common?'

'Because we both spend our every working moment striving to get into the mind of another.' Goodman nodded slowly. 'You, Inspector, into that of the perpetrator of a crime to work out the why, the when, the how, and thus the who. And myself, to hone and test my hypotheses, to analyse, to discern and record man's true capability as a species.'

Seldon held his hands up. 'Fair point. Yet with very different aims.'

'And methods.'

Eleanor gestured at Goodman's briefcase. 'And somehow you manage all that while lecturing and instructing the next generation of impassioned psychologists.'

'And my patient practice also, yes.'

'Then my even greater admiration. May I ask, though, if the capacity of the mind is as vast as you described, surely the field of psychology should be comparably so?'

He gave her an appreciative smile. 'Very astute, Lady Swift. It is, in fact, branching rapidly for that very reason. I myself have moved across from the Freudian personality study into the still very new, in scientific terms, field of behaviourism.' At Eleanor and Seldon's collective shrug, he continued. 'The theory that a person's set of behaviours are created through conditioning has come a long way in the short time since Pavlov started with his dogs.'

'"Conditioning" is?' She'd quiz Clifford later about who this Pavlov chap might be.

'"Conditioning" is why we act the way we do. Behaviour, in simplified terms, Lady Swift, is actually at its root a *response*.

Nothing more. A person is "conditioned" through repeated exposure to a certain stimulus to respond in a certain way. Which means one can explain why someone behaved a certain way after the event. Or even predict how they will behave beforehand.' He glanced at Seldon. 'I can see, Inspector, you are not convinced of the merits of the belief I subscribe to. The belief that all human behaviour can be predicted. Conviction in your evidently illustrious career only comes with hard evidence. That evidence convinces you. You convince the court. But I think also, the basic concept of my field of psychology goes against your experience?'

Seldon nodded. 'My experience with felons, certainly. And victims. And witnesses. In fact, my experience has led me to the belief that people often act as erratically and incomprehensibly as this boat.' He waved around the room. 'Which constantly lurches around for no discernible reason!'

Goodman eyed him with seeming amusement. 'Do you include yourself among those who act "erratically and incomprehensibly", Inspector?'

Seldon's brow creased. Eleanor stepped in.

'It must be amazing working with people from as many different walks of life as your patients; from bank managers to opera stars and more.'

Behind his spectacles, Goodman blinked slowly twice. 'A very odd profession, opera singer, to pluck from the air, Lady Swift?'

'Is it? Signor Marinelli gave us all such a treat serenading the passing of the *Auriana*, you've obviously helped him a great deal.'

His eyes widened slightly. 'Lady Swift, I have given no suggestion that Signor Marinelli is, or ever was, a patient of mine.'

'No, you haven't. Where did I learn that now? Hmm.' She drummed her fingers on her forehead and then held Goodman's gaze. 'But we do know it is the case. Signor Marinelli came to you for help. Expert help.'

'We?' He turned his gaze to Seldon.

'Yes, we,' Seldon said. 'Professor, there is a very good reason for the request I am about to make. We need you to tell us why Marinelli came to you.'

'Impossible.' Goodman reached for his briefcase. 'Patient–therapist confidentiality can never be broken. The field of psychotherapy would be in tatters in an afternoon. To say nothing of the patient.'

'So he *was* a patient of yours?'

Goodman leaned further into Seldon's gaze. 'I say nothing, Inspector. Trust is everything in my world. A court judge could sentence me for contempt and I will still divulge nothing.'

'Although he wouldn't, as I believe you are well aware.'

The professor's eyes narrowed. 'Let us stop playing games with each other, Inspector. I will not break client confidentiality, whether Signor Marinelli was a patient of mine or not.'

Time to level that playing field, Ellie. 'That's very good to hear. And exactly what we hoped for.'

Goodman looked from Eleanor to Seldon and back, his brow wrinkling. 'Then why make the request?'

She spread her hands. 'Because, Professor Goodman, it means trust and discretion really are at the heart of your ethics. And both of those are vital if you are going to help us.'

He looked between her and Seldon again. 'Please explain. What precisely is it that you want?'

'A crime has taken place on the *Celestiana*, Professor,' Seldon said. They'd agreed not to reveal the true nature or extent of the crime, or crimes – two murders! 'A number of suspects have already been identified. But with only a day and a half remaining until we dock on Thursday morning, time is against us. Hence, the need to resort to des—'

'Less orthodox methods,' Eleanor said quickly. 'Professor,

we need your psychological expertise in detailing anything you can about the suspects. There is no need to interrogate them. Just to see what you can observe through normal contact. Although, as the chief inspector said, time is not on our side, so you may have to increase your normal contact with them, as it were.'

Goodman stroked his beard, indecision in his eyes. Seldon offered his hand again.

'Will you help the police in this matter, Professor? You may spot something vital I, without your expert knowledge, might miss.'

Goodman hesitated again and then shook Seldon's hand. 'I agree, although I must stress in these circumstances, and with such a time restraint, I cannot give you the detailed analysis I would normally offer.'

Seldon held up a hand. 'I promise you, Professor, whatever you can do will be greatly appreciated.'

He slid a sheet of paper across the lectern. Goodman took his time to look down the list of names.

'Ah!' He glanced at Eleanor. 'Since all of these people were present at the captain's table, I assume that was by design?' She nodded. 'Good, then, as the captain must have already agreed to my part in this, I have no further objections.'

'That's excellent, Professor.' She kept her face neutral. *Well, Ellie, Bracebridge would probably approve if he knew. But, then again, he might not!*

'Now, if you will both excuse me.' Goodman lifted the flap of his briefcase and slipped the list carefully into the rear pocket. 'This lecture theatre and I might have seen a little too much of each other for two long evenings. To the point I missed the chance to observe one of psychology's most interesting phenomena.'

Eleanor was the one to be confused now. 'What exactly did you miss, Professor?'

'Why, the passing of the *Auriana*, Lady Swift. If you remember, I was forced to decline your gracious post-dinner invitation because I needed to prepare my lecture.'

'That's a shame. It was a spectacle I will never forget,' she said sincerely, the image flooding back to her.

'No, Lady Swift. I was referring to the passengers' collective behavioural response. Two thousand-plus people surging en masse in such euphoric agitation!' Professor Goodman adjusted his spectacles and peered harder at her. 'To herd might be innate to humankind, but to experience such a rush of emotion as to be compelled to trample all regard for social decorum underfoot? What could possibly produce such a remarkable response?'

Eleanor shrugged. 'Only a remarkable stimulus?'

'Correct. But tracing that to its very foundation would be a life's work in itself.'

'Well done, Eleanor!' Seldon said in a low voice once they were alone. 'I don't know exactly what he can do for us, but it was still an excellent suggestion of yours.' His deep brown eyes gazed down into hers. 'You know, Eleanor, you are wonderfully...'

She leaned forward. 'Wonderfully what, Hugh?'

Gently tucking a stray curl behind her ear, he laughed. 'Wonderfully Lady Swift.'

Her heart skipped. 'That's quite the turnaround, Hugh. You've always said I was impossible.'

'And you are that too. Wonderfully impossible!'

33

The snap of Clifford's pocket watch closing only seemed to deepen Seldon's troubled air. They were in Eleanor's cabin and had been discussing the case for what seemed like hours to her. Gladstone's exuberant attempts to offer the inspector some licky solace weren't helping.

She laughed. 'You do know Hugh's pockets aren't filled with sausages, don't you, old friend?'

Seldon looked bilious. 'Ugh! No one mention food to me!' He shook his head. 'And it's nonsense. That can't be correct, Clifford.' He paused in his unsteady pacing and glanced at his own watch. 'This infernal ship's relentless lurching and heaving must have damaged our watches' mechanisms.'

'If you say so, Chief Inspector,' Clifford said. 'I will look for another that tells a more cheering time.' He vanished into the butler's pantry. Eleanor slid her beloved late uncle's timepiece back in the pocket of her skirt, throwing Seldon a wince across the mahogany table.

He groaned. 'Blast it, you two. It is correct, isn't it? We're only thirty-six hours from New York.'

She tutted. 'Come on, Hugh. You knew that already. It's

only the seasickness and exhaustion talking. You haven't had a decent sleep since we left port. It's not as bad as it seems.'

He broke off rubbing his temples to stare at her. 'Don't tell me among the other wonders your butler is capable of that he actually has the ability to turn back time? Because that's all I can see is going to help us solve this terrible mess before it's too late, Goodman's help or not.'

She shook her head, eyes closed. 'Losing heart can only push the finish line out of reach forever, darling.'

A rush of butterflies filled her chest at the feeling of Seldon's athletic frame stepping in close. 'Umm... darling?' His deep voice tickled her ear.

'It's one of only a few of my mother's sayings, I remember.' She opened her eyes to stare up at him.

'Ah!'

They looked away.

'It's alright, Clifford,' she called towards the pantry door. 'It's quite safe. Hugh and I haven't actually ripped each other's heads off.'

He reappeared, eyes twinkling mischievously. 'Heartening news, my lady.'

With harmony restored and further comforted by the delectable rich roast coffee Clifford had produced, she marshalled her thoughts to the matter at hand.

'Right. The results of my speaking to the delightful Miss Rosamund Swalecourt.' She recounted what she'd been told.

Seldon looked up from taking notes. 'And your assessment?'

'I honestly think she was telling the truth. I know she's a headstrong nineteen-year-old, desperate to get back at her over-bearing mother for not allowing her any freedom, but it still rang true.'

Seldon nodded. 'Good.'

'Good?'

'Yes, because it takes a truly wilful donkey to recognise another, so we can relax on that score.'

'You total rotter!'

He didn't hide his amusement. 'What Miss Swalecourt told you fits with what even I knew of Marinelli before seeing him in the flesh here. He's a complete... whatever the polite word is for a grown man living an extravagant lifestyle, always parading around in showy excess.'

'A *braggadocio*, Chief Inspector?'

Seldon shrugged. 'Probably.'

Eleanor tapped his page. 'So how does your observational assassination of Marinelli fit?'

'Because when he retired, he must have lost most of his income.'

She clicked her fingers. 'Ah, but despite that, he continued his lavish way of life, you mean?' She frowned. 'But how do you know that he has, Hugh? I didn't have you down as an opera fan, if I'm honest.'

'I'm not. At least, I've never been to one to find out if I would be. Maybe I'll give it a go one day.' He looked away. 'If I can find the right person to take along.'

She hid a smile. 'That's a yes.' As he turned back, looking hopeful, she pointed at Clifford. 'My impossibly learned butler would love to explain every minute detail of it to you for however many excruciating hours it lasted.'

Clifford coughed. 'Ahem. I believe, my lady, the chief inspector was surmising that Signor Marinelli spent a great deal of the monies from his contracts in advance of receiving them.'

'Ah! Which would explain then why he had to borrow money from Mrs Swalecourt. To pay for Professor Goodman's treatment to regain his confidence. And to secure new contracts so he could pay off the debts he'd run up for the lavish lifestyle he continued to keep even though he had no income. A most vicious cycle.'

'Exactly!' Seldon said. 'If only we had someone who knew how those musical evening things go at country houses.' He gave her a pointed look.

'Hilarious. And Clifford knows precisely how they go, as you are well aware. Besides, I'd be hopeless at all that formal entertaining stuff.'

Clifford nodded. 'Most assuredly.'

Seldon raised his hand with a smile. 'Moving on. The next important question is why Mrs Swalecourt would "lend" Marinelli anything in the first place?'

Eleanor closed her eyes and then opened them wide. 'Of course!' Gladstone, roused from a deep slumber at her feet, staggered up and collapsed with a whimper, his head in her lap. 'Rosamund said she heard her mother saying to her father that the problem wasn't with the *information* Marinelli gave them, but with his wunderkind whose name Rosamund thinks was Dawson.'

Seldon slapped the table. 'Morrison Dawson! One of Yeoman's aliases I mentioned before. So what information was Marinelli passing to the Swalecourts and/or Yeoman, that the Swalecourts believed was worth paying handsomely for?'

They thought for a moment, Clifford being the first to break the silence. 'Naturally someone of Signor Marinelli's fame would draw the cream of society...'

Eleanor nodded eagerly. 'And the cream of society would have to show off the cream of their jewellery boxes!'

'Quite. The overall value of gems sported at such an event would be significant indeed.'

'And Signor Marinelli would be perfectly placed to pass on whatever information Yeoman needed to gain entrance to the establishment where the event was being held and steal the jewels.'

Seldon rubbed his chin. 'So Mrs Swalecourt could have been the one in league with Yeoman. And Marinelli their inside man on the payroll, as it were. Certainly, as a known patron of the arts, Mrs Swalecourt's "loans" to him would never be questioned if they came to light. Then the items Yeoman stole, mostly jewellery one imagines, could have been fenced through her husband's antique shop, the black market side of Golden Age Antiquities.'

'We've got it, Hugh,' she cheered. 'That all tallies—'

'No. Blast it!' He slapped the table. 'Excellent deduction, but think about it. That doesn't work at all. It can't be that Marinelli drew the wealthy guests to these country houses and then fed Yeoman information so he could break in and steal their valuables. Because, they'd have been wearing them at the concert. Yeoman was a brilliant burglar, not a magician. No one could lift jewels that valuable directly off a person unnoticed.'

Eleanor and Seldon's gazes slid to Clifford. He arched a brow.

'Ignoring any slanderous inferences, the majority of these elite musical soirées take place over three, or even four, days. Guests are accommodated throughout. Most valuables would therefore be kept in each of the guestroom's safes whilst not worn.'

'Where Yeoman could lift them from. Excellent.' Seldon jotted down a note on his page. 'However, none of this gives Mrs Swalecourt a motive for killing Yeoman. Unless it was a falling-out of thieves?' He shook his head. 'Of course, Eleanor! You said Rosamund heard her mother say the problem wasn't on her side with Marinelli, but on her husband's side with his wunderkind.'

'Yes. Dawson. Or Yeoman to us.'

'And the problem could have been him getting greedy and wanting a larger cut, for example.'

Eleanor, who had been staring into the distance, blinked and nodded to herself.

'The black opal. Suppose Yeoman stole it to order from one

of those musical gatherings and then decided he wouldn't hand it over to the Swalecourts to... What was it, Clifford?'

'To fence, my lady.'

Seldon shook his head. 'Excellent deduction again, Eleanor. But if a gem like that had been stolen, we'd have heard about it at a headquarters' briefing. We have a list of the most expensive, and at risk, jewels in the country and who owns them. I can't recall seeing a black opal of that immense value being on the list. If it was, normally we would be made aware if it was going to be paraded in public. I—'

Eleanor grasped the table as the floor seemed to slide away. Opposite her, Seldon hung on grimly. The floor then changed its mind and slid violently the other way. After growing up on a boat, she was ready for it. He wasn't.

34

A moment later, the boat righted itself. From outside there came the sound of cursing as someone fell against the door. Eleanor helped Seldon up as Clifford let go of the rail he'd been holding on to and opened the door. He stood to one side before announcing, 'Professor Goodman.'

Goodman stepped forward, brushing his clothes down.

'Are you alright, Professor?' she said.

He nodded and walked to the table, his pace as collected as the cadence of his words. 'I am fine, thank you. We seem to be experiencing some rougher seas. I trust this is a good time, however, Lady Swift? Inspector?'

'Absolutely, Professor.' She stumbled as the ship swayed again. 'Please join us. You'll probably be safer sitting down!'

'Thank you.' He carefully settled himself into the chair opposite her and Seldon, who was now back in his seat, gripping the chair's arms. He accepted a black coffee from Clifford, shaking his head at the proffered cream jug. He glanced at him and then back at her.

'Ah, Professor, this is my butler. And so much more besides. Please speak freely.'

'Very good, then. I thought you might wish to hear my
assessments before...' he steadied himself as the boat rolled
again, 'before we are confined to our cabins with the worsening
weather.'

'Wonderful!' Seldon muttered. He waved a placatory hand.
'Sorry, Professor. I meant being confined to our cabins, not your
assessments.'

Eleanor glanced at him in concern and then hurriedly back
to Goodman. 'Please, Professor, fire away.'

Seldon turned to a new page in his notebook, pen at the
ready.

Goodman cleared his throat. 'If I might first outline the
format of my assessment? It goes against my professional code to
report what can only be described as a hasty summation to a
colleague without explanation of the methodology.'

Eleanor now felt even more sure that involving him had
been a good idea. 'Please detail whatever you need to, Professor.
We're just immensely grateful for any insights.'

He nodded. 'As with any branch of science, in order to
make informed judgements, one must first establish a baseline.
Here, that required noting the subjects' ordinary behaviour
markers, speech patterns and general level of information
sharing so that any deviations could be observed.' He produced
a sheaf of notes from his briefcase and took a moment to look
through them.

'Didn't that take hours in itself?' Seldon said.

'Not after twenty-two years in my field, Inspector,'
Goodman said affably. 'Three commonplace conversational
questions presented as one would expect when meeting an
acquaintance for the second or third time. Followed by six
more. Three designed to elicit the truth, three, the untruth.
That being enough.'

Impressive, Ellie!

'My approach then,' he continued, 'was to determine the

indicators of truth and those of falsehood, by asking the subject's greatest passion and their most ardent urge.'

'Wow!' Eleanor felt more dim-witted than ever. 'That sounds so systematic. I simply blunder into such conversations and come away again, reliant entirely on my intuition.'

Goodman's intelligent grey eyes held no disparagement, only good-natured interest, she noted appreciatively. 'Which, Lady Swift, has frequently reaped you successful results, I'd wager?'

'It has,' Seldon said. 'Now, on to the suspects?'

'Subjects, to my mind, Chief Inspector. But yes, of course.' Goodman glanced at the first sheet in front of him. 'Sir Randolph. The gentleman's tone lowers and softens when being truthful. However, he employs ambiguous words or a strident delivery to mask lies. His cane is as much a prop for his deceptions as it is for his gait. He dismisses as disinterest that which he does not wish to discuss. His greatest passion is his personal reputation, which he sees as inseparable from his business one. The urge which drives him onwards and upwards every day—'

'Is securing his family's happiness and safety?' Eleanor couldn't help chipping in.

'That is what he would have the world believe, yes. But, in truth, winning is his strongest impulse. And at any cost, I would go so far as to suggest.'

'Mmm.' Seldon tapped his notebook. 'So if someone had, say, done him a bad turn. Something that might affect his business reputation...?'

Like robbing a succession of his hotels so they are seen as unsafe to stay in by the rich and famous, Ellie?

Goodman was nodding. 'He would take that as a personal affront. He would not rest until he had beaten them, such that they would never try again.'

'Interesting.' Seldon finished his note and gestured for Goodman to continue.

'Next then, Mrs Swalecourt. Repeated truth-telling indicators were jutting of the jaw, leaning forward, calmed breathing
and a detailed account offered. Conversely, lying was accompanied by a barely perceptible shoulder twitch, a less comprehensive account, and most interestingly, a proliferation of truthful
hand gestures throughout.'

Seldon paused in making notes. 'That sounds rather well
practised.'

'Categorically so, yes. The lady's greatest passion is her
home. Her driving urge, however, is one she will never attain, I
predict.'

Eleanor shared a puzzled look with Seldon.

'A title, Lady Swift. Mrs Swalecourt spends her life
compensating for the lack of one.'

*Not too much help there, then, Ellie. Unless she intended to
buy one from the sale of the black opal.* No one talked about it in
the upper echelons of society, but everyone knew for the right
price certain titles were always up for sale.

Goodman took a sip of his coffee. 'No questions? Miss
Swalecourt junior, then. Truthful indicators, widened eyes,
brushing hair away from cheeks and spreading of hands. Lying
behaviours predominantly included hair tossing, lack of any use
of "I" or "we", a detailed account and leaning forward.'

'The last two being the opposite of her mother,' Seldon said.

'Yes. I noted several aspects of the young lady were in direct
opposition. To the point, I found her greatest passion to be a
desire to be independent. Her driving urge, though, is rightful
justice. But I would add, from atypical morals.'

*So, Ellie, maybe she really does want to do the right thing by
exposing her mother's actions, even if her motive is a
little... selfish?*

Goodman waited until Seldon's pen had finished flying
across his page. 'Miss González, I found most interesting of all.
Lying indicators are dilated pupils, tapping of collarbones and

smiling. Her greatest passion is having her heart sated. Her driving urge is jealousy.'

'Sorry, I missed you spelling out her truth-telling signs,' Eleanor said.

'No, Lady Swift. I did not list any because none were displayed.' He nodded at their shocked expressions. 'Miss González did not utter one honest word.'

But Seldon was sure she was Yeoman's fiancée, Ellie. Was everything she told you really lies?

Goodman closed his folder. 'I'm afraid that is all I've been able to observe so far. Nevertheless, I hope that might assist in some way. I will continue to study the four subjects until we dock.' He rose. 'I bid you good—'

'Five suspects.' Seldon waved him back down. 'Professor, you haven't told us anything of Signor Marinelli?'

'No, I haven't, Inspector,' Goodman said firmly. 'And neither shall I. As I believe I made clear to you before.'

Seldon shrugged. 'No harm in trying, Professor.'

'No harm at all, Inspector.'

Eleanor stepped forward. 'Professor. If you can't talk about Signor Marinelli because he was a patient of yours, perhaps you can just satisfy my curiosity? When he was on deck and the *Celestiana*'s sister ship passed us, he broke into an aria. My butler informed me that it was from...' She turned to Clifford.

'*Der Fliegende Holländer*, my lady.'

Goodman nodded. 'Ah! *The Flying Dutchman*. A masterpiece of German music and storytelling, based on Heinrich Heine's 1834 *From the Memoirs of Herr von Schnabelewopski*.'

Clifford coughed discreetly. 'Although it has been noted that as early as 1790, the English writer John MacDonald wrote about a ghostly ship called the *Flying Dutchman* in his *Travels, in various parts of Europe, Asia, and Africa*.'

Goodman momentarily looked daggers at him, before his face broke into its customary serene expression.

Seldon grunted. 'Did that answer your question, Eleanor?'

She laughed uneasily. *What was that about?* 'Not exactly. I just wondered why Marinelli would have chosen that particular aria. I mean, the *Celestiana* is hardly a ghost ship, is it?'

Goodman shrugged. 'I assume because the *Auriana* passing the other way in the night reminded him of that scene from the opera. Now, I really must be going.'

'Right,' Seldon said once they were alone. 'Let's discuss—'

The floor, which had been tipping one way and then the next, lurched wildly. He grabbed the table with both hands, his face ashen. He swallowed hard. 'Perhaps we need to continue this conversation when this infernal machine has stopped bucking like a mule!'

As she steadied herself, she glanced outside at the squalling rain now lashing the portholes. 'Good idea. We can discuss the professor's findings when this... this, er...' *Don't say storm, Ellie, look at him.* 'When we meet up again. Say, here in two hours? After we've all had some time to rest.'

As Seldon stumbled down the corridor towards second-class, Clifford closed the door and she reached for her drink. She swayed as the room tipped again and the lights flickered. *It really is getting rough out there.*

A knock on the door interrupted her thoughts. Clifford opened it. Out in the corridor, the former stowaway, his rake-thin body swamped by his new cabin boy uniform, braced himself against the wall.

'Sidney. Step inside.' He gestured for the young boy to enter.

'If you're sure as that's in the rules, Mr Clifford?' he stammered, seemingly unable to will his legs forward until Eleanor had waved him in too. Clifford closed the door behind him. 'It's alright, Sidney.' He smiled, trying to ease the lad's obvious discomfort.

Eleanor's heart swelled. *I wonder if he sees his younger self in the boy?* It was an odd thought that her ever-composed and ever-confident butler could once have been such a shy, timid soul.

Clifford dropped to his haunches. 'You look quite the part in your new uniform. Very smart. And I'm sure you're here as part of your duties?'

The young lad stared at him like a frightened rabbit. 'I ain't shirkin', I promise, Mr Clifford. I was just told to check that her ladyship was in her cabin as the seas is gettin' rougher and report straight back.'

'Very dedicated of you, Sidney, well done. Please return, taking particular care of yourself among all the ship's lurching, and say her ladyship—'

The pounding knock on the door made the young boy jump to the side.

Clifford opened it to find the master-at-arms bracing himself with a stout boot in each corner. From across the room Eleanor stared at him in surprise.

'Lady Swift, you are to remain in your cabin until further notice.'

She frowned. 'Rather an unnecessary trip for you to make. My cabin boy informed me of that only' – she glanced at the young boy behind the door – 'a few minutes ago.'

'This is no longer an advisory, Lady Swift. This is an order. All passengers are being so instructed. The situation has deteriorated swiftly. The *Celestiana* is heading into a severe storm.'

He scanned the room before striding off, swaying with the ship's motion. Clifford closed the door. 'Well, Sidney, where were we?' She saw a look of concern pass over her butler's normally inscrutable face. He knelt down and took hold of the young boy's shoulders. 'What's the matter?' The young lad was visibly trembling.

'Shouldn't tell,' he mumbled.

Clifford looked into the young boy's eyes. 'Sidney, if something is worrying you, it's alright to tell me.'

'Really, it is? Because it's eatin' me up tryin' to do the right thing, Mr Clifford. No matter the barrel of trouble I'll be in.' His chin fell to his chest. 'But it'll be a mighty big barrel, I know it.' His gaze slid to the door. 'It's him.'

'The master-at-arms?'

On the settee, Eleanor's mind jumped back to the awful scene when the boy had been found. Clifford had obviously had the same thought.

'Ah, I see. It's alright. He's not going to arrest you again, Sidney, I promise.'

He shook his head. ''Taint that, Mr Clifford. I seen his temper first hand.'

Anger flashed across her butler's face. 'Did he try and hurt you?'

'Not me. That man what went overboard. I seen the master-at-arms arguing so fierce on deck with him in the dark. Then he stomped off in a terrible temper and the other man did too. I slipped out the back of me lifeboat hidey-hole and ran in case they returned.' His eyes turned to saucers. 'He's as bad as they come, that master-at-arms!'

35

Eleanor frowned. 'Well, he never mentioned it to us, did he?'

Seldon shook his head. 'Most definitely not!'

Along with Clifford, they were in her cabin discussing what Sidney had told them. Seldon had re-joined them a few minutes earlier. He'd taken care to make sure he wasn't seen as passengers were still confined to their cabins, even though the rough seas had calmed. Eerily so.

The calm before the storm, Ellie. The real storm.

She shook the idea out of her head. 'I mean,' she continued, 'it's most puzzling. After Professor Goodman's summary, and given what we've learned before, I'd have thought Miss González was our main suspect.'

Clifford nodded. 'I concur, my lady. But then this latest revelation—'

'Is damnably confusing!' Seldon shook his head. 'Why would the master-at-arms have a stand-up row with a passenger on the first night of the cruise? And why Yeoman? And why on a deserted deck in the dark?'

A noise outside interrupted them. Since being officially removed from the case, they had become increasingly paranoid about being overheard. Clifford opened the door a crack. After a few moments, he closed it, a puzzled frown on his face.

'Problem?' Eleanor said.

He shook his head. 'No, my lady. Merely crew entering the Regal Suite.'

Seldon glanced from him to Eleanor and back. 'Then why the frown?'

'Both were carrying concealed weapons, I believe.'

Seldon shrugged. 'Hardly surprising. There have been two murders. And there is obviously someone very important in there.'

Clifford cleared his throat. 'I had observed, Chief Inspector, that several members of the crew were armed when I first boarded the *Celestiana*. Before Mr Yeoman or Count Balog were murdered.'

Eleanor shrugged. 'Well then, that must have been because of the royal guest, as Hugh said.' She nodded towards the door.

Clifford aligned his perfectly straight cufflinks. 'My obser-vations might suggest otherwise, my lady.' He opened his note-book at a meticulous double-paged list. 'There are a number of discrepancies. The main one being that food is delivered to the Regal Suite, but nothing consumed.'

Seldon's brow furrowed. 'How can you know that?'

'A loaded salver, Chief Inspector, is not carried in an equal manner to an empty one. Nor even one partially reduced of its contents. A person's posture always varies slightly.'

Seldon looked doubtful. 'But the occupant, whoever he, or she, is, might just be fussy? Guaranteed if they are royalty.'

Clifford held up four fingers. 'After almost four days since the *Celestiana* left berth, the occupant, royal or not, would eat his or her own hand.'

'Fair enough. So what's your conclusion?'

'That there is no one royal, or indeed non-royal, staying in the Regal Suite's staterooms.'

Eleanor tried to rub away the confusion furrowing her brow. 'I hate to question your usually infallible reasoning, Clifford, but I saw all the royal's luggage being brought into the suite by the master-at-arms and his men.'

Seldon looked thoughtful. 'Did anything about it strike you as odd, Eleanor?'

She thought hard. 'Not beyond the fact that there was a uniformed sailor flanking every porter, as Clifford just mentioned there is now. And there was an exceptional amount of luggage. All double padlocked.'

Seldon tapped his notebook. 'Why would the master-at-arms store luggage in the Regal Suite and then pretend it was occupied when it wasn't? And what is in that luggage that it needs to be double padlocked and escorted by an armed guard whenever someone goes in or out of the suite?'

'Not luggage,' Clifford said slowly. 'Valuable cargo.'

'You're right!' Seldon tried to leap up, only then realising his legs were pinned by the weighty Gladstone who'd snuck onto his lap. 'Ships like this are sometimes used to carry precious cargo for merchants or governments. Gold or gems, or the like. But it's never advertised, obviously. I've come across it occasionally in investigations colleagues have worked on.'

'Which would account for the sailors carrying guns even before Mr Yeoman was murdered,' Clifford said.

'Absolutely.'

Eleanor waved a hand. 'Wait, though, chaps. Any cargo that valuable would surely be stowed way down in a strongroom, or whatever they have on ships like this?'

Seldon nodded. 'Yes, but supposing Bracebridge had been informed that criminal elements had found out about the shipment?'

'Then...' Clifford grabbed a handhold as the ship pitched. *The storm's back, Ellie.*

Clifford waited until the ship had righted itself and then

continued. 'The master-at-arms might have suggested they hide it somewhere unexpected?'

Eleanor had been watching the two men's exchange like a tennis match, her hands thrown wide. 'That's all very interesting, but surely the only thing of import is that...' Seldon's words came back to her from when they'd found out who had been instrumental in getting them thrown off the case, 'that "at least we know who our enemies are now!"'

Seldon looked up sharply and on seeing her expression, frowned. Almost immediately, however, his eyes widened in comprehension. 'Such as the very man who would have organised the security for the – we now think – valuable cargo? And probably suggested, and definitely arranged, for its new home in the Regal Suite!'

Clifford held up a white-gloved finger. 'The very same man who was so furious at her ladyship and yourself, Chief Inspector, being assigned to the investigation of Mr Yeoman's death.'

'The master-at-arms,' Eleanor breathed.

The squalling rain lashed at the portholes again, this time even heavier than before.

Seldon nodded. 'Which would also explain why he took so long to provide us with background information on each suspect. And why most of it was so perfunctory.'

'Indeed, Chief Inspector,' Clifford said. 'And why he ensured you were both thrown off the very same investigation as soon as possible.'

She nodded grimly. 'Which is why he was grinning like a Cheshire cat when I left Bracebridge's office after getting kicked off the case. And don't forget he was seen arguing with Yeoman on deck in the dark the night of his murder! Yeoman, who just happened to be an expert jewel thief.' She shook her head. 'It's just all too coincidental.'

Seldon slapped the table and then winced. 'It's genius, that's what it is! The master-at-arms arranges for a supposed security breach about the valuables he is charged with keeping and then organises that, instead of the stronghold, they are transferred to the Regal Suite. Yeoman, meanwhile, secures a cabin on the same deck. With inside information and help from the master-at-arms, he steals the opal—'

'And then the master-at-arms shoots him and pushes him overboard!' She shook her head. 'Not only does he get the whole fantastically valuable gemstone to himself, but he also eliminates the only person who might have been able to lay the finger of blame on him...'

She stopped at Seldon's look. 'What is it, Hugh?' Then it hit her, too. She nodded slowly. 'Only, after the master-at-arms killed Yeoman, he couldn't lay his hands on the opal, could he? Because it was too well hidden in the cologne bottl—' She gasped. 'Oh, Hugh! Too well hidden until, that is—'

'We found it and gave it to him!'

She groaned and hung her head. 'No wonder when we told the master-at-arms we'd found the opal he wouldn't believe us until we'd shown it to him. I imagine he couldn't believe his luck.'

'Or how gullible we were!' Seldon buried his face in his hands.

Over the course of the conversation, Seldon had looked worse and worse as the erratic motion of the boat increased. It was plain he was at the end of his tether. Eleanor laid her hand on his arm.

'Hugh, there's nothing we can do right at this minute. We have absolutely no evidence. Bracebridge would laugh us out of his office. Besides, we're basically confined to our cabins until the worst of this storm passes. Please go and lie down again until the weather improves in a couple of hours and we'll regroup and come up with a plan of action.'

'Blast it!' he muttered weakly. 'I suppose you're right. As usual.'

Hauling himself up with difficulty, he declined any help from Clifford and staggered out of the cabin. She watched him make unsteady progress to the stairs, and then nodded to Clifford to close the door. However, as the lights flickered off, and then on again, he hesitated.

'My lady, before we officially confine ourselves to our cabin, may I check on the ladies?'

She nodded vigorously. 'Of course. I imagine Polly at least will be terrified. Especially if the lights go out altogether. In fact, please stay with them until the storm has died down.'

As the door closed behind him, the ship lurched violently as another squall hit.

Eleanor grabbed the nearest support and hung on grimly.

How much worse can it get...?

36

Alone in her cabin, Eleanor's emotions pitched and rolled as violently as the *Celestiana* in the grip of the increasing storm. The three of them had only just identified the murderer and yet patience needed to prevail. They had no tangible evidence the captain would believe, and the storm made it impossible to get any until it had abated. Even then, she could hardly imagine how they were going to find any before they arrived in New York.

Assuming this storm doesn't get any worse, Ellie. Because if it does, it will surely be a hurricane!

She'd been in some severe storms on her parents' forty-five-foot yacht that had made the whole boat pitch and yaw like a toy, but the *Celestiana* was eight hundred and sixty-seven feet long. And yet, it was being tossed around like a toy as well.

Despite her best efforts, images of the *Titanic* filled her head. Even though she'd been abroad at the time, it had made headlines around the world. *But that was an iceberg. There are no icebergs here.* She wondered if the captain of the *Titanic* had been thinking exactly the same thing just before... She shook the thought out of her head. She just hoped the ladies and

Gladstone were alright. Even with Clifford's calming presence they would be terrified.

She forced herself to concentrate. Grateful for her innately resilient sea legs and her childhood years of experience aboard her parents' yacht, she paced around her cabin in a drunken zigzag. The murderer had killed twice. And fooled them all. Balog's words the first evening she'd met him came back to her. 'We are locked in a box. A pretty floating palace of a box, yes, but a box nonetheless. We cannot get off. Neither can we choose who else is in the box that we must sit, eat and play along beside. All we can do is protect our corner...' She shook her head in frustration. *But how can you protect your corner when the killer holds all the aces?* She stopped pacing, something flashing across her mind. An inkling of a thought she'd first had when she'd examined the two playing cards at the scene of Balog's murder.

No, Ellie! It couldn't be?

37

The increasingly unpredictable careering of the *Celestiana* crippled her progress. The faster she tried to reach Seldon's cabin, the harder the elements seemed against her. Vases and paintings sporadically smashed at her feet, making her leap and dodge as best she could with the ship's now wildly sideways rolling.

A huge potted palm crashed to the ground just as she passed the door to the first-class lounge. Only her lightning reactions letting her sprint out of harm's way. Scrambling over the palm, her legs were whipped out from underneath her as a waiter's trolley shot across the polished floor, spewing plates and cutlery like a spitting cobra. As she scrambled back up, a tangle of tables and chairs slid past, narrowly missing her as they slammed into the opposite wall. She dodged them on their return journey.

Rounding the entrance to the staircase, she looked over the rail in horror. A section of roof had been torn away by the increasingly ferocious wind. Water poured in, forming a debris-laden deluge that now cascaded down the main steps like rapids in a fast-moving river. Slipping would result in a broken leg if she was lucky. A broken neck, if she wasn't.

The scene that greeted her in the second-class lounge was even worse. The few crew she could see were clinging helplessly to doorways or pillars, the lighter, lower quality furniture flying across the room and back as if hurled by opposing armies of invisible giants. A petrified man spun on his knees towards her, pursued by what looked like a section of the bar. Failing to grab anything solid in time, he threw his arms wide as he hurtled into her. Grabbing him around the chest, she stopped him from sailing back the other way by clutching the rail beside her so hard she thought her fingers would break.

'Oh my, you're hurt.' Blood poured from the man's temple. 'HEAD WOUND OVER HERE!' she bellowed to the nearest senior-looking crew member. Battling the next wave of speeding detritus to join her, the sailor looked little better given that his own knuckles were bleeding as profusely as her casualty's head.

She left them and stumbled into the corridor leading to the cabins. As she drew level with Seldon's, the ship's lurching flung the door open. The first thing she registered on pulling herself into the cabin were the two narrow bunks, both empty. An indent in the left one, however, showed Seldon had at least made it back to the cabin. The wardrobe doors were flapping open, three white shirts, an evening suit, and a spare jacket swinging wildly in and out with the malicious swell of every wave. The long toes of a pair of black dress shoes poked out from underneath a suitcase, which had crashed down on top of them.

'He can't have gone far,' she groaned. 'He could barely stand before, and now none of us can.'

She stared in horror at the porthole as a slab of grey water rose up the glass as if the ship were sinking. *Get a grip, Ellie.* Given the pitching, she realised it was more a case of the boat nosediving into a trough left by an enormous wave. But the savage force that threw the *Celestiana* back onto her hindquarters also made Seldon's familiar dark-grey brogues cascade onto the debris on the floor in front of her.

She was about to turn away when something caught her eye. She fell to her knees and grabbed the item as it was thrown to the other side of the cabin in the relentless seesawing. It was soaking wet, a jug of water having crashed onto the floor along with the rest of the cabin's contents. *Hugh's watch, Ellie! The one his wife gave him before he went to the Front. He never takes it off.* So how had it come to be here? There was only one answer. He'd dropped it on purpose!

Kneeling in the carnage of her beau's belongings, everything finally fitted together: the ring, the black opal, Marinelli's impromptu aria, the dropped playing cards in Balog's cabin, Professor Goodman's summing up of the suspects and Sidney, the young stowaway's account of seeing the master-at-arms arguing with Yeoman. She shook her head violently in frustration. But how? How could—

She blinked and slowly turned her hands palm up and looked at them. *They're wet, Ellie. And... cold!*

'MAN OVERBOARD!' a voice yelled. She scrambled up and hurled herself out into the corridor. 'You!' she cried. 'Who is missing? Quick!'

The sailor, battered and bruised, stood as straight as he could. 'Sorry, miss, the passenger who reported it didn't know. Just said he was tall and sporty-looking. Curly dark hair.'

Her heart lurched. *Stay calm, Ellie! That could describe a hundred men aboard. It doesn't mean—*

'And I'm sorry, but you should be in your cabin. Captain's orders. I'll—'

She grabbed his arm. 'Damn that! Who reported it to you?'

'Didn't stop to ask his name, miss,' he said, staring at her. They were thrown against the wall. The sailor stared at her, wide-eyed. 'We're in the midst of a storm! No one should have been out on deck. They must have been mad!'

'What did he look like?' she shouted. 'The one who reported the man overboard?'

Before the sailor had even finished describing the person, she was running for the stairs.

It was him, Ellie. The killer!

'Captain!' she cried breathlessly, having fought her way up to the bridge.

The sailors at their stations all turned except Bracebridge, who kept his eyes fixed on the heaving, swollen sea in front of him.

'What are you doing here, Lady Swift? Passengers are confined to their cabins for their own safety. That is an order.'

'You have to turn the ship around.' She staggered forward to stand beside him. The bridge, being one of the highest points of the ship, was swaying and dipping even more wildly than below. 'There's a man overboard. It's—'

'I heard,' Bracebridge said firmly, staring forward. 'We cannot turn around.'

'But, Captain!'

A sailor who had been standing looking at several brass instruments interrupted with a swaying salute as he stepped between them. 'Wind speed sixty-two knots. Rising rapidly. Pitch angle fifty-four degrees, Captain.'

'We have to go back!'

Bracebridge nodded to the sailor and waved him back to his instruments. 'Categorically not, Lady Swift. If the wind speed reaches seventy-four knots—'

'I know! It means the storm has reached hurricane classification. And sixty degrees pitch is probably the *Celestiana*'s limit. But we have to try.'

Bracebridge was the only one not to cower back as a wall of water slammed into the bank of windows in front of him. 'Lady Swift, as you well know, whoever has fallen is dead already.'

'But it's Chief Inspector Seldon. The—'

He half turned. 'Then I am truly sorry. However, my decision stands.'

'Captain—'

'Lady Swift!' he barked. 'There have been three reports of ice and we are in the middle of the worst storm I have ever encountered in these seas. I will not jeopardise the lives of thousands of passengers and hundreds of crew, yours included. You need to leave. Now!'

His gesture to an armed sailor made it clear that the brig was waiting if she refused.

'You know I have no choice!' he called as she stumbled back out.

But as she paused to gain her breath in the corridor, things became clear again.

He's right, Ellie. He has no choice. But you do!

Her heart pounded harder than she knew it could as she sprinted along the corridor. Obstacles that flew in her path she shoved aside, caring nothing for the cuts and bruises. Cries to stop by the crew she shrugged off. Corridors strewn with sumptuous debris came and went. Even the cascading waterfall that used to be the central staircase couldn't slow her. Only the magnificent brass clockwork model of the solar system in the oval room made her falter. It had crashed free of its dome mounting, its guardian cherub lamps mere headless wrecks of porcelain. Even the gods and goddesses had succumbed. The last, and greatest, testament to the *Celestiana* being protected by the heavens had fallen.

38

'Where? WHERE!' she shouted through the tears flooding her heart. She threw the first mattress to the floor, tipping its bedding off before attacking the other.

'My lady.' Clifford's measured tone cut in from the door to Seldon's cabin. 'This is not the time.'

She stumbled over Seldon's dress shoes. The ones he'd taken her dancing in.

'Isn't it? The murderer must – *will* – be stopped!'

'My lady,' her butler repeated more urgently.

The washstand drawers flew out behind her. 'Where is it? Where? WHERE!' The picture covering the safe joined the rest of the mess on the floor. But all it had obscured was a miniature iron stronghold, which was as unlocked as it was empty. The writing desk gave up nothing but a snowstorm of *Celestiana* notepaper as she yanked the whole thing free to turn it upside down.

In the doorway, she could see Clifford was no longer just trying to reason. He was urging, pleading. But his words were lost in the blood rushing through her ears. She jerked to a stop. *Hugh, talk to me. Tell me where to look.*

A vision of her beau filtered in through her tear-filled thoughts. 'Blast it, Eleanor,' she heard his familiar rumbled lament. 'Will you ever put your own safety first?'

'That's it!' She righted the desk roughly and scrambled on to it. Balancing precariously, she scrabbled to prise the air vent cover free. The one set above the framed safety notice.

Pulling the cover off and dropping it among the debris, she reached in to the duct and seized what she was looking for. Jumping down off the desk, she spun around to find her path blocked by her butler.

For the first time, breaking his own immutable rule, he reached out and physically restrained her. 'On no account, my lady. To pursue the killer now, in this storm, is madness. You – *we* – are already in dire danger.'

'That's the point!' she shouted. 'If the *Celestiana* sinks and the killer gets into a lifeboat, and that sort always do, they'll be rescued along with the other passengers and then what? In the confusion, they'll disappear when the rescue ship docks and start their murderous career all over again!'

The room seemed to tip upside down, throwing them both to the floor. As it swung back, she struggled up.

'Go back to the ladies, Clifford. Keep them safe no matter what happens. And' – she swallowed hard – 'make sure they are in a lifeboat if...' She didn't need to finish the sentence. Ducking through the door before he could clamber up, she ran along the corridor and swung down the staircase.

In the next corridor, her only companion was her staccato breathing as she jumped obstacles like a trained hurdler, the lights around her flickering like deranged fireflies. To a man, every other passenger was huddled in their quarters, the eight hundred-plus crew miraculously vanished, the magnificent cruise liner a ghost ship.

A ghost ship! Just like the Flying Dutchman, *Ellie!*

A flash of blue caught her eye. She spun around, grabbing the rail as the boat juddered as if wounded.

'STOP! Or I'll shoot.'

'I don't think so, Lady Swift,' came the cool reply. The figure continued advancing, a smug smile adding to the malevolence of his unflustered stride. 'We are who we are. You won't pull that trigger.'

Her eyes narrowed. 'You don't know who I am!' Her arm recoiled with the force of the shot, which rang out inches above his head. With an unexpected turn of speed, her quarry spun around and ran.

Damn it, Ellie. If you lose sight of him now...

Through the endless warren of corridors on deck eight she pursued him, doggedly matching his every turn, just keeping his blue-clad form in view. She cursed his superior grasp of the boat's layout as he double-backed through the starboard passageways towards the stern and down more stairs to the seventh deck, unknown territory for her.

Knowing that any more commands to stop or warning shots would be fruitless, she grimly hung on to the flash of blue ahead of her. Clearing the stairs down to the sixth deck in two jumps, she landed hard. As she straightened up, pain shot up her leg. *You've twisted your ankle, you fool!* She staggered for a moment, then ran on, ignoring the burning sensation. *The blue. You've lost it.* She stared down the empty corridor, then intuition threw her through two swing doors to find she was in the massive kitchens. Ahead, the rap of running feet on tiles spurred her on despite the pain in her leg.

Devoid of staff, the colossal space used to cook and prepare food for thousands seemed even more vast. As she sprinted on, the increasing sway of the ship sent the last of the plates and bowls crashing in front of her. With the floor already awash with shattered china, the minefield of sharp crockery shards kicked up viciously at her calves. She sped past the bank of enormous boilers, shielding her face from the intense heat, cheeks burning.

As she reached the hundred-foot range Clifford had delighted in telling her about, she was thrown to the ground with such violence she was sure the *Celestiana* had cracked in two. A split second later, she rolled under the enormous steel table as three giant cast-iron pans of boiling water crashed to the ground. Rolling out the other side, she jumped out of the way as the scalding water swamped the floor.

Scrambling on, she caught another flash of blue, but the *Celestiana* lurched as if hit by a giant fist, knocking her sideways again. Only instinct saved her by ducking as the knife blocks on the preparation tables sent their deadly load flying across the room, one pinning her sleeve to a chopping board.

Tearing herself free, she spotted her prey scrambling out through the far doors. On she raced down decks five and four, through the maze of steerage class. Deck three threw up new obstacles, its storerooms awash with smashed crates, the contents littering the heaving floor.

Am I descending through Dante's Nine Circles of Hell? she cursed as the clenching stench of damp and steam stole her lungs of oxygen. She smiled grimly as she briefly caught his rasping breath ahead.

He's tiring.

But so was she. As she fought her way through the drying area of the *Celestiana*'s immense laundry room, hundreds of wet hanging sheets, swaying wildly like demons, exhausted her even further as they wrapped her in cloying arms of restraint. Finally she broke free to see her prey staggering down the staircase at the end of the corridor.

She reached it moments later and started down just as the flickering lights finally went out, plunging her into darkness.

Undeterred, she felt her way, hardly slowing. But the stairs seemed to plunge into the very bowels of the ship, the 'thud,

thud' of the *Celestiana*'s colossal engines increasing as she descended the staircase until they filled her ears like the beating heart of some immense beast.

At the bottom she gasped. With the lights out, the huge space before her was illuminated only by a hundred fiery furnaces. *Surely this is Dante's last Circle of Hell?* She gritted her teeth. *The one reserved for traitors!*

But surely hell had nothing on the heat that sucked all the air from her already burning chest as the furnaces fed two rows of giant boilers. And the demonic noise! The cacophony of clanking metal and hissing steam reverberated around the cavernous two-storeyed engine room, disorientating her as she spun on the spot. Rising on every side, narrow gantries ran between a densely packed confusion of massive spinning shafts and belted flywheels, many towering over twenty feet. Raised platforms filled with banks of yard-long levers and stopcocks crowded the floor, offering even more hiding places for her quarry.

Just then she glimpsed him threading his way over to a series of rungs set in the wall that acted as a ladder to the second level of the engine room. Behind her, a duplicate set did the same. But those at the opposite end also ran on up to a hatch in the riveted metal ceiling. An open hatch.

You'll lose him for sure if that's where he's heading and you don't get there first.

But you'll lose him for sure if it isn't and you're waiting up there as he tricks you by doubling back.

She had no time to decide. Intuition took over. She slid Seldon's gun into her waistband, turned, and put her foot on the first rung. As she heaved herself up, pain ripped through her leg. For a moment, she almost tumbled backwards. Somehow hanging on, feeling light-headed with the pain, she pulled herself up the remaining rungs one at a time.

At the top, she saw stars as she lay on the metal gangway. Forcing herself up, she limped to the other side.

Wait, Ellie, wait. Be patient. You know you can't go any further. You'll only get this one chance.

As a long shadow crept up the wall opposite, the furnaces below surrounding it in a fiendish red glow, she stepped out.

'It's over.'

The shadow stopped as it stepped off the ladder onto the gangway. Slowly, it turned towards her.

'Is it though? I've come too far to be thwarted by *you*.'

Somehow, she held her rage in check. 'You're a murderer. And a traitor!'

'Very impressive, Lady Swift.' Professor Goodman's tone was so matter-of-fact a wash of ice ran down her spine. He clicked his heels together. 'I did indeed work for the British government, outwardly at least, but in reality, I worked for the Germans.'

She gritted her teeth in disgust. 'So, you passed on secrets to the enemy!'

His unruffled tone didn't flinch. 'With relish as I am, in fact, German, as I believe you may have guessed as well.'

She recalled Seldon's words. *Even at the place my wife worked during the war, she mentioned they had a psychologist.*

'You were working in military intelligence in Ardwycke Manor, weren't you?'

'Why, yes!' His tone rose in appreciation. 'Shrewder and shrewder, Lady Swift. As you have evidently deduced, I worked there during the war. With Chief Inspector Seldon's wife. He'd dropped her off at the gate a few times. I saw him from my window, but he did not see me. Which is how I recognised him as I was boarding the *Celestiana*.' He looked at her quizzically. 'Ah! So, you are not quite as clever as you think, though. You have not guessed, no?'

'Guessed what?'

Goodman laughed cruelly. 'That Yeoman did not kill her. *I* did.'

Suddenly, the world turned upside down. She was thrown like a rag doll onto a nearby boiler, the hot rivets driving into her arm and face like shot pellets. She gasped in pain and tumbled onto the floor as the ship righted itself. For a moment she lay there, the pain too much for her to think of moving or opening her eyes.

The gun! She forced her eyes open somehow, scouring the surrounding area. *There!*

She tried to lunge for it, but the pain in her leg was too great. Scrambling forward, she reached out as another hand whipped it from her grasp.

Looking up slowly, her gaze was met by the barrel of Seldon's gun.

39

Goodman's lips twisted into an evil smile. 'Lady Swift, it seems that the tables have turned.'

He wedged himself against the opposite tank as the ship rolled again, this time less violently. 'You should have shot me when you had the chance. But your mind will not let you kill a man in cold blood. Some men, and women, have the killing gene. You do not. No matter how much you may think you want revenge, morality will always be your weakness.'

He raised Seldon's gun.

It's over, Ellie. You lost. She felt an overwhelming sadness. Not for herself, but for Hugh. And his wife. And the others Goodman had killed.

'Quite fitting, don't you think, Lady Swift? To be shot by the very weapon I only possess because you never handed it over to the authorities when you should have. You see what happens when you make one bad moral decision?'

She closed her eyes. She'd promised herself she'd finish this for Hugh and—

Losing heart can only push the finish line out of reach forever, darling, a soothing voice whispered in her thoughts. Not needing to look, she knew her mother stood behind her with that serene smile that made everything seem alright. And anything possible.

She reopened her eyes. 'Thank you, Mother,' she murmured.

Goodman cocked his head and looked at her questioningly.

The ship rolled once more and then settled. The storm was receding. She stared into the killer's eyes.

'I said thank you. For reminding me that even if you cannot correct a past mistake, you can still make amends. I *will* see justice done.'

He laughed coldly. 'All you are going to see, Lady Swift, is a bullet.'

'Then before I do,' she said calmly, 'tell me why. Why did you kill the inspector's wife?'

He hesitated, then shrugged. 'To satisfy your curiosity, she was getting far too suspicious and I couldn't risk she wouldn't soon report those suspicions.'

Her mind was working through what she knew, and what she had guessed. 'But Yeoman was the one who broke into the building, yes?'

'Of course. I needed a patsy. A fall guy. I had my contact arrange for a break-in the very next night after I saw the troublesome Mrs Seldon sifting through files she had no business to be looking at. And while he was robbing the floor Mrs Seldon was working on, I swiftly dispatched her. Yeoman, on hearing the shot, fled as I knew he would. When the police investigated, they came to the conclusion, as intended, that she had disturbed the burglar and he'd killed her.'

She didn't mask the contempt in her tone. 'It must have seemed very tame after the war, though. No more treachery to commit. So, you reinvented yourself as Professor Daniel Goodman, the master of the new science piquing the public's interest: psychology.'

He shrugged coldly. 'It made sense. It had always been my field. And my book is exemplary.'

Her mind was fitting the last pieces of the jigsaw in place. 'So, you killed Yeoman because you thought he'd trailed you onto the *Celestiana*? To what? Blackmail you? And then you tried to frame Hu—' her heart clenched, 'the inspector for Yeoman's murder.'

Goodman shrugged. 'Yeoman was an "inconvenience" from my past I could not afford. I did not wait to find out if he was going to blackmail me or not. I killed him before he had the chance.'

She shook her head. 'The irony is, Professor, I don't think Yeoman was interested in small game like you.' Goodman's eyes flashed with anger. 'He was after a bigger prize than that.' *Stealing the opal from the Regal Suite.* She shook her head again. 'So why did you kill Count Balog?'

'Because Yeoman may not have recognised me, but Balog did. He wasn't half the fool he delighted in playing.' He waved the gun, but quickly brought it back to bear. 'His government supported Germany in the war and he was seconded in for a brief while to train the likes of me.' He frowned. 'But how did you know I killed Balog? Or Yeoman, for that matter?'

She laughed curtly. 'Because I knew who the gun that killed Yeoman belonged to.' *Hugh, Ellie.* She forced herself to continue. 'And I knew he wasn't a murderer. So why hadn't the real killer thrown it overboard and destroyed the evidence? Because the gun was planted, that's why. To incriminate the inspector. And then there was the ring with the bee on.'

He smiled smugly. 'The one I wrenched from Yeoman's finger just before I shoved him overboard, yes.' He tapped his forehead. 'Do you see how quick thinking and superior my brain is?'

She shrugged. 'Perhaps, but it niggled me. It was just too easy to find. The master-at-arms' men should have found it. The answer? Like the gun, it had been planted by the killer. The really odd thing, though, was it didn't point to the same person as the gun. Why not? Because the killer must have known, or guessed, when he saw the inspector still freely wandering around the ship that his plan had gone wrong. The gun hadn't been discovered. Or, if it had, it hadn't been linked to the inspector. So, he had to choose another passenger on D deck to incriminate. And it worked. To start with.'

He gestured with the gun for her to go on.

She took a calming breath. 'The ring led us to Miss González, as did the cards dropped in Balog's cabin, if you took her as being the Queen of Hearts. But again, I had a niggle. Why were there only a few cards on the floor and not the whole deck? The only explanation seemed to be Balog grabbed those particular ones as he was dying, to give a clue to his killer. But right next to the remaining deck on his desk was a pen and pad of paper. He could just as quickly have written down a name! The answer, like the ring, was that the cards had been planted to throw more suspicion on Miss González. But inadvertently, you led my mind in another direction. The right one. You see, the cards were from an old German deck. Balog had decks from every far-flung country, so if the dropped cards *were* planted, why did the killer choose that particular pack? Because, in the heat of the moment, he picked up the most familiar one. And when you betrayed your anger when my butler pointed out the story of the *Flying Dutchman* was based on an English, not German, story, I knew you were German. Only a German would have known and cared about such things!'

Anger flitted across his features again, but he said nothing.

'And then your summations of the suspects. They all rang so true. Except your assertion that everything Miss González said was a lie. Because I knew she was the only suspect who was telling the truth! She confessed she was Yeoman's fiancée and our information backed this up. The only thing she did lie about was being over him once he was dead, poor girl!'

Goodman laughed mockingly. 'How touching!'

Her eyes glinted. 'Which meant you were either a bad psychologist, which your reputation refuted, or you were trying to make us believe she was the most likely suspect. Which was exactly what the killer had been doing. And then I remembered...' she swallowed hard, 'the inspector mentioning there was a psychologist where his wife worked. It had to be you! That was how you knew Seldon by sight, as you told me.'

His lips curled. 'So, Lady Swift, why didn't you tell the master-at-arms to arrest me?'

'Because several things muddied the waters. The first was the opal. The only clue we'd found up to that point that you *didn't* plant. But ironically, it wasn't a clue as to who murdered Yeoman. It did, however, explain what Yeoman was doing on board the *Celestiana*; robbing it, naturally, as that was his profession. Which started us on the path to believing the master-at-arms was actually the killer. It wasn't until a witness told me he'd seen, and heard, him arguing ferociously with Yeoman on deck the very night he was murdered I began to doubt it.'

Goodman scowled. 'Why so?'

'Because if the master-at-arms was of a mind to murder Yeoman, he would have done so right then and there. It was the perfect opportunity. He had no idea he was being watched. Why return and risk killing him later? But then... when I saw... Hugh's watch.' Her heart clenched so hard it stopped her words. She hugged her shoulders. 'Then, I knew for certain at that moment Yeoman's ring and Balog's cards had also been dropped on purpose. By the killer.' She shook her head. 'But I still couldn't understand how you could be the killer because we were sure whoever murdered Yeoman also murdered Balog—'

'And I had a watertight alibi!' Goodman crowed.

She nodded grimly. 'Your having an alibi for the time of Count Balog's death threw us all off originally which is why we dropped you as a suspect. Cyanide works so quickly once it is ingested, it seemed the only person who could have added it to Balog's whisky was someone who was with him moments before. *Unless*, that is, the cyanide was added to *ice* that was then added to that already in his drink. The devious method you employed, aided by the *Celestiana* having every luxury in the first-class cabins, including ice buckets!'

He clapped one hand against the gun. 'Fiendishly well worked out, Lady Swift. Like my plan itself, you must admit. Boring a hole in two ice cubes, filling them up with cyanide and then refreezing them again. The cyanide wasn't released until the ice melted. This gave me five to ten minutes after slipping them into Balog's drink, which had ice in anyway, to leave the lounge and establish my alibi. Pure genius!'

'Maybe. It certainly explains why you excused yourself straight after dinner. But you see, when I shook your hand when you left to rehearse your lecture, I thought it was just naturally cold. But it was cold because it had just been wet. Wet with ice!'

Goodman's expression had been growing increasingly dark as she spoke. Now he raised his arm. 'Enough! You have been too much of a meddlesome nuisance, Lady Swift. I shall enjoy killing you even more than I did—'

His eyes went blank. For a moment, she thought he would pull the trigger. But instead, the gun fell from his grasp as his legs buckled. He sank to his knees, looked up at her in confusion, and then collapsed full length on the gangway.

40

The most welcome voice she could ever hear whispered in her ear, 'Why can I never have you to myself for even a moment? Especially when I need to hold you the most, blast it!' Seldon's strong fingers slid out of hers as he reluctantly nudged her towards the door in front of them. That he hadn't released his tender grip of her hand once until now meant everything. He'd even been uncharacteristically demonstrative while Mrs Butters had fussed over her every cut and bruise. But all she wanted was to be wrapped tightly in his arms. The arms of the man she finally admitted to herself she loved more than life itself.

Her thoughts raced back again to that heart-stopping moment when she thought it was all over. Over, that was, until Goodman had collapsed on the floor, revealing an enraged Seldon behind, bleeding copiously from his forehead but still wielding a wrench as long as his arm.

She shook her head, still not quite believing he was really there alongside her. Goodman hadn't shot and thrown him overboard like Yeoman but forced him at gunpoint to the lower decks and then knocked him out and left him tied up in a store cupboard. Just like Eleanor, though, he'd underestimated how much Seldon would fight for what he loved. Coming to, he'd broken free of his bonds and tracked Goodman to the furnace room.

He nudged her forward again.

She looked up at him. 'Tell me, again, I'm not hallucinating. You're still here?'

He nodded as he buried his chin in her fiery curls. 'I thought... I thought I'd lost you forever.'

She laughed. 'Likewise, Hugh. But here we are.' She turned and stared at the door. *Time to face the music.*

Sharing a wince, she ran a hand over his bandaged head before they stepped inside.

'Good evening, Captain Bracebridge. Here we are post storm and mostly in one piece.' She cocked her head as she gestured around his largely back-to-rights office. 'I rather thought, though, you might be ripping me to shreds somewhere far less comfortable. The brig, perhaps?'

Bracebridge nodded, but a smile played about his lips. 'A fitting suggestion in the main, I agree, Lady Swift, since you deliberately withheld pertinent evidence from me. Namely, that it was the chief inspector's gun which dispatched Mr Yeoman.' He waved both of them to take a seat. 'However, I believe I can leave the full admonishment for your further impetuous actions to another.'

He nodded over at the door to where her butler was being ushered in. She stared up into his ever-inscrutable expression.

'I fully deserve every telling-off you're itching to chastise me with, I know. But I rather hoped we might not spoil the last shred of my birthday trip with all that just now?'

'Indeed, I would not dream of such, my lady.' He produced his leather pocketbook. 'I have recorded everything in meticulous detail to chastise you with at a later date.'

She laughed with the others. 'You terror! For that, you'll

have to take a seat along with the rest of us. At least I can enjoy seeing you squirm.'

Bracebridge had been watching all of this with clear amusement. He turned to Seldon with a questioning look.

He shook his head. 'Oh, this is nothing, Captain, trust me.'

Over the rim of her tot of rum Bracebridge had insisted they all join him in, Eleanor's cheeks coloured at his endless praise for her courage and quick thinking.

She flapped a hand, hastily swiping her sleeve back down over the bruises and injuries tended to by Mrs Butters.

'Oh, it's nothing. Anyone would have done the same. Besides, the inspector was the one who apprehended the professor in the end.'

'Nothing? Nonsense,' Bracebridge said as sharply as Seldon and Clifford shook their heads. 'You were the one who had the brute cornered. Modesty is a noble quality, Lady Swift, but in your case it is entirely unfounded. As Mr Walker and I agreed wholeheartedly when I contacted him this morning with the news the murderer was securely under lock and key.'

Eleanor's face lit with a fond smile for her old boss. 'How is he?'

'Overawed by your exploits, as ever.' Bracebridge smiled. 'He asked me to pass on his personal thanks and I am as delighted as I am honoured to also deliver a second heartfelt mark of gratitude. Blue Line's board of directors, and yes, it was voted through unanimously, have hereby invited you to enjoy free passage on any of their ships. In perpetuity.' His gaze flicked to Seldon and back. 'With a companion, naturally.'

Seldon gaped. 'On one of these floating nightmares!' He ran an anxious hand around the nape of his neck. 'What I meant was... oh, blast it!'

Eleanor laughed. 'Please pass on my sincere gratitude for the board's incredible generosity.'

Bracebridge nodded. 'I will do so. Oh, and let me return

your notebooks.' He reached around to the long table running along the back of his settee. 'Although they are no longer needed, given you've identified the guilty parties just in time before we reach New York in the morning.'

'Almost,' Eleanor said, catching Seldon's eye.

Bracebridge frowned. 'Almost?'

'During the investigation, we did unearth some other goings on, Captain.' Seldon's tone was every inch the efficient chief inspector. 'With your permission, I shall be requesting that the New York authorities detain Mrs Swalecourt and Signor Marinelli. I wish to question them further over a possible series of organised robberies at large country estates.'

Bracebridge shook his head. 'I fear what else you might have discovered had our journey been longer! Really, this has been an eye-opener. But yes, of course, request whatever you feel is appropriate, Chief Inspector.' Bracebridge's manner became more earnest. 'But if I might add my own indebtedness to you all. All the more so for your discretion over the other shameful matter.'

'You mean with your master-at-arms?'

'Yes. He is... *was* a good man. However, he ruined a hard-won reputation and lifelong career with one act of greed. He will be tried in a naval court and they will decide his fate. Now.' His face broke into another smile. 'I need to let you know that during the storm, your young Sidney the stowaway proved himself beyond selfless in helping passengers and crew alike. And even respectfully challenged my order that he retire after fourteen hours of heavy labour in righting the *Celestiana*'s fixtures and fittings.' He nodded at Eleanor's hopeful look. 'Yes, Lady Swift. Rest assured, the young fellow has more than earned his permanent place on my crew.'

'Thank you, Captain. That has made my entire trip.' She glanced at her butler and despite his impassive features, his shining eyes told her it had made his, too.

Bracebridge leaned back in his seat. 'And please know, I have also actioned your other request. Everyone in third class will receive the best and largest meal the *Celestiana*'s somewhat storm-damaged supplies can muster. Particularly one Lebanese family, I understand.'

Eleanor's smile widened. 'Then I can assure you, Captain, you have also made two young maids very happy!'

Bracebridge shook his head. 'I am not sure, Lady Swift, if you or last night's storm have made the biggest impact on myself. And the *Celestiana*. And I still cannot fathom exactly how you knew beyond reasonable doubt who the killer was?'

Seldon laughed wryly. 'It's called feminine intuition, Captain.'

Bracebridge looked between him and Clifford. 'I've spent my life mostly among men, naval at that. What is this mysterious beast that seems to rule the way ladies operate, gentlemen?'

Clifford's lips quirked. 'As the astute Mr Oscar Wilde noted, Captain, "Intuition is a strange instinct that tells a woman she is right, whether she is or not."'

Bracebridge roared with laughter as Ellie folded her arms in a mock huff and fixed Clifford with her best steely stare.

Seldon leaned forward. 'However, Captain, in Lady Swift's case, I can wholeheartedly vouch that she invariably is!'

She gasped. 'Thank you, Hugh! Surely that smarted a little to admit it, though?'

'Not a bit. It was agony!'

Bracebridge's laughter followed them to the door, where Eleanor turned to him.

'To New York in the morning, then, Captain.'

'Oh, surely to the *Celestiana*'s final celebration first.' Bracebridge's gaze flicked once more to Seldon and back to her. 'It is tradition, after all. And storm or no storm, nothing stands in the way of a ship's traditions. And on this occasion, your staff are all invited too. Captain's orders. You wouldn't miss that, would you?'

41

Clifford melted away as if pulled by an invisible force as the three of them neared the first-class lounge.

'Can't we just go somewhere quiet for a moment?' Seldon pleaded in a whisper to Eleanor. He slid her arm gently over his. 'I need to convince myself that you really are still here and in one piece after... after that awful moment in the engine room. Perhaps, venture down to a corner in second class with me?' He flushed from his neck up to his lean cheeks. 'Oh lord, if that isn't too forward of me to ask?'

'Well, since my scallywag chaperone has disappeared, we could just nip—'

'Lady Swift!' a silken voice called from behind.

'Blast it!' he groaned quietly.

They both turned to see Miss González hurrying over, her curves catching only Eleanor's eye it seemed, as Seldon stared into space beyond her silver silk-shoulder-strapped form. She stopped in front of them. If there had been a chair behind her, Eleanor would have fallen into it as she reached out and took both of her wrists.

'This ghastly trip. It's nearly finished!'

Eleanor smiled. 'And I thought you were so busy ticking off all the things to do and see, silly me.' She stared between the dark pools looking back at her from the flawlessly beautiful face. 'How are you doing, though? Really? You lost someone you cared for.' She looked up at the clearly still distracted Seldon. 'And I know how much that cuts your heart in two.'

Miss González sighed. 'I'll get over it. Eventually. And I've stopped railing against the truth and wishing it was different.'

Eleanor patted her arm. 'We can't help who we are.'

She nodded. 'And we can't help who we fall in love with.' She drew Eleanor into a hug. 'I hope you're brave enough to try again. I will.'

Am I?

With a wave, she sashayed away, leaving Seldon looking bemused. 'What was that she was saying? I confess, I tuned out the minute she called your name.'

'It doesn't matter.' She shook Miss González's words from her thoughts. 'Now, what was that you whispered about nipping down to somewhere quiet? Because you'll have to help me negotiate any stairs.'

Just as they reached the last turn in the staircase, Seldon fell backwards onto the step behind as a whirlwind hit him.

'Oof! Gladstone, old friend. Really, every time?' He tried in vain to dodge the exuberant, greeting. 'Ugh!'

'Oh, my stars!' Eleanor caught her cook's familiar voice hiss below. 'You'll never guess who Mr Wilful has bowled over on to his magnificent behi—'

'Ahem!' Clifford's firm interruption from above made her smile.

'Hello, troops,' she called over the banister rail. 'Come on up. What a great meeting spot this seems to be.'

'Can I disagree on one count?' Seldon groaned, now flat out along the stairs, pinned by the bulky bulldog who was trying to balance on his chest.

'Oh, Butters, just look at that.' Eleanor caught Mrs Trotman's whispered chuckle to her housekeeper as their heads emerged up the steps. 'There's a policeman who's going to need mending like all the things we've had to fix in our cabin after that there storm!'

'Master Gladstone!' Clifford commanded. 'And, ladies,' he added with a firm look. 'Stand down, all!' With the bulldog coaxed off Seldon, he helped the inspector up and brushed down his jacket.

'Butters could mend that, Mr Clifford, sir,' Mrs Trotman jumped in.

He tutted. 'As can the ship's laundry, thank you. Which I will arrange forthwith after her ladyship has finished enjoying seeing you all. For whatever reason, that is,' he added teasingly.

'M'lady, 'tis our treat to see you.' Mrs Butters stepped forward and waved a concerned hand over Eleanor's leg. 'How's it holding up? And what are we going to do if Mr Clifford and the chief inspector can't keep you safe?'

'They can. And they did. Please don't worry. And your ministrations on my leg, and everything else, are helping marvellously.' She noticed that Lizzie and Polly were unusually quiet, seemingly in another world together. The younger of her two maids, particularly, looking on the verge of tears. 'Polly?' she said gently. 'Is something the matter?'

Polly's gaze flew up to Clifford. Receiving his nod that she could speak up, her bottom lip trembled. 'Not to be ungrateful for all the magical days so far, your ladyship, but 'tis hard to think of... of...' A tear rolled down her cheek. 'These dream days in wonderland is almost over.'

'But there's still our time in New York and the return trip. And we'll have other holidays together.' Eleanor meant every word as she looked around the group, who felt more like family than ever after the recent events. 'Besides...'

She caught Clifford's eye, noting his own expression had softened. He nodded with a rare smile.

'Yes, my lady, I think it would be entirely appropriate. *If* the ladies' behaviour is also such.'

'Thank you,' she mouthed. She turned back to them. 'What I was going to say is, this holiday is not over yet. I need to pass on a personal invitation to a party in first class tonight from the captain himself.'

'Did you hear that, my girl?' Mrs Butters cried, pulling Polly into her side.

'The likes of us! In first class? Can't be true,' Mrs Trotters said. 'But say 'tis, m'lady?'

She laughed. 'It is. After all, you helped enormously with our investigations as well. So, it's glad-rags time for all of us. And whatever you have with you will be wonderful. However, Mr Clifford will pop down with a little envelope for each of you and you can ask him to slide along to the shopping arcade to purchase any extras you need.'

'Oh, m'lady, thank you!' the three of them chorused, Polly too overcome to join in.

'That will be all, ladies.' Clifford swished them away back down the stairs with the waft of one finger.

'Actually,' Seldon said awkwardly. 'I need to... to...' he faltered, 'to dig out something suitable for later. So... I'll see you in a bit, Eleanor.' He hastened off, his long stride taking him out of view in a trice.

She stared after him with a sigh. 'Dash it, Clifford!'

'Patience, my lady,' he said gently. 'However, I believe you have a celebration evening to prepare for. Captain's orders!'

And what a celebratory spectacle the *Celestiana*'s staff had pulled together, even after the storm had wreaked havoc throughout the ship.

'So beautiful,' she breathed, having apparently arrived last since the room was full of elegantly turned-out passengers already chatting in cosy twos and fours with flutes of champagne. She stared around at the stunning expanse of the ballroom, every inch of the walls painted with one long fresco of heavenly deities dancing in celestial paradise. Only the occasional missing chandelier told of the previous evening's terror.

An ocean of white marbled flooring led down to the fifty-strong horseshoe of immaculate, if rather bruised and bandaged, waiters bearing more champagne bottles at the ready. On the right, a small orchestra had already started up, filling the wondrous space with serene music. The indigo ceiling twinkled with a thousand tiny lights, making it seem there was no roof at all. She hugged the emerald silk shoulders of her floor-length beaded gown, wishing—

'Eleanor,' a tantalisingly deep voice rumbled behind her.

Wishes do come true, Ellie.

'Hello, Hugh.' She turned around carefully, her leg still aching. Her shoulders rose in delight at the far too handsome man looking down at her. 'Gracious! Is that really you? Because dash it, in evening wear even with that bandage, you look too, too...' She tailed off, floundering for the right word.

'Awkward?' He pulled on the collar of his black velvet jacket with a worried frown. 'Formal? Ridiculous?'

She laughed. 'Delicious, actually. But that's probably not a very ladylike thing to say.'

Seldon's eyes shone. 'It's a very Lady Swift unladylike thing to say, though. And what else could I wish to hear this evening? Or any other?' He offered her a courtly bow as couples walked onto the floor and the orchestra slid into a romantic waltz. 'May I?'

'I didn't actually think you'd ask,' she stuttered. 'Clifford and the ladies are here somewhere.'

'They are over there.' He nodded left. 'So, let's give them a spectacle they can ooh and aah over in the kitchen during those long winter nights.' Scooping her up as gently as a butterfly, he led her off around the ballroom, his strong arms more than compensating for her injured leg and making her heart skip so hard she thought it might actually stop.

By the second dance, she felt her body was floating. By the third, Clifford had run out of handkerchiefs to offer the ladies.

She looked up at him. 'How has a policeman who's spent too many years and definitely too many nights working overtime had the time to learn to dance like this?'

'He hasn't. He's letting his heart do it for him.' He held her gaze, his deep brown eyes filled with concern. 'Just as he did when he asked it to show him where you were in danger.'

She pulled back in surprise. 'That's how you found me in the engine room? By following a... a feeling?'

'Yes. And it told me you'd be in the most dangerous place, in the most fearful trouble. You are an incorrigible influence.' He brought her to a gentle stop. 'I really shouldn't believe... blast it, Eleanor!' he mumbled as he took her hand.

'Believe what?'

'That you'll forgive me.' He hesitated and then seemed to decide. 'Come with me, please.'

Outside on the forward deck by the sleek pointed bow rail, he tucked his jacket tightly over her shoulders.

'Hugh?' she coaxed. 'I don't need to forgive you anything. You saved my life. If it hadn't been for you, I'd be—'

'Don't say it!' He pulled her into his chest. 'Don't say it, Eleanor, please, not now. Not ever. Besides, you saved my life the Christmas before last, remember.'

'Then we're even.' She smiled as she gazed into his eyes. 'But if you want to say something, say it.'

'I don't,' he blurted out. 'I mean, I do. But it will come out all wrong. Everything always does when I'm with you.'

She laughed, trying to ease his nerves, totally flummoxed by what had caused them. 'Well, we're definitely equal on that score. Every time I've even tried to apologise to you, it's ended up making things worse.'

'This is different. This is... unforgivable of me.'

'Can't I be the judge of that?' She leaned against the rail, now fearful of what was to follow.

He took a deep breath. 'Eleanor, I need to confess I used up all my savings... my special savings, pursuing Yeoman and purchasing the ticket on this nightmare of a boat. I had to buy both berths in my cabin, you see, and...' He sighed. 'It will take me another two years to save up a sufficient sum again.'

She smiled in confusion. 'Is that all? You had good reason, Hugh. You did it for your wife. For love.'

He hesitated. 'Yes. My savings were for... love.'

'I don't understand,' she said falteringly. 'What are you saying?'

He groaned. 'That ridiculously, I've been putting aside every possible penny and pound since...' He scrabbled in his jacket pockets, his fingers tingling against her hips. Pulling out a sheet of *Celestiana*'s notepaper, he unfolded it and held it up. In his short efficient strokes, it simply read, 'Yes, man. Do it!'

'I wrote this when I dashed out of the room we had as our base of operations. Right after you'd made me feel so much better.' His handsome face broke into a smile. 'And given me hope we might actually understand each other one day. At least a little.' He turned her around to stare out to sea and nestled in behind her, his arms through hers, holding her hands. 'Eleanor, I've been saving since the day I met you, in the ridiculous hope.' He sighed. 'The trouble is we're both so awfully—'

'Hopeless with each other?'

'Not any more.' He turned her gently back. 'What I'm trying to say is it's fearfully cheeky, but it would have to be a long one. Well, until I'd saved enough up again. And all the more so because you're a titled lady and I'm just a policeman.'

He leaned in so close her breath caught. And then he took it away altogether as he kissed her longingly. 'But, Eleanor, when I have saved up enough again to treat you like the princess you are on the most important day of your – *our* – life, would you?'

'Would I what? Oh my,' she breathed.

Down on one knee, he looked up at her. 'Lady Eleanor Swift, will you marry me?'

'Hugh! Marriage!' she gasped falteringly. 'Me? And you?'

'That's traditionally how these things work, I've heard.' He swallowed hard, looking panic-stricken. 'Have I got it all—'

'Yes!' she cried. 'I mean no, you haven't got it wrong.' She clasped his hand in hers. 'Yes, I will marry you.' Tears of happiness ran down her cheeks. 'And, Chief Inspector Seldon, I would wait until the ends of the earth to be your wife.'

A LETTER FROM VERITY

Dear reader,

I want to say a huge thank you for choosing to read *Death on Deck*. If you did enjoy it, and want to keep up to date with all my latest releases, just sign up at the following link. Your email address will never be shared and you can unsubscribe at any time.

www.bookouture.com/verity-bright

I hope you loved *Death on Deck* and if you did I would be very grateful if you could write a review. I'd love to hear what you think, and it makes such a difference helping new readers to discover one of my books for the first time.

I love hearing from my readers – you can get in touch on my Facebook page, through Twitter, Goodreads or my website.

Thanks,

Verity

www.veritybright.com

facebook.com/veritybrightauthor
twitter.com/BrightVerity

HISTORICAL NOTES

HISTORY OF FORENSIC FIREARM IDENTIFICATION

As Eleanor rightly says, when Goodman leaves Seldon's gun at the scene of Yeoman's murder, he is assuming Seldon has registered the gun when boarding with the ship's security and therefore when the murder weapon was found, it would be traced to Seldon. However, even though Seldon didn't register his gun, he tells Eleanor he would never lie under oath.

The truth is, it would have been hard to prove his gun was the murder weapon otherwise. Fingerprinting was still in its infancy and a man as calculating and careful as Goodman would have worn gloves, which would have overlaid Seldon's fingerprints anyway. On top of that, the science of matching bullets to certain guns (forensic ballistics) was also only just emerging and the only bullet they might have been able to prove came from Seldon's gun anyway went overboard along with Yeoman.

PLAYING CARDS

Playing cards have been used for centuries and Germany has one of the oldest histories dating back to before 1450. In the 1920s (and even now in some parts) the pack of cards used in Germany were different to American or English packs. They had thirty-two or thirty-six cards and the four sets weren't clubs, diamonds, spades and hearts but acorns, bells, hearts and leaves as Clifford states, correctly as ever.

Erotic playing cards have almost as long a history. In the 1800s the French produced translucent playing cards that showed noblemen and women apparently going about their normal daily life, but when held up to a strong light revealed they were doing anything but!

PASSPORTS

The first 'modern' British passport was a single piece of folded paper with a photograph, signature and brief description of the holder's distinguishing features. It was simple to forge and was replaced in 1920 by the 'Blue' passport book. European passports followed a similar pattern. However, they were still easy to forge, and after the war it was easy to obtain originals to alter. All of this meant that it was perfectly possible to reinvent yourself as someone new without much difficulty and travel under an alias as Miss González does. And all with very little chance of being discovered.

PASSENGER LINERS

Officially, the largest ocean liner in the world in 1923 was the *RMS Majestic*, built in 1914, a title she held until 1935. She had a gross registered tonnage of 56,551, compared to the *Titanic*'s 46,328. A little-known fact is that before WW1, most of the largest liners in the world were actually German and were ceded to Britain after the Treaty of Versailles. *RMS Majestic* was actually built in Germany and called the *SS Bismarck* before being handed over to the British and rebranded.

FIRST-CLASS PASSENGERS

The first commercial flight to operate regularly across the Atlantic from London to New York wasn't until 1939, so absolutely everyone had to go by sea. The grand liners of the day,

such as the *Celestiana*, carried kings, film stars, millionaire businessmen and heads of state in first-class luxury that rivalled even the famous hotels of the day. The estimated wealth of the first-class passengers on the *Titanic*, for instance, was around half a billion dollars.

One oddity that Eleanor encounters and might seem strange to us today, is that first-class passengers often boarded last. And the *Celestiana*'s first class was very luxurious for the day. Many ships still had shared toilet and bathing facilities in first class, with the shared baths using seawater to preserve fresh water supplies, whereas Eleanor is treated to her own private facilities.

SECOND CLASS

In contrast to first class, most second-class passengers were from the professional classes; teachers, clergy, etc. The price of second-class tickets was quite variable, with the most expensive being not that much cheaper than first class. Indeed, in some liners, some second-class cabins could be converted to first class by rolling out carpet over the linoleum and upgrading the furniture, and vice versa.

Staff of first-class passengers were also accommodated in

second class and ate in special dining rooms waited on by stewards. Being such a time of turmoil in terms of class structure, the staff of first-class passengers were considered above the crew of the ship, but did not really have the kudos of first- or second-class passengers. On the *Titanic* they ate with silver-plated cutlery, but the napkin holders bore the word 'SERVANT'.

THIRD CLASS

Third class, or 'steerage', as that's where the ship's steering equipment was originally located, was mostly made up of immigrants from Europe and beyond. As well as Irish, there were many Scandinavians and Lebanese, including the family Polly and Lizzie get to know. Usually, no meals were provided in third class, which is why the family had to fend for themselves. However, on some boats, the *Titanic* included, simple meals were available.

EATING & DRINKING

Luckily for Eleanor, the food on board the *Celestiana* rivals that of any fancy hotel or restaurant. Meals are served three times a day; breakfast from 8.30 a.m. to 10.30 a.m., lunch from 1 p.m. to 2.30 p.m., and dinner from 7 p.m. to 8.30 p.m. And each meal was heralded by a trumpet. On board the real liners of the day, things were much the same, breakfast being considered the most important meal of the day. Even twelve years earlier on the *Titanic* the breakfast menu was vast:

Fresh Fruit
Baked Apples
Stewed Prunes
Oats
Boiled Hominy

Puffed Rice
Herring
Haddock
Salmon
Sirloin Steak & Mutton Chops
Grilled Mutton
Kidneys & Bacon
Grilled Ham
Grilled Sausage
Lamb Collops
Cold Meat
Vegetable Stew
Fried, Shirred, Poached & Boiled Eggs
Plain & Tomato Omelettes
Mashed, Sauté & Jacket Potatoes
Rolls
Scones
Corn Bread
Buckwheat Cakes
Black Currant Conserve
Honey
Marmalade

How they ever fitted in lunch, let alone dinner, is a mystery, although Eleanor manages it!

BLACK OPALS

Black opals really are among the rarest gemstones on the planet. Found almost exclusively in one small area of Australia, Lightning Ridge, they can fetch prices as high as $6,000 per carat, more than most diamonds.

SHARKS

Marinelli and Sir Randolph are correct about sharks in the Atlantic. There are dozens of species. Even the UK coastal waters have almost two dozen native shark species, including the thirty-foot basking shark (which is actually harmless). However, few, if any, ever attack people. Conversely, in 1916 there were a series of fatal shark attacks off the New Jersey coast and a fatal attack off the Yorkshire coast in 1922. (The only reported fatality from a shark attack ever recorded in UK waters.)

DANTE'S INFERNO

Written by Italian Dante Alighieri, a favourite of Clifford's, *Inferno* (Italian for 'Hell') is the first part in a three-part work called *The Divine Comedy*. *Purgatorio* (Purgatory) and *Paradiso* (Paradise) are the other two parts. *Inferno* involves the journey of Dante through the 'nine Circles of Hell'. Each circle is reserved for a certain type of crime, or sin:

1. Limbo
2. Lust
3. Gluttony
4. Greed – if there was a doggy version of Dante's Hell, Gladstone might be found here.
5. Anger
6. Heresy
7. Violence
8. Fraud
9. Treachery – where Professor Goodman resides.

ACKNOWLEDGEMENTS

To the team at Bookouture who make sure my readers actually have something to read.

Made in United States
North Haven, CT
10 November 2023

43858632R00178